I0671130

PRAISE FOR BROOKLYN ANN'S BOOKS

His Final Girl

"Brooklyn takes the reader on a rollercoaster ride through the horrors that lurk in the woods, yet keeps it light, before terror strikes. Full of pop culture references, horror, romance, enjoyable characters, and twists and turns to keep you wanting more, HIS FINAL GIRL has something for everyone. If Friday the 13th was a love story, this would be it." ~Anthony Northrup, Through the Black Hole

Gripping suspense, action, fabulous vivid scene descriptions, praise-worthy engaging characters and an awesome happy ending for the hero and the heroine. Enthralling page-turner that keeps you guessing who the ancient killer is. The author has done a fabulous job fusing horror and romance. Linnea and Wes are a perfect match; love them together. ~midniteink

Her Haunted Heart

"Another excellent, amazing read. I started today and finished it this morning because I couldn't put it down, it's that great, the ending will blow you away because it gives you a clue to another book this writer writes. Which I totally loved. Great characters and exceptional writing plus a lot of history that's fascinating. Highly recommend this book." ~Roxane

"This story was a cross between Supernatural *and* The Amityville Horror. *Creepy with a 1980's background it was a fun and interesting story."* ~Gina Johnson

"Hearts of Metal is a rock series that is not to be missed."
~Kara's Books

Kissing Viciöus

"KISSING VICIÖUS is a sensual, rockin' romance with a hero to die for." ~Fresh Fiction

"This is not your usual rocker romance. I thank the author for creating strong characters and taking a different course from usual. We really need more strong characters like Kinley and Quinn in the romance genre." ~The Romance Reviews

With Vengeance

"I was hooked the minute I started reading!! This is a totally different rock star book, but that's not a bad thing at all!! It's refreshing to see a rock star not be all about the 'rock star' lifestyle. Klement and Katana's relationship is pure and genuine and I can't say enough good words about it!" ~B1tches N Books

"Plenty of kicking ass, hilarious moments, and one hell of a romance." ~Librarian by Day, Reader by Night

Rock God

"This story has the right mix of sex, sweet and romance. I fell in love with the characters from the very first page." ~Bramley, Emma, Obsessed Book Reviews

"Brooklyn Ann weaves us another amazing story fill with drama, angst, passion, and inspiration. Her characters are so realistic and

written with so much depth... it's hard not to become emotionally attached to them all!" ~Rachel, Behind Closed Doors Book Reviews

Metal and Mistletoe

"Another winner. If you haven't read this author you're missing something." ~LuvLeeLorraine

"I will definitely read this one again when I want to feel warm, fuzzy and hopeful for my own happy ending." ~Fan Forever

Forbidden Song

"This is my favorite Bleeding Vengeance story. I was a little emotional as this story unfolded with happy tears at the end. I highly recommend this book and series." ~Christine Woinich

"Brooklyn Ann has created another great read in her Hearts of Metal series. Brooklyn writes in such a way as to show you the character development. Well worth reading." ~All Things Book

Tempting Beat

"The author is smart enough to keep the reader hooked - the characters are terrific, and even the secondary characters are well drawn. So read this book and slip into your Cinderella shoes - and fall in love with a young, handsome rock star who is more than he appears to be!" ~JennM

"I always look forward to a new book by Brooklyn Ann! I know I'm in for a treat and a fantastic read long into the night. I've read all her books, I've never been disappointed. This is book 6 in the Hearts of Metal series, but each book can definitely stand alone. Though you will want to go back and read about the other characters lives and how they came to be together. They are not typical romance

books. There's something special about each one, making each one different. More than five stars!" ~ginger@thebeach

Heart Throb

"I don't want this series to end because I need more from all of the bands! I loved the way each character was not only depicted as skilled at what they did but also as imperfect, vulnerable, normal human beings. This was a fabulous read, with well-developed characters and a fascinating setting." ~BookLover

*"Hot chemistry, romance, drama, and perceived betrayal make up this gripping rockstar romance. **Heart Throb** is an entertaining read that moves at a good pace, thus keeping you entertained until the very end. Both Brand and Lexi are likable characters and are well developed. I really enjoyed this book and I am definitely going back to read the rest of the series."* ~AT_202

HIS SCREAM QUEEN

B Mine Book 3

Brooklyn Ann

www.BOROUGHSPUBLISHINGGROUP.com

HIS SCREAM QUEEN
Copyright © 2020 Brooklyn Ann

ISBN: 978-1-951055-69-1

To Karen Ann
06-11-62 ~ 02-14-09
Thank you for nurturing my love of horror films

And to Hans Curtis
Thank you so much for helping me research for this book,
and introducing me to the fascinating world of giallos

ACKNOWLEDGEMENTS

Thank you to my agent for believing in me. To my editors for helping me polish this book up as best as it can be. To Layla J. Omorose for critiquing every chapter as I went, and for keeping up my enthusiasm throughout this project.

Thank you to Kent for being my real-life romance hero, and to Micah for being the best son ever. Thank you to my friends and family for cheering me on. And thank you to Bad Movie Club and Halloween Horror Club for helping me with intensive research for this project.

Most of all, thank you to my readers.

AUTHOR'S NOTE

When I set out to write the B Mine series, I only had a vague concept of where I wanted to go. For book 1, I wanted to write a summer camp slasher story. Book 2 would be a haunted house story, and book 3 would be a prom-themed horror story. Book four...well, you'll see what that one will be based on soon enough.

Back to this book though: When I started writing *His Scream Queen*, I had only a vague idea of what a prom-themed horror would look like. I knew that I wanted to pay a few tributes to the most infamous prom horror of all, *Carrie*, but I sure as hell didn't want to rip it off. My movie club helped a lot with where to go. We watched *Prom Night* and all the sequels, a bevy of high school horror films and rom coms, including my guilty pleasure, *Ten Things I Hate About You*.

Those all helped, but the real breakthrough came when my friend and fellow movie club admin, Hans, decided that January's theme month would be *giallo* films. In the simplest terms, *giallo* films are a class of Italian horror that focuses heavily on mysterious murders and feature an art-house stylization, whether sensual, supernatural, bizarre, or all three. *Giallo* films were the precursors to American slasher films.

Like destiny, I'd already named the hero of this book after two of the most famous *giallo* directors: Lucio Fulci and Dario Argento. I devoured more films, which inspired me to pepper this story with more *giallo* homages, especially with the kills. I did Argento-style kills, a Fulci kill or two, and, of course, a common Mario Bava device.

The result became the book you are about to read, a mishmash of American '80s high school angst, *giallo*-style kills, and a hefty dose of my own usual weirdness.

I hope you have as much of a blast reading *His Scream Queen* as I did writing it.

HIS SCREAM QUEEN

Chapter One

January 1984

Brittney Shaw allowed Brandon Teller to kiss her as the clock struck midnight. He'd be the perfect candidate to be her king at the prom if only he went to Amteep High instead of Sunnydale Prep. Looking at the glittering throng gathered in the Skeetshue Country Club ballroom, she wondered if she should have asked Daddy to transfer her to Sunnydale. But no, she'd gone to public school with the same classmates since kindergarten, and they'd witnessed her transformation from a dull, stringy-haired, middle-class girl to the rich, beautiful, popular princess she was today. And before graduation, those peers would see her change from a princess to a queen.

Brandon snapped her attention back to the present. "Hey. My parents are still in Cabo. I can have my driver take us to my place if you want to go somewhere where we can...talk alone." He trailed his fingertips across her collarbone.

"That's *very* tempting," Brittney purred. "But I have a headache. Maybe next time."

Brandon's protests chased her as she left the dance floor and had one of the club employees call her driver and bring her fur from the coatroom. The employee brought the luxurious mink and even placed it over her shoulders.

Brandon didn't take the hint, instead following her out onto the shoveled patio and down the slick flagstone steps. Rock salt crushed under the heels of her red leather Oscar de la Renta shoes as Brittney thought of how easily she could silence him forever if she felt like it.

Once she was delivered home to the gorgeous mansion on Lake Skeetshue that her father had purchased two years ago, Brittney kicked off her shoes and raced up to her room. She only had a few more hours before her parents would return home from the party.

Quickly, she changed out of her puffed-sleeve red chiffon gown and into a ski outfit that was so two years ago. Something she could easily throw away if things got too messy.

After grabbing the suitcase that she kept hidden in the back of her walk-in closet, she went back out into the winter night. Her boots crunched over the frozen snow. Her nose and cheeks stung from the cold, but it couldn't be helped.

This was the first day of the new year. A time when she had to give thanks for all she'd received the previous year and ensure the fortunes for this one.

The gardener's shed was unused in the winter, which made this ritual easier. In the summer, she had to store her sacrifices elsewhere.

The animal whimpered when she opened the door but didn't try to escape. It was too weak for that now. Instead, it allowed itself to be led to the birdbath in the backyard. Brittney set her suitcase on top of the glass-hard ice surface of the marble birdbath and opened it to reveal the tools that had helped her grant her every heart's desire.

With practiced ease, she withdrew a large dagger and carved a pentagram in the snow around the birdbath. Then she placed red candles at every point and lit them. Opening one of the books she'd stolen from the library three years ago, Brittany chanted the words that summoned her own personal genie.

Scar rose up in front of the birdbath, looking more solid than he had the first time she'd called him forth from the netherworld. Long, sharply pointed horns extended from his large head. His eyes glowed yellow, and his massive jaws were filled with sharp teeth. The animal let out a piteous squeal and tried to flee, but Brittney was used to this part of the ritual. Still gripping the knife she'd used to carve the pentagram, she slit the creature's throat.

Steaming blood sprayed through the air, glittering in the moonlight. As she'd expected, crimson droplets splattered on her ski suit, more than a stain removal spray could handle. She shrugged. She'd have to burn the outfit.

Brittney extended her hands and chanted the ritual words, "Oh, Scarlionapskhis, scourge of the soulless, most infernal, please accept this blood sacrifice as a token of my gratitude for the favors you've bestowed on me, and as a gift in exchange for making me beautiful."

The demon inclined its head sardonically and fell upon the still-twitching body of the sacrifice.

Brittney used to gag when Scar devoured the animals she'd killed, but after so many years, she was used to the sight and aftermath. Now, she only wiggled her numbing toes in her snow boots, impatient for the ritual to be over with.

When Scar finished dining, he fixed Brittney with yellow glowing eyes. His growling voice sounded like a rabid dog coughing up shards of broken bones. "Do you have a wish you want me to grant?"

"Not tonight." Brittney did not fall into the trap. She'd quickly learned not to get too greedy with the demon. Not only because it would grow angry with her if she demanded too much too soon, but also because she didn't want to owe a debt before she was ready to pay it.

Wishes called for careful consideration, cautious wording, meticulous ritual, and a proper sacrifice.

"This night, I gave you this gift, and now allow you to return to your realm in peace." Brittney then said the guttural words that banished the demon before she blew out the candles. She then lit a sage bundle and trailed the smoke behind her as she kicked snow over the pentagram. After packing her candles and knife away in the suitcase, she hauled the grisly remains of the sacrifice over to the edge of the cliff where the backyard ended and kicked it over where it sank into the black waters of the lake below.

Back inside, she stripped off the bloody clothes and tossed them in the fireplace. The smell of burning nylon wrinkled her nose. She hoped it dissipated before her parents got home.

After a luxurious soak in a hot bubble bath, Brittney changed into a nightgown and settled into her king-size four-poster bed.

Her parents' drunken laughter carried up from downstairs.

Mother spoke in a fake, Zsa Zsa Gabor wannabe voice she'd been affecting lately. "Can you believe that Cora Neery dared to show her face at the gala tonight? I would have thought that she would be persona non grata after the incident at the charity ball last month. Some people have no sense of class."

Brittney's father cleared his throat and spoke in a grating, patronizing tone. "The Neerys have more money than us and are friends with Mr. Hogadane, punkin'. They'll always be able to behave as they like, unlike us, who weren't allowed among their ranks before my promotion."

"Well, I still think she's a tacky hussy," Mother sniffed. Daddy must have made some sort of expression of disapproval, for Mother's voice shifted back to normal. "I *am* of course grateful for the improvement of our circumstances. You've worked so hard for our family."

They have me to thank, Britney thought furiously. *If I hadn't learned the mysteries of the occult and called forth Scar, Dad would still be a junior at Woodward & Paulson instead of a full partner, and Mother would have been getting her manicured nails dirty working at the jewelry counter at J.C. Penny. We still would have lived in that ugly subdivision on Locust Lane, and the doors of Hogadane's country club would still be slammed in our faces.*

But it wasn't her parents' misfortunes and mediocrity that had motivated Brittney to check out that book at the library on casting spells. It was the desire that every fourteen-year-old girl had.

To be pretty.

Brittney still didn't know if the spells from that first book had actually worked, though just enough things that she wanted had happened and made her think it wasn't coincidence. Her acne had cleared, and her hair *did* seem a little thicker, and the other girl competing for a spot on the cheerleading squad had indeed suffered a terrible fall and had broken her ankle. That was enough of an impetus for Brittany to delve further into the occult.

That first book mentioned the possibility of summoning spirits to do one's bidding, so she looked up books on that. Most were full of useless ghost stories, but one directed her to exactly what the spell book had promised. Only this book referred to the spirits as demons. Brittney had felt one icy shiver prickle the back of her neck before tossing her hair and deciding that it didn't matter what they were called, only that they gave her what she wanted.

Months of chants, arcane symbols and a pentagram drawn on her bedroom floor beneath her rug, three dead mice and four dead rabbits later, she brought forth Scarlionapskhis for the first time. All the demon's names were impossible to pronounce, that was the first challenge in summoning them.

Brittney called her demon "Scar" for short but learned quickly that demons did not appreciate nicknames.

The first wish Scar granted was for her dad to have enough money to buy a new wardrobe from the J.Crew and Esprit catalogs she and her friends pored over. That wish was granted when one of the partners of Woodward & Paulson Law Firm committed suicide, and her father was made into a full partner.

The wardrobe got Brittney a foot in the door with the A crowd at school, but since the queen bees, Heather Price and Jennifer Armstrong, were part of the country club set, Brittney's family had to be as well.

That wish was granted when her grandmother died shortly after visiting, leaving Brittney's mother a small fortune, and around the same time, her father landed a prestigious client, gaining the Shaws their coveted invitation to Hogadane's country club.

Wayne Hogadane was the richest man in Amteep, maybe even the entire northwest. He owned the most prestigious country club, two giant lake cruise boats, the Amteep Resort, the Amteep Press, and, some said, the entire town. Becoming part of Hogadane's social sphere guaranteed high social status.

Brittney never returned the library books. She couldn't stand the idea of someone else gaining the power she had. Besides, she reasoned, if these books fell into the wrong hands, good people could be hurt. Demons demanded sacrifices. And while Brittney only offered up creatures that wouldn't be missed and people who were bad, like her father's mistress, someone else might not be so discerning.

***

The return to school after Christmas break had Brittney energized. She'd spent an invigorating morning at cheerleading practice in the gym, demonstrating that extra edge of agility that Scar had given her, and examining the loyalty of her friends who'd been away for the break, making sure there were no cracks in their devotion to her as their leader.

After practice, she showered and changed into one of the new outfits she got for Christmas, an oversize, off-the-shoulder cashmere sweater of the palest pink with a large matching hair ribbon, high-waisted acid-washed Guess jeans with rolled-up cuffs, a pink Swatch, and tons of new bangle bracelets. She blow-dried her hair and sprayed it until she had amazing volume.

On the way to first period, her best friend, Heather Price, leaned over and asked, "I heard you dumped Lucio Argento after Christmas."

Brittney shrugged, trying to ignore the pang of envy at Heather's new burgundy blazer. "He was beginning to bore me. Men of his breeding simply cannot understand the importance of the finer things in life."

While Heather nodded in sympathetic understanding of the vast chasm between those who had class and those who didn't, her other friend, Jennifer Armstrong, stared at her with wide, curious eyes. "Is it true that Lucio's dad is a mobster?"

She shrugged. "He's a restaurant owner. I barely saw the man. Besides, if I'd learned the truth, I wouldn't be alive to tell it, now would I?"

Later, at lunch, Brittney couldn't fight off a pang of bittersweet regret when she saw Lucio in the cafeteria looking decadently gorgeous with his long black curls, and eyes dark as sin, which perfectly complemented his Mediterranean complexion.

The narrow arching upper lip made him look a little wicked, while his full lower lip promised sensuality. His square jaw and broad shoulders made him look powerful and dangerous. And his large hands… She bit back a sigh, remembering how they felt on her bare skin.

He was fun while he lasted. Her friends had been amusingly awed that she was dating "a bad boy," and the popular guys had been driven crazy by the fact that Brittney had passed them over in favor of "slumming with a dumb…" She'd never heard so many slurs for Italians in her life until she'd agitated the WASPs' nest.

Ah, but Lucio had been fantastic in bed and treated her like a queen. Brittney wasn't so sure that she'd be treated as well when she began dating someone who was her social equal. And being with him was hardly slumming.

Lucio's father owned Bava's, one of the fanciest restaurants in town, and if Mr. Argento really was a member of a crime family, then he and his son weren't poor. Hell, Lucio drove a Trans Am, albeit an older one, and had motorcycle.

But Brittney wanted to be prom queen. Therefore, she needed a worthy king. And no one would vote for an Italian delinquent who'd been held back a year in tenth grade.

Her musings broke as she crashed into Jamie Blair, a friend back in Brittney's middle-class days, now a pariah who must be avoided at all costs.

Brittney fixed her with a glower. "Watch it, trailer trash."

Jamie backed away, her black hair falling forward to hide her reddening face. But her light brown eyes flashed a hint of defiance and accusation. "Watch yourself, bimbo," Jamie's retort was barely audible as she retreated.

If I hadn't been staring at Lucio like an idiot, I wouldn't have bumped into her. I need to focus on finding my king.

But Brittney couldn't let Jamie's defiance stand. "Do you want to be dumped into a trash can again?" Her friends were dutifully laughing at Jamie's retreating form.

Brittney noticed the strong arms of Chet Morgan wrapped around Heather Price's waist. Now *there* was an excellent candidate.

His sun-bleached hair and tanned skin attested to a Christmas vacation spent in a warm paradise. His eyes were the color of aquamarines, shining nearly as bright as his perfectly white, straight teeth. His shoulders were broader than Lucio's, and since Chet was quarterback of the Amteep Devils, he was also more muscular.

And he was definitely more fashionable, looking like he stepped out of the latest L.L.Bean catalog, with his sandy-blond Ken Doll hair, popped-collar polo shirts, and loose-fit tan slacks.

Yes, Brittney mused as she appraised her best friend's boyfriend. *Chet would be a perfect prom king. A lot of people would vote for him because he's the quarterback. He should be with me anyway since I'm head cheerleader.*

She closed her eyes and pictured him being crowned beside her. It should be easy enough to snare him, either with her charms or with magic if she needed to.

And if Heather decides to get in my way, I can get rid of her. The demon likes human flesh better than cats or dogs anyway.

Chapter Two

Lucio watched Brittney shove Jamie, a quiet girl who had English and auto shop class with him.

"Watch it, trailer trash," Brittney snarled while her sycophantic friends laughed. Jamie's retort was so quiet that Lucio couldn't hear. Whatever she'd said made Brittney threaten to throw her in a garbage can again.

Again? Lucio frowned. His ex-girlfriend was a bigger bully than he'd realized.

He watched Brittney flutter her eyelashes at Chet Morgan and favor him with one of her sparkling smiles before she joined the quarterback and her fellow cheerleaders at the table they always dominated.

Lucio still couldn't believe he'd allowed a monster like her to break his heart.

As if to punish such idiocy, the memory of that depressing Christmas Eve tormented him again.

"You want to break up?" Lucio hated the weak crack in his voice. *"I thought we—"* were in love, *he'd almost said, but swallowed the words,* "—had something good going on."

Brittney closed the velvet box holding the emerald pendant that Lucio had gotten after busting his ass at his dad's restaurant for months. She barely even glanced at it before handing it back and announcing that she no longer wanted anything to do with him.

She placed her soft hand over his rough one, and gave him a pouting look that was supposed to convey sympathy, but her sky-blue eyes were empty. "I care a lot about you, and what we had was very special. But Lucio, don't you remember that we talked about this? You know this wasn't going to be forever. I want to be prom queen."

"Prom?" Lucio couldn't believe she was bringing up something so petty now. "That's a whole five months away."

Brittney rolled her eyes and spoke slowly, as if Lucio were a child instead of a year older than her. "To win the crown, I'll need a proper king. That will take time."

No, it wouldn't. Brittney could wrap any guy around her little finger. And although the last thing Lucio wanted was to become one of the jocks or country club yuppie types who'd qualify to be prom king, the reminder that she didn't consider him worthy to be with her and never had still stung.

At least Lucio hadn't fallen on his knees and offered to try to change for her. Nor had he tried to convince her to stay with him a little longer to delay the inevitable. Not even when she'd tried to climb on his lap and asked him to take her up to his room one last time.

No need to embarrass himself further.

Instead, he'd let her walk out the door into the snowy afternoon and immediately went back to the jewelry store to return the necklace. Sure, he'd spent the rest of Christmas vacation alone and heartbroken, thinking of the midnight kiss on New Year's Eve he'd been anticipating and of how pathetic he'd been to have almost wasted his savings on that expensive necklace for a shallow bitch who didn't love him.

But by the time Christmas break ended, and he found himself back in the hellish halls of Amteep High, Lucio felt like an invisible lead cloak had been lifted from his shoulders. No more tense lunches with Brittney's friends where they regarded him with patronizing smiles and pointed remarks about his social standing and criminal record. No more being dragged to even more uncomfortable parties at the country club, where his long hair had been scrutinized in an entirely different way than usual, and people inquired about his religion and ethnicity in hushed tones and then sighing in relief to learn that he was Italian.

When Brittney had explained that certain classes of people were barred from entry, Lucio had been sickened. It took all her cajoling to make him stay, and even more wheedling to convince him to return.

Now he'd never have to go back to that cesspool of prejudice, snobbery, and ridiculous clothes. And he'd never have to hear

Brittney ask him to cut his hair, or to wear one of the stupid polo shirts and lame slacks she'd convinced him to buy. He'd already donated all those clothes to the Humane Society Thrift Store.

The ache in his heart gave way to relaxed muscles and easier breathing. *Freedom.*

And yet his pride still stung. Bitter anger took place of the hurt. Brittney's utter callousness in breaking up with him for a petty title in a stupid high school dance that wouldn't matter even a month later made him realize how shallow she was. She'd used him up and tossed him aside with no regard to his feelings.

And now, watching her shove Jamie Blair and snarl, "Watch it, trailer trash," and threaten her, Lucio's fury morphed into new determination. Brittney had dumped Lucio because she wanted to be prom queen. So Lucio would do everything in his power to make sure that the crown went to another girl.

How he would accomplish such a thing, he had no idea. The details would be figured out later. Except for the first thing. He needed to enlist a girl who'd not only be a worthy contender for prom queen, but who would be willing to cooperate with his plan.

As he watched the most beautiful and popular girls at Amteep High grin at Brittney and point and laugh along with her at Sally Fenton, a heavyset girl who was kind to everyone and shared her history notes with him, Lucio knew he couldn't bear to team up with any of those malicious snobs.

But, as he'd reminded Brittney the night that she broke up with him, prom was five months away—plenty of time to find a diamond in the rough.

The bell rang and he left the cafeteria on his way to shop class, but he was intercepted by Stacey Johnson, who purposefully dropped her books in front of him.

"Hi, Lucio," she purred when he bent to help her pick them up, giving him a great view of her cleavage beneath her oversize sweatshirt.

There was no denying Stacey was a beauty, with her chocolate ringlets and baby blue eyes. And she wasn't in Brittney's circle of friends. Maybe...

But then she said, "I hear you're a free man again. I've always wanted to take a walk on the wild side. I'm free this weekend if you want to give me a thrill."

Lucio shoved her books into her arms. "If you want a thrill, go spend the night in the Raimi House."

He tried to tamp down the sudden, visceral burst of disgust that boiled in his gut. He'd never been bothered by his reputation as a dangerous rebel before. Hell, he used to encourage such talk. Better than them learning that he only had bad grades because he had a learning disability. Better to be seen as dangerous instead of dumb.

And yet, having a girl pursue him for the same reason Brittney had, for the so-called thrill and cred of being with a bad boy, now felt dehumanizing as well as dishonest.

Sure, he'd spent a few months in Juvenile Detention and had gotten picked up by the cops for a few random offenses that his wealthier peers got away with, but it wasn't like he was a murderer or a drug dealer or anything.

Lucio shook his head. He'd worry about his own dating prospects later. Way later, like maybe after college. In fact, the girl he recruited to win the crown at the prom needed to be someone who wasn't interested in him because he'd have to find her a different guy who could be prom king.

Brittney had been right that he was not the right guy for that.

As he entered the auto shop and grabbed his coveralls from his locker, Lucio wondered if maybe he should focus on finding a prom king first. After all, a more likeable guy would probably have better luck pitching the plan to a suitable girl.

His gaze scanned the guys in his shop class. Not many letterman jackets and Ivy Leaguers here. Except for Todd Banks. He was a varsity track star and was well liked by almost everyone because of his class clown antics. The girls seemed to adore him too.

Except for one.

A feminine growl rang out. "What the fuck, Todd?"

Lucio turned to see Jamie Blair, the only girl in their shop class, holding a dead mouse by its tail.

Todd laughed, though disappointment glimmered in his ice-blue eyes that he hadn't gotten a squeal of fright out of her. "What's the matter, ragamuffin, can't take a joke?"

Todd had it out for Jamie ever since she embarrassed him in the beginning of the school year by pointing out that the way he had the multimeter hooked up to an alternator would break his tester. He hadn't listened and there'd been a loud pop and an expensive piece of school equipment was destroyed.

Jamie glared up at Todd. "I fail to see the humor in having a health hazard dropped down the back of my coveralls."

A few more guys laughed.

"Health hazard?" Mike Bronson quipped. "You should be used to that, trailer trash."

Trailer trash... that's what Brittney and her friends called Jamie. Lucio had often wondered why Brittney was so hostile to Jamie in particular. She was mean to other girls, but with Jamie there seemed to be an extra degree of malice.

Their teacher, Mr. Hobbs, broke up the argument, urging them all to go to their assigned seats at the table at the back of the garage. They were having a quiz on steering systems.

Lucio groaned with dread. He *hated* tests. Hated the way the words on the paper jumbled around as his heart pounded in time with the ticking clock.

Taking a deep breath, he tried to slowly read each word of the questions by dragging his pencil under them. But the tactic failed most of the time, leaving him to guess at the multiple-choice questions, and bomb the one-sentence answers.

Afterward, he wiped the sweat from his brow and met his shop partner at their assigned toolbox. They were going to learn how to change wheel bearings.

As they gathered around one of the practice cars to watch Mr. Hobbs demonstrate, Lucio's eyes kept straying to Jamie. Todd was badgering her again, but whatever she said back to him made Todd flinch. Her light brown eyes blazed like burnished amber.

She was really quite pretty, Lucio realized with a bit of shock.

Her hair, pinned up in a messy bun to avoid getting grimy from the shop, was a shiny blue-black that looked like it would be silky to the touch. Her skin was smooth over high cheekbones, and her lips formed a perfect cupid's bow that reminded him of Snow White.

Her figure was tough to determine in the shapeless coveralls, but working from memory, Lucio pictured her in a shimmering formal gown.

Jamie would be a knockout.

But she was practically a pariah. Did he dare take on what would be a likely impossible challenge of turning a not-so-ugly duckling into a beautiful, celebrated swan?

Memories of Brittney shoving Jamie and calling her trailer trash flashed through Lucio's mind, along with other repulsive incidents where Jamie had been bullied.

Yes.

Jamie would be his prom queen, Lucio decided. If the girl Brittney spent all of high school looking down at stole her crown— that would be like salt in a wound.

Chapter Three

After shop class was finished for the day, Jamie shrugged out of her coveralls and bent down to unlace her shoes to get them off.

But someone stepped on the back of the coveralls, making her pitch forward. Strong arms caught her shoulders and steadied her. She looked up to see Lucio Argento peering at her with mingled concern and something else. Those dark chocolate eyes looked past her shoulder and narrowed on the asshole who'd tripped her.

"Leave her alone," he growled with such menace that Jamie shivered.

No surprise, Todd's voice whined behind her. "Aw c'mon. I was just having a little fun. If she wants to be one of the guys, she's gonna have to be able to handle a little joking."

"And since when do we put dead animals inside another guy's clothes?" Lucio asked with a raised eyebrow.

Todd's tanned face reddened. "Whatever. Wops have no sense of humor."

Jamie frowned at the slur he'd called Lucio as Todd slammed his locker shut and retreated. She turned back to Lucio and fought to speak past the fluttery feeling in her stomach. "Thanks for defending me, b-but I can take care of myself."

"I know you can." Instead of seeming like he was humoring her, he sounded sincere. "But I'm sick of watching him be a prick to you every day."

The warmth in his eyes made her belly flip-flop.

"Okay, thanks." Jamie slung her backpack over her shoulder, wincing as the worn canvas made a noise of protest. "I'll see you tomorrow in English class."

He stopped her with a light tap on her shoulder. "Hey, do you want to get some burgers at Topper Too after school?"

White-hot lightning seemed to strike her chest. Was Lucio Argento asking her out? What if it was a trick? The time Shane Lowry asked her to homecoming and stood her up as a joke back in sophomore year still stung. No, she couldn't risk it.

"I... um..." She took a deep breath and spoke in a rush. "I have a lot of homework to catch up on, then I gotta go to work."

Before he could reply, she fled.

As Jamie wove through the mass of students in the hall, her mind spun with shock and confusion at Lucio's asking her out for burgers.

What if it's not a joke? A tempting voice whispered in her head. *After all, he stood up for you in shop class and never joined Brittney in taunting you. Maybe he really likes you.*

Another voice countered cynically. *He also didn't do anything to interfere when his girlfriend at the time was giving me shit, so maybe not.*

Jamie trudged into her next classroom, rubbing her temples in an effort to silence the arguing voices. *I don't have time to worry about Lucio, no matter how gorgeous he is. I need to get through this class.*

Thankfully, instead of a pop quiz or a lecture, Mr. Davis, the government teacher, had them watch a documentary on the progress of Reagan's War on Drugs.

Allison Winthrop, Jamie's friend since sixth grade, leaned over. "You look dazed. Did something juicy happen since lunch?"

Jamie squirmed inwardly before spilling. "Lucio Argento asked me if I wanted to get burgers with him."

"Holy shit," Allison breathed. "Brittney Shaw's ex-boyfriend asked you out? What did you say?"

"That I was too busy." Jamie's low whisper was directed at her folded hands. Her shoulders tensed as she braced herself for her friend's response.

Allison abandoned all efforts to whisper. "Why would you say that?"

Mr. Davis rose from his desk and his stern voice rang out. "Miss Winthrop, would you and Miss Blair like to continue your conversation in detention?"

"No, Mr. Davis," Allison answered with sufficient humility.

Jamie was grateful for the darkness of the classroom. No one could see that she was probably bright as a tomato.

After the teacher settled back into the swivel chair behind his massive desk, Jamie opened her Trapper Keeper and tore out a sheet of notebook paper to finish the conversation in writing. Allison did the same.

Jamie wrote out a reply and passed it to her friend: *I don't want to be the butt of another joke.*

Allison's pen moved like the wind before she passed the paper back to Jamie: *Has he ever joined Bitch-ney in bullying you?*

No. Once more, she thought of how he stood up for her in auto shop class and felt warm all over.

Then maybe he actually likes you.

That stupid swoony feeling threatened to return as her inner voice jumped at Allison's agreement with her earlier positive analysis. Jamie's jaw clenched as she scrawled her reply.

I don't think it's a good idea to get involved with him.

Allison smirked and wrote lightning fast.

Is it because he was held back a year, or because he's a delinquent? I heard he vandalized a lot of businesses and destroyed some property. But it's not like he held up a gas station or killed someone.

Jamie shook her head.

Honestly, she'd admired Lucio's graffiti on the otherwise barren walls in the alleys. Her favorite had been a well-detailed painting of a guy with a mummified face wearing an old English redcoat military jacket, and holding a British flag.

And when he'd toilet-papered part of Mr. Hogadane's mansion, she and her mom had cheered when they'd seen it on the news. Mr. Hogadane pretty much owned the town of Amteep and did everything in his power to cater to the rich people who had summer homes, and the rich people who lived here year-round, and, of course, the rich tourists. To make things more appealing to those rich people, he trampled the poor.

Jamie had egged his mailbox one Halloween.

No, Lucio's so-called criminal record didn't bother her in the slightest.

The bell rang before she could write a response to Allison. Jamie shoved her Trapper Keeper in her bag and tried to flee, but Allison wasn't going to let her off so easily. She gathered her stuff and stayed glued to Jamie's side as they made their way out of the classroom and into the chaotic hallway.

"You should seriously say yes and go out with him," Allison said. "I'm begging you. You would drive Bitch-ney crazy."

"I'll think about it, okay?"

Allison gave her a quick hug. "Call me tonight."

Through the rest of her last class, Jamie struggled with her resolve to avoid Lucio, and the temptation to change her answer and go out with the bad boy of Amteep High. To have a chance to reach out and touch one of those long dark chocolate curls of his and see if they were as soft as they looked was an itch that needed to be scratched.

After the final bell rang, she ran out the door into the cold January wind like a demon was chasing her. Her speed didn't dislodge the devil that was already on her shoulder, but at least she got to the senior parking lot and into her car before the lot turned into a disaster.

A familiar car revved its engine behind her. Jamie looked in the rearview mirror to see Lucio Argento looking wickedly handsome behind the wheel of his black 1978 Trans Am. For a moment, it looked like he'd block her in her parking spot, but then he zoomed on, the dual mufflers growling.

Maybe breaking up with the most popular girl in school had made him crazy. Jamie shook her head and flipped on the radio to drown out her thoughts. The Clash's "Rock the Casbah" came on and she sang along the best she could.

When she got home to the Springwood Trailer Park, her heart sank as she saw a bright new missing pet sign.

"Oh no," she breathed. "Not Ralphie."

Her neighbor's white and brown terrier mix hadn't come home last night. Mrs. Ambrose had been frantic this morning when she'd intercepted Jamie on her way to school, asking if Jamie had seen him.

Her neighbor's worry was more than valid. A *lot* of animals, mostly dogs, had been disappearing from the trailer park for the past couple years and, more recently, in other neighborhoods. Maybe longer, since few people kept track of the stray cats.

Jamie's mom and a few other residents of the trailer park had been bringing up their concerns in city council meetings, but their stories fell on deaf ears because nobody cared about trailer park residents losing their pets.

But when some animals were found mutilated in the woods near a suburban development, the city of Amteep began to pay attention. Whispers about the supposed rise of Satanism began to circulate, and the police now combed the cemeteries and abandoned houses looking for a rumored cult. But all they did was disrupt the spooky kids who wore all black, and some poor homeless people.

Jamie gave the missing poster of Ralphie one last fearful glance. She hoped with all her heart that the sweet dog would be found alive and in one piece.

The rickety steps to her trailer groaned as she made her way up to the chipped front door. She needed to see if she could scavenge good boards somewhere to replace the rotting wood.

Mom called a cheerful greeting from the kitchen as Jamie shrugged off her backpack and hugged her fat fluffy black cat, Shadow. The smell of chili made her salivate.

"Did you know that Ralphie's missing?" Jamie said, worry for the dog surpassing all thoughts of her strange day.

Mom shook her head. "I hope he comes home. Mrs. Ambrose adores that little mutt. I don't know what she'd do without him."

Jamie went into the kitchen and stirred the chili. "Do you think they'll ever catch the person who's doing this? I don't believe the news stories about a satanic cult. I think it's some sicko."

"Me too." Mom shuddered. "It's a good thing Shadow is too lazy to go outside much. Anyway, I don't want to talk about those poor animals. Do you work tonight?"

"Yeah." Jamie couldn't hide her sullen tone. The last thing she wanted to do was go back out into that snowy cold.

"Damn. I was hoping for a movie night with you." Mom pouted. "I have the night off and I got some microwave popcorn."

Jamie studied her mom, worrying at the exhaustion revealed in her voice. Despite the smile lines around her full lips and the dark circles around her blue eyes, Leigh Blair was still a beautiful woman with a slim, slightly muscled figure.

Her long, golden blonde hair was shot with strands of silver at the roots, though Jamie knew she'd dye it soon. Leigh worked as a waitress down at The Shanty Bar, and though she was well liked and often brought home good tips, Jamie knew she was burnt out from the job. Especially when assholes were at the bar. There was always at least one.

Jamie wished she could skip work, but they couldn't afford it. She managed a smile. "We close at nine on weeknights and I can use one of my free rental credits to get us a new release. And in the meantime, you can have a nap."

Mom laughed lightly. "You're the one who looks in need of a nap."

After rushing though her homework, Jamie devoured two bowls of chili and changed into her work clothes that were supposed to make her look like a concession stand worker at an old-fashioned movie theater: a crisp white linen button-up long-sleeve, burgundy vest, and black slacks.

The uniform did little to shield her from the winter chill on her drive to work, even with her heavy blue peacoat and gloves.

Prime Time Video was bright and chilly this afternoon. Mr. Bay never had the heat up high enough since he liked to dress up as an old-fashioned movie theater usher in a dark red double-breasted coat of thick velveteen with brass buttons, which hid his growing belly that strained his black slacks. The topper to the outfit was a round dark red hat trimmed with a gold braid.

As she headed to the popcorn machine to make a fresh batch for the incoming, albeit scant, weekday crowd, Mr. Bay interrupted her. "The new releases came in. Would you be a dear and apply the rewind stickers? And speaking of, there's a stack of tapes that didn't get rewound. I'm considering charging a fee when they do that, but I don't want to drive people to that accursed Family Video that's already cut into my business."

Jamie bit back a groan. She loathed putting the "Be Kind, Please Rewind" stickers on the tapes. She always screwed up a few and it was such a pain in the ass to redo them.

But she did like rewinding the movies. Especially when the boss left and she could rewind them the slow way, where she could see the scenes of various movies running backwards. If they looked intriguing enough, Jamie would use her employee discount to bring them home to watch with Mom.

Unfortunately, Mr. Bay lingered for an eternity, examining the racks for dust, grousing over tapes shelved out of order, and uneven lines on the carpet from the vacuum.

When he finally shut the door behind him, Jamie ejected the store copy of *Wizard of Oz* that the boss seemed to want to play daily, and put a copy of *The Blob* in the VCR.

She had only three more tapes to sticker before she could move on to rewinding. She peeled another rewind sticker off the roll, prepared to put it on the third store copy of *Porky's*, and jumped as the bell over the door chimed.

Lucio strolled into the store, his dark eyes glimmering with triumph and some other emotion she couldn't place. He looked dark and dangerous in his black leather jacket, distressed jeans, motorcycle boots, and Dokken t-shirt. He smiled at her, revealing gleaming white teeth.

"Fuck," Jamie burst out as the rewind sticker got stuck to her finger. Her face heated. "I'm sorry, that wasn't directed at you."

Lucio's dimples deepened with his broadening grin. "I had no idea that *you* had to put those stickers on those tapes. But then again, I suppose someone has to. I'd never thought about it before."

Jamie refused to allow herself to melt under the force of that smile. "How did you know I worked here? Did you follow me?"

"Whoa." Lucio held up his hands in mock surrender. "I've been renting movies here for years. In fact, I was here last Saturday night. You were pretty busy putting tapes back on the shelf, but you rang me up."

Oh shit. She *did* remember that. She'd been a nervous mess and screwed up on the register because she was too busy ogling him. Then there were the times where he'd been in here with Brittney Shaw and she'd overheard them bickering over what to rent. Brittney's choices were always horrible, and she treated Jamie like a lowly servant.

"I'm sorry," Jamie said, trying not to get lost in Lucio's eyes. "C-can I help you find anything?"

Lucio acknowledged her apology with an incline of his head. "I was gonna browse the horror section and catch up on all the ones I've missed over the past six months."

Bitterness laced his voice and Jamie put together the timeline. That was how long he'd been dating Brittney. Was he bitter because he wasn't over her, or because he couldn't rent horror movies when he was with her?

She reprimanded herself for hoping it was the latter. "Well, I definitely recommend *The Howling*."

"Sold." Lucio strolled to the horror section and grabbed the newly released horror movie. Jamie admired the muscles in his back and shoulders shifting beneath the tight black T-shirt he wore. But when he returned to the counter, he banished her relief that he was only here to check out a movie. "But also, is there a way I can convince you to reconsider my offer to talk over dinner? Or lunch. I'm not particular."

"We're talking now," she said desperately, trying to focus on the cash register. "That'll be a dollar and sixty-seven cents."

Lucio shook his head and counted out the correct change. "I don't think it's fair to have this particular conversation while you're working." Right on cue, the bell dinged as a middle-aged couple walked in. "And now you have customers. But we could go tomorrow for lunch if you're still too busy after school."

Damn it. She didn't have much of an excuse. "Okay. Lunch at Topper Too tomorrow."

Once more, that brilliant, dimpled smile stole her breath. "Great. I'll meet you in the parking lot and we can take my car."

"I'll take my own car." No way was she going to incite a bunch of unnecessary gossip at being seen in his Trans Am. "Um, that way I can make sure to get back to class."

One of his dark eyebrows rose. "You don't trust me?"

She crossed her arms over her chest. "I don't trust anyone."

He cocked his head to the side. "Pretty cynical way to be."

Jamie shrugged and waved him aside so she could help the next customers. Lucio's low laughter tickled her senses as he walked out the door.

She spent the rest of her shift in a distracted daze, burning with curiosity as to what Lucio wanted to talk to her about. Did he want to date her? Or was it something mundane, like a request to help him with one of his classes? And if it was the latter, why didn't he bring it up in shop class? He worked near her often, since the shop only had four bays and two hydraulic lifts.

It was only when she closed up for the night and locked the door that her inner heat turned into a chill.

The telephone pole she'd parked next to was covered with new missing pet signs.

Chapter Four

Lucio fidgeted at the table at Topper Too, a 1950s-themed diner famous for their burgers and milkshakes. In the summer, you could order your food outside from your car and have a cute girl on roller skates bring it to you. In the winter, everyone huddled inside and fought over the jukebox and pinball table. Someone had put on that annoying Madonna song, "Material Girl." Brittney adored it and had abused his tape deck with the cassette.

He twisted his paper straw wrapper into various shapes as he watched the parking lot for a sign of Jamie's car. She wouldn't stand him up, would she? There was plenty of snow falling from the iron-gray sky to give her an excuse.

Then, her red 1973 Honda Civic hatchback puttered into the icy parking lot, the holes in its muffler making the thing audible even through the windows of the diner. Still, the little car was kind of cute, even if it looked like a roller skate and its paint was faded and chipped. He wondered what it would take to restore it.

All thoughts of the car dissolved like morning fog when Jamie stepped out of the car. Like her vehicle, her clothes were old and faded.

The blue jeans she wore resembled the distressed ones at the mall that rich girls spent fortunes to get. But the tears and lightness on the legs of Jamie's jeans clearly came from being worn during hard work and being washed constantly. However, the supple hips and shapely legs that the denim hugged were more interesting.

As she walked into the diner, Lucio forced his gaze up, past the patched blue wool peacoat that concealed her curves, and up to her face.

The obnoxious song ended and "Earth Angel" played on the antique jukebox, completely fitting for her entrance.

Yes, those high cheekbones rivaled those of Olivia Newton John's in *Grease*, and Jamie's shiny black hair framed her heart-shaped face, providing a contrast to her pale ivory skin and light brown eyes that almost looked gold.

With a few changes to her clothes and makeup, Jamie Blair would be a stunning beauty. One who could outshine Amteep High's elite, and most importantly, the reigning beauty, Brittney Shaw.

Jamie's voice interrupted his musings. "Why are you looking at me like you've never seen me before?"

His gaze swept over the snowflakes melting in her hair like captive jewels before he blurted, "Because you're beautiful."

Roses bloomed on her cheeks as she sat down, then her lush lips quirked in an adorable frown. "You've been in classes with me since sophomore year. What's up with your sudden interest?"

He cleared his throat and tried to sound professional. "I have a proposition for you."

Those blue eyes widened with horror and she shook her head. "Oh no, I'm not going to be your rebound ride."

"No, it's nothing like that," Lucio assured her quickly.

"Then what is it?" She crossed her arms over her chest, visibly trembling with defensiveness.

She was so prickly that he was torn between the urge to flinch and the urge to hug her. Lucio weighed his words, trying to figure out the best way to explain what he wanted. However, he was never good at dancing around a subject, slowly warming someone up to a topic. He'd always spoken plainly.

Even the server giving him more time by taking their orders didn't help.

"I want to help you to become prom queen," he said bluntly.

"What?" Her outburst was loud enough to make every head turn in the diner. She hunched over and lowered her voice, maintaining her suspicious glare. "I don't want to be prom queen."

Lucio blinked at her, taken aback. He thought all girls coveted that crown and prestigious high school milestone. His mind raced, trying to figure out what to say next. "Would you consider it as a favor to me?"

Her pretty mouth twisted in confusion. "How would me being prom queen help you?"

Once more, he settled on blunt honesty. "Revenge on Brittney Shaw."

Fighting back embarrassment, he told her why Brittney broke up with him. In the midst of his story, their food was delivered: burgers, fries, and a shake for him, a mere basket of fries for her. Lucio wished he would have insisted on ordering for her, but he hadn't wanted her to get the mistaken idea that this was a date.

"Damn, that's messed up," Jamie said when he finished his tale of the breakup. Her eyes softened slightly.

To avoid getting lost in those amber depths, Lucio brought the subject back to his plan. "I want to see her lose the crown and be crushed."

"Then why not spread the word and convince people to vote for one of her biggest rivals?" Jamie squirted some fry sauce into a paper dip cup. "I mean, Stacey Johnson or Heather Price could easily win."

"At first, I was going to go that route." Lucio remembered the predatory way Stacey had looked at him yesterday. But he didn't want to get into that with Jamie. "But then I saw Brittney pick on you in the cafeteria. I know she bullies you constantly, so if you won prom queen, it would be giant salt in her wound."

"Bullying is sometimes an understatement." Jamie's mouth twisted in a bitter frown as she dipped her fry. "I wish I knew why she and her friends are so awful to me."

"It's because you have the one thing they can't buy." Lucio pointed a French fry at her. "Natural beauty. Jeez, girl. When's the last time you looked in a mirror? Your hair is thick, shiny, and a shade of black that can't be bottled without looking fake. Your skin is perfect, and your nose and cheekbones can't be duplicated with plastic surgery. Your eyes are a unique color. Seriously, how do you not know that you're beautiful?"

Jamie shrugged, but the flush of pink in her cheeks and the tips of her ears belied her composure. "I d-don't feel beautiful. And in the long run, it doesn't matter what I look like. I mean, I'm trailer trash, and no one at that hellhole of our school is going to forget that."

Lucio flinched at her blasé, self-deprecating description of herself. Coupled with her resignation to remaining trapped, Jamie's words squeezed his heart and fired his will to prove her wrong. "I disagree. I think that if I can get you the right clothes and makeup, the perception will change. Besides, it's not like you're going to stay in that trailer park. You'll go to college and get a good job. You're brilliant and talented. I've seen that enough in auto shop and all the other classes I've had with you over the years."

Jamie didn't reply. Instead, she stared at him as she ate her fries in quick, furtive movements, like an adorable mouse.

Lucio polished off his burger and returned to his plan. "I really think we can do this. Now, Brittney's probably right that I'm not prom king material, so we'll have to find a king for you as well, but when I'm done with you, you'll have candidates lining up."

Was it his imagination, or did she look disappointed that she wouldn't be dating him? For a moment, disappointment panged him as well. She certainly wasn't the type to dump someone because they'd impede her efforts at a superficial prize.

"Wait, what do I get out of this?" Jamie fixed him with a narrowed gaze. "You get your revenge on Brittney, and though I'd love to see her face when she loses the crown, that doesn't mean *I* want to be prom queen, if such a ridiculous thing were possible. And I certainly wouldn't want to date any of the guys who'd be the type to be nominated as prom king. They've all treated me like shit since elementary school."

Lucio held up his hands in surrender. "Okay. There's no law that you have to be dating. Only your date for one night. I can call in some favors if need be to get the right guy on board. But we have months to work that out. Right now, we need to focus on you. Wardrobe change… makeup, accessories—"

"Wait." Jamie cut him off. "I didn't say yes to any of this. I think your plan is insane. I'm not going to be your Eliza Doolittle and let you be my Henry Higgins. I wouldn't be surprised if you're also doing this to win a bet and your story about wanting revenge on Brittney is bullshit. If you were telling the truth, you would have picked someone better, like Heather or Stacey, to play *Pygmalion* with."

"Who's Eliza Doolittle? Or Henry Higgins?"

One of her dark brows rose. "*My Fair Lady*? We had to read the play in English class last semester."

"Oh." Shame crept into his tone. Lucio had struggled so badly with reading the play that he'd relied on the movie to aid him with the related assignments. "Well, now you know why I'm failing that class...again."

"I didn't mean—" Jamie broke off and rose from the table. "Never mind. I'm going back to class. Find someone else to play your game with."

She took her tray with the single empty cardboard French fry container and paper dip cup of fry sauce to the garbage in the corner and disposed of them with prim neatness before walking out the door, head held high like the queen he wanted her to be.

Lucio rose from the table and disposed of the remnants of his lunch. His shoulders slumped with defeat.

As he got in his car and headed back to class, he tried to tell himself that he should take Jamie's advice and return to his original plan to recruit one of the already popular girls in his mission to make anyone but Brittney the prom queen.

And yet... he didn't want to give up on Jamie. Not because her victory would spite Brittney the most, but Jamie's tired resignation to remaining an outcast niggled him like a mournful song stuck in his head.

Lucio had never been anything resembling popular, but his social standing was different. People feared him instead of bullying him. And Jamie had probably never been in a school situation where she felt welcome. She didn't fit in with the popular crowd because of her economic status, but he didn't see her with most of the nerds either, even though he knew she was smart and got good grades: probably why his troublemaker crowd didn't embrace her either.

The scorn in Brittney's voice when she'd called Jamie "trailer trash" superimposed itself over Jamie's tired tone when she called herself that.

That's why Jamie wanted to meet me here during lunch instead of having me pick her up after school. She didn't want me to see the trailer park where she lives. It was probably either Springwood or Whispering Pines.

Lucio's hands tightened on the steering wheel. The movie *Carrie* popped into his head. Could he be like Tommy Ross and give Jamie the prom she deserved and the victory over those who scorned her? Minus the pig's blood and telekinetic apocalypse, of course.

If he was going to get Jamie on his side, he needed to change his strategy. Find a way to spend more time with her so she knew he wasn't lying about wanting revenge and wouldn't make her part of a bet or the butt of a joke.

As he pulled into the senior parking lot, an idea began to form in his mind.

Chapter Five

Jamie drove home from school, shoulders slumped, and shivering behind the wheel of her little Honda. Winter was the only time she didn't love this car. The heater rattled ineffectually, bringing only enough warmth to keep the windows from fogging up. Her gloved hands gripped the fake leather-wrapped steering wheel, her mood as gray as the January sky above. Snow fell relentlessly, her mind darting in tandem with the windshield wipers.

Humiliation burned beneath her ribcage, warming her more than her car's feeble contributions. Here she'd been thinking Lucio Argento wanted to date her. She'd smugly planned her refusal to let him seduce her, to use her as a rebound. Oh, he wanted to use her, all right, but as a tool of revenge against his ex.

Why that stung so much, she didn't know.

Okay, fine. She'd melted at the way he'd looked at her when she'd walked into the diner. For a moment, she'd forgotten all about the few classmates who'd seen them having lunch together, and what they'd say about it in school later. Instead, she'd basked in the heat of his gaze, knees weakening when he called her beautiful that first time.

Then he'd thrown ice water on her dreamy daze when he'd revealed the reason for his interest in her.

And yet, her heart had stuttered again the second time he'd called her beautiful.

The clinical way he'd said it had given her heart an unbidden twinge of pain. If he'd called her beautiful, talked about her hair and lips with any warmth in his tone, the careful shield she'd maintained around her heart may have punctured. Maybe it was just as well. The last thing she needed was to become part of Lucio's deranged revenge and rebound plot, and while he was doing it, get her heart broken.

She wondered why he'd looked so bitter when she'd clarified her *My Fair Lady* reference. Then she remembered that he got held back in tenth grade. Maybe the reminder that he wasn't smart hurt him.

Guilt squirmed in her belly like eels.

But, come to think of it, Lucio didn't seem dumb. Except for dating Brittney, but all guys were morons when it came to beautiful girls. Was he really telling the truth about wanting revenge on his ex?

Reluctantly, Jamie had to admit that she would be the perfect candidate to make Brit losing prom queen a bitter pill. Brittney had been mean to her since the first day of sixth grade. Before that, they'd sort of been friends, through a mutual friend, Margaret Chelan. They'd have occasional sleepovers at Brittney's house or in Margaret's tree house.

Then, Margaret moved away and Brittney's dad got a job at a law firm and they'd moved from their run-down apartment to a nicer neighborhood. Brittney decided she was too good for Jamie, first telling her to get away from her at school because Jamie's presence embarrassed her, then, when Brittney's family got richer, she became outright cruel to impress her new rich friends.

Jamie still had nightmares of the time back in ninth grade when Brittney and Heather Price beat her with wet towels in the locker room until her skin was red and raw.

But would taking the crown from Brittney at prom be worth it? Jamie still felt conspicuous and vulnerable after all the stares and whispers she'd gotten since she was seen at Topper Too with Lucio. Heather Price had stared at her the whole time, making it nearly impossible to concentrate on Lucio's proposition. Maybe it would have been better to go out with him after school like he'd wanted. She had tonight off, so there was no excuse.

No. Being with him in the darkness of night would have made it way too intimate. Why, she couldn't say. And the idea of being intimate with him scared her.

Finally, she pulled into the Springwood Trailer Park and guided her car into the narrow driveway. All she wanted was a hot bath and then to talk to Mom for advice on what to do when a devastatingly handsome guy wanted to make you into prom queen.

Ice mixed with dirt crunched beneath her snow boots. The trailer was dark because Mom was at work, and leaving a light on cost money. The thermostat was kept down to sixty for the same reason.

Her heart heavy with the need to confide in someone, her body shivering and aching with the need to be warm, Jamie trudged up the creaking wood steps.

"Jamie," a voice called. "Wanna come in for a hot toddy?"

Some of the tension gripping her released as she turned to see Mrs. Miller and her daughter, Arlene, beckoning her two trailers down. Arlene had been in a lot of Jamie's classes since elementary school. But then she'd had to drop out at the end of junior year 'cause she got pregnant.

Jamie hesitated in her driveway, longing tugging her back from her dark, unwelcoming porch.

Mom wouldn't be home for another two hours, and leaving the lights off and the thermostat down would save money.

Some tension in her shoulders eased as she succumbed. "Gladly. I'll be right there."

The Millers' trailer was a scene of comfort and chaos. Baby toys littered the otherwise well-vacuumed gray carpet. The small black-and-white television set played a videocassette of *Snow White and the Seven Dwarfs*. Jamie smiled, remembering rebuilding that VCR with Mom, and gifting it to Arlene for her baby shower.

Mrs. Miller passed the hot toddies around in mismatched mugs. Jaime sat on the faded couch and inhaled the sweet scent of rum, honey, and lemon. For a moment, she held the steaming mug, letting the warmth seep into her hands.

Arlene sipped hers and leaned forward. "You have to tell me what our old pals at Amteep High are up to these days."

Acid laced the word "pals." Jamie was one of the only friends to visit Arlene since she dropped out.

"Same shit, different day." Jamie took a deep drink of the hot toddy, savoring the taste, and enjoying the warmth the rum brought to her chest. "Still working at the video store, and I'm trying to help Allison Winthrop pass government class, but she won't listen to my study tips. And Lucio Argento has some harebrained scheme to make me prom queen to get revenge on Brittney Shaw, the other mundane stuff—"

"Whoa, rewind that," Arlene interrupted. "Lucio Argento wants to make you prom queen? Isn't he the long-haired super-senior who spent three months in juvie last year, and whose dad is a mob boss?"

"The same, though I don't think his dad is mafia. Not all people who own Italian restaurants are crime bosses. I think that's just a thing in the movies."

Jamie had forgotten all about Bava's, one of the fanciest restaurants in town. She'd never be able to afford to eat there, a fact that stung worse whenever she had to pass near the place and smell the heavenly scent of garlic and herbs. She shook her head and took another sip of her drink. "I think those three months cost Lucio because he got held back."

"I always thought he was kinda cute," Arlene said. "But he also sorta scared me with his dark, heavy metal looks and his criminal record. What did Brittney do to him?"

"She dumped him because he wasn't prom king material."

"Well, she's right. No one would vote for him." Arlene paused and her mouth gaped comically for a moment. "Brittney Shaw was dating Lucio Argento?"

Jamie nodded. "I guess she liked the notoriety of his 'bad boy' status. Now that he's not useful to her, she tossed him away."

"So where do you fit in? No offense, but you're not exactly prom queen material. You're pretty enough, but…"

"I'm from Springwood Trailer Park," Jamie finished.

"Yeah." Arlene's voice rang with resigned knowledge. "But what if you could do it? I mean, it would be pretty awesome to see Brittney and girls like her knocked down a peg or two. And you *are* gorgeous. Who knows? The right guy could notice you and be your ticket out of this dump."

"No one escapes this dump," Mrs. Miller said coldly. She held her grandbaby over her shoulder, rubbing her back. "It's one of the biggest lies we're told. That if we work hard and pull ourselves up by our bootstraps, we'll be living the good life over in one of those cookie-cutter housing developments. Bullshit."

"That's not always true for everyone," Jamie protested. "Eric Travers managed to get that teaching job in Spokane. And Irma Quinn married a lawyer and moved to a house on Lake Skeetshue. Edward Speller joined the army and—"

"Eddie will be back here or somewhere worse, unless he makes a lifetime career out of the military. You're both too young, but I've seen our boys come home from Vietnam, all broken and poisoned from the chemicals they dropped on the jungles and poor villages that didn't deserve it. The government promised to take care of our boys when they came home. That their training would give them good jobs, health care for life. But Uncle Sam lied. Same as Craig Mendelson lied to our Arlene when he told her he'd sweep her away from here and move her into a nice house. All this time the lyin' son of a bitch was married and had another mistress on the side."

Arlene held up a hand. "Jamie already knows my tale of woe. No need to rehash it again. Besides, Jamie's definitely going to get out of here. She's smart, and has a whole plan to get a business degree and land a good career."

The confidence in Arlene's voice warmed Jamie far more than the hot toddy or the baseboard heaters in the Millers' trailer. Even better, the reminder of the stakes of her future put this prom queen thing into perspective. In less than six months, she'd never have to see any of her classmates again. Then she'd take as many college classes as she could afford, and get a business degree. What type of business she'd end up in, she didn't know, but she'd figure that out later.

The cuckoo clock chimed six and Jamie rose from the couch. "I wish I could stay longer, but I want to have the house warmed up and dinner ready for Mom."

Mrs. Miller nodded. "You tell Leigh not to be such a stranger. She's working herself too hard these days. And if she wants a hot toddy, our door is open."

"I'll tell her." Jamie put her empty mug in the sink and gave them both hugs good-bye.

Outside, the temperature had dropped at least four degrees. Farther down the lane of trailers, angry shouting carried through the chill air. The Rusks were arguing again. Jamie first hoped that the cops wouldn't come, but mostly hoped that Tina Rusk wouldn't be walking around with another bruise tomorrow. Jamie wished Tina would leave Paul. He was a drunken prick.

Inside Jamie's trailer, it was almost as cold as outside. She heard a thump as Shadow jumped down from wherever he was perching.

He mewled pitifully in that tone that told her his food bowl was empty.

She flicked on the living room light and practically ran for the thermostat, cranking it up to the blissful seventy-one degrees that she and Mom had compromised on. She scooped up Shadow and gave him a hug. His soft fur warmed and soothed her as images of missing pet signs danced in her head. If someone took him and harmed him…

Reluctantly, she put him down to turn on the kitchen light and feed him. Then she made supper. The frozen lasagna wasn't anything like one that would be served at Bava's, but it would still be delicious. Too bad there wasn't any garlic bread. But she could improvise with regular bread, Country Crock spread, and garlic salt.

By the time Mom got home, Jamie's stomach was growling.

"I have some good news," Mom said as she set down her purse. Her cheeks looked like bright red apples from the cold. "Ralphie came home. Mrs. Ambrose told me this morning. A man over on Seventh Street found him trapped in his toolshed."

"Thank God," Jamie breathed, even though she didn't believe in any deities. But she still worried about all the other missing animals. How many would turn up dead before the monster was caught?

The oven timer beeped and Jamie made her poor version of garlic bread. They tore into their dinner, eating in contented silence. When the edge of Jamie's feral hunger had been slaked, she talked about visiting the Millers. She didn't mention Lucio. Even though part of her yearned to talk to her mom about him, her smarter half worried about how Mom would react to a guy offering to buy her clothes and attempt to transform her.

Instead, she asked Mom about her shift at the bar and got a hilarious story about Grouchy Bill and Crazy-Eye Bill winding toilet paper around Sleeping John. There were about four Bills, three Johns, two Deans, and two Jeffs who were regulars, so they all had nicknames to tell them apart.

After dinner, Jamie had a blissful bubble bath. Then, she went to bed and fell into a contented sleep, soothed by the soft purrs of the cat curled up beside her.

In the middle of the night, Lucio invaded her dreams.

They danced together under glittering lights and he bent down to kiss her…

***

By the time she got dressed for school the next day, Jamie was determined to avoid Lucio Argento at all costs. Sure, auto shop and English class might be tough, but if she didn't look at him, didn't let those dimples scramble her brain, she could make it through the day.

All went well until lunch, when Lucio slid next to her. Damn him, he somehow looked even more gorgeous. His black leather jacket framed his broad shoulders and his Iron Maiden shirt was a little tight, emphasizing the muscles in his chest and stomach. And those long dark curls looked silkier than ever.

Jamie straightened her spine and forced a stern tone. "I told you yesterday, I'm not interested in trying to be prom queen."

"That's not what I'm here for this time." Lucio's tone was soft, like he was trying to calm a frightened rabbit. "I was actually wondering if you could help me pass English."

Jamie's shield cracked. "Depends on how you want me to help. I won't write your papers for you, or let you copy my answers on the tests or anything. I need my diploma more than you do."

"What's that supposed to mean?"

"My mom doesn't own a business that I can go work at."

Lucio's eyes narrowed and his jaw tightened before he spoke in a slow, furious tone. "First you accuse me of wanting to cheat, and then you say I don't need the diploma that I'm suffering another year in this hellhole to earn. Who says I want to work at Bava's all my life? Maybe I want to be a firefighter, or a lawyer or something." His scowl turned deadly. "I'm beginning to see why you're not popular."

Shame burned her worse than the heat in his gaze. "You're right. I'm sorry. I didn't mean to imply that you'd cheat. It's just that every guy who asks me for help with a class always wants exactly that. I also shouldn't have declared that your future is set in stone. I don't know you that well, so it was wrong of me to assume."

The stiff set of his jaw softened and he shrugged. "Well, you didn't literally accuse me of wanting to cheat, and I suppose I do have options that others don't. But could you try filing down that chip on your shoulder? I promise I'm not a bad guy with nefarious intentions. I only want to pass English."

"You *do* want to use me for your elaborate revenge scheme," Jamie reminded him. "And I still won't be part of that. I will help you with English though. What parts of the class are you having a hard time with? The essays, test anxiety?"

"Reading." His cheeks darkened as he blushed. "I mean, I know how to read, but I have dyslexia so it makes getting through the assigned materials difficult. Same with test questions. I don't think you can help with those, but maybe we can meet up after school and you can read the chapters out loud and I can follow along."

"I can do that on days I don't work." Jamie's heart clenched with sympathy at his embarrassment. Her cousin was dyslexic and struggled all through school. "And if you don't mind hanging around the video store and waiting while I help customers, we can do it there too."

"Great." He gave her one of his knee-weakening smiles. "Where should I meet you today?"

"How about the library?" There was no way in hell she wanted him to see where she lived.

Lucio shook his head. "I'm too embarrassed to do the reading thing in public. Come to my house. I'll give you my address."

As he pulled out a pen and paper and wrote slowly in precise block letters, it occurred to Jamie that after vowing to avoid him, she'd just agreed to spend time with him.

A *lot* of time with him.

Chapter Six

Brittney frowned when she saw Lucio sitting across from that trailer trash, Jamie Blair. They'd been spending a lot of time together the past couple days.

Jealousy roiled her gut as she watched his white teeth flash as he grinned at Jamie. Brittney forced the childish feeling down. He was definitely on the rebound. Jamie didn't mean anything to him. How could she after he'd been with Brittney? Lucio probably couldn't get a date with a better girl since none of Britney's friends would take her leftovers. Plus, he was a loser anyway. Held back because he was dumb.

She wasn't even sure he was interested in hooking up with the trailer trash. All she'd seen them doing was sitting together today, and him following her around the school a lot. Heather Price had said they'd had lunch at Topper Too yesterday, but that they'd taken separate cars and Jamie hadn't looked happy.

In sixth period algebra, Jennifer Armstrong eased Brittney's stubborn remnants of attachment to Lucio by telling her that she'd overheard him asking Jamie for help in passing English class.

"Little good it will do him," Brittney sneered. "He's as dumb as a rock."

Still, the assurance that they weren't dating helped Brittney pass by Jamie and Lucio without looking at them after school. They were taking separate cars. A couple would ride together.

Brittney chided herself for paying them the slightest bit of attention. She needed to focus on getting her prom king.

Her target in mind, she headed for the gym. Heather had an optometrist appointment this afternoon, so she wouldn't be in the way.

Brittany found Chet Morgan jogging laps with his teammates. She settled herself on the bleachers, making sure to sit at an angle where her skirt rode up on her thigh. Every guy who jogged past her cast her an appreciative look. Except for Chet.

This wouldn't do.

Maybe she needed closer proximity to work her charms.

After the workout was done, she hopped off the bleachers and followed the team to the locker room. A few players gave her inviting looks as if they hoped she'd follow them in. She gave them coy smiles and remained outside the door. While waiting for Chet, she fluffed her hair, styled like Madonna's, and applied another coat of hot pink lipstick to her lips.

Slowly, the football players trickled out of the locker room. Many had "forgotten" to put their shirts on, silently pleading with her to admire them.

Evan Legard tried to flirt, but she let him down gently while still giving him a dash of hope, because if things didn't work out with Chet, he was a suitable candidate.

Finally, her target emerged, his blond hair damp from his shower.

"Hello, Chet," she purred.

"Brittney, what are you doing here?" Chet didn't look pleased that she'd waited for him. "Is Heather okay?"

His concern for Heather instead of joy to see her made Brittney want to scream in fury. She forced a sweet smile. "Heather is fine. She had to see the optometrist. I think for colored contacts."

She congratulated herself for hinting that Heather's green eyes weren't natural.

"Well, you tell her to call me if I don't hear from her first. We usually go bowling on Wednesdays."

Brittney eased herself closer to him until their bodies almost touched. "I'll go bowling with you, Chet."

His face reddened. "Um… Thanks for the offer, but it's not the same without Heather. I gotta get home. Have a nice night."

As she watched him walk away from her, she clenched her fists. How could he turn her down like that? She was a lot more beautiful than Heather Price.

At this rate, Chet and Heather would be voted prom king and queen.

"No," she whispered as she left the gym. "I won't allow that to happen."

After getting into her sleek yellow Porsche, Brittney made her decision. Though she liked Heather and appreciated their friendship, she couldn't afford to have her as a rival. That meant Heather had to be removed from the competition.

Unfortunately, that also meant that she'd have to deliver another sacrifice to Scar. He was hungry and already grumpy with her when the dog she'd promised him escaped. She'd have to make up for that failure and get him something bigger.

Her mind raced as she wondered what she could capture. There was no way she could wrangle a larger dog into her car and then to her shed in the backyard. The smaller ones were hard enough to restrain when they sensed Scar's presence. She needed to find something that was either dumber, more compliant, or both.

She steered away from the commercial section of town and went in the direction of the various farms on the outskirts of Amteep.

Brittney had an idea.

Chapter Seven

Two days later

Jamie's voice shook as she read the newspaper article to Lucio:

"Yesterday afternoon, a group of elementary school children discovered a mutilated goat at the Berry Hill Park. What was supposed to be a carefree afternoon of sledding became the stuff of nightmares when Greta Bowie, age 8, Patrick Kasprak, age 7, and Veronica Rogan, age 6, ran to their homes to tell their parents. The police were called to investigate, along with the local game warden.

"'The wounds on the poor animal are not consistent with an attack by a predator,' Garland Cooper, enforcement chief officer of Idaho Fish and Game said in his statement. 'At least, not of the four-legged variety.'

"This is the seventh case of animal mutilation found in the past year, but the first incident where livestock—" Jamie broke off. "Seventh? I remember them reporting only three cases."

Lucio snorted sarcastically. "They probably didn't want to cause a panic. As if we weren't all frantic about our pets disappearing."

Jamie nodded. "I hug my cat as soon as I get home every day."

"I'd like to meet your cat. His name is Shadow, right?"

"Uh-huh." Jamie tensed. She still didn't want him to come to her trailer, even though he and his father had been welcoming and nonjudgmental since the first night she came over to help Lucio study.

His house wasn't a mansion or anything close, but it was a nice, pure white two-story Victorian over on Bourbon Court, not too far from the infamous Sazerac House and some other homes that could be classified as mansions.

He lived in one of the "good" neighborhoods, a far cry from Springwood Trailer Park.

Jamie was intimidated that first evening, both by the nice house and worry that he could turn out to be a skeeze and try something with her. But the moment she'd stepped inside the warm, well-lit house that smelled of garlic and herbs, she'd felt cozy and safe.

And hungry.

Her stomach had growled and Lucio had fed her some leftover chicken parmigiana that tasted like something from a magical world.

Then, they'd done as he'd promised. Settling in the dining room under an old hanging crystal globe light, they'd opened up their copies of *To Kill a Mockingbird*, and Jamie read aloud while he followed along, tracing the text with his finger and mouthing the words.

Two cats, one fat and orange, the other a thin tabby, and a Shih Tzu dog eventually emerged, and Jamie pet them while she read. Later, Lucio had introduced the fat orange cat as Bruce, the tabby as Steve, and the Shih Tzu as Fulci.

Lucio's father had come home and introduced himself with a warm boisterousness that melted her heart. Mario Argento was nearly as handsome as his son, with silver-streaked black wavy hair, those same dark eyes, and dimpled cheeks his son touted.

"I brought home some cannoli," Mr. Argento sang when he'd strolled through the front door. "Enough for you and your *bellezza*."

"Dad," Lucio had said in a scolding tone, his cheeks slightly red. "Jamie is helping me study for English class. That's all."

"That does not mean she can't have cannoli," Mr. Argento had said, though the teasing glimmer in his eyes had faded. He'd looked disappointed. Had he disliked Brittney?

The cannoli had been a revelation and Jamie had a fascinating conversation with Mr. Argento about how they were made. Too bad ricotta and mascarpone were so expensive. She'd longed to ask about the breading and sauce used in the chicken parmigiana, but the clock struck ten and she'd had to get home.

Now she was back in this delicious-smelling haven, with Steve purring on her lap, reading the newspaper with Lucio instead of helping him study. They had a worksheet to do on the first three chapters of *To Kill a Mockingbird*, but neither seemed in a hurry to work on it.

"We can study at your place too, you know," Lucio said.

"I'd rather work with you here and at the video store." Jamie fumbled quickly for an excuse. "I have nosy neighbors."

At least that was true. The Millers would be merciless if they saw Lucio going into Jamie's trailer.

"Fine." He tapped the newspaper. "Do you believe that some satanic cult is killing the animals?"

Jamie shook her head. "I think it's a budding serial killer. They almost always start with animals and move on to people."

"That's what I think too," he said. "I hope they catch the bastard before he hurts a person."

"Me too." She set aside the paper and reached for her backpack. "Should we get back to our homework?"

He shook his head. "I'd much rather keep talking with you. But we can move on to something other than those poor animals."

Jamie considered steering him back to the homework, but she wanted to keep talking to him too. As she learned each new facet of his personality, she liked him more. A guy who cared about animals couldn't be all that bad.

"Okay. What motivated your big crime spree in your sophomore year?" She kept her tone light so he didn't think she was judging him.

He shrugged his broad shoulders. "I was bored."

Somehow, she knew he was lying, but she wouldn't pry. "I like those paintings you did in the alleys. Especially the one with that mummified guy with the British flag. What inspired that?"

Lucio's eyes lit up with joy "That's Eddie from Iron Maiden. What I painted was the design for the song 'The Trooper.' Come upstairs and I'll show you."

Jamie's mouth went dry. Go up to his bedroom? That wasn't a good idea. And yet, her heart skittered with excitement as she followed him up, burning with curiosity to see what posters he'd hung on his walls, what stuff he collected.... What his bed looked like.

Lucio's bedroom was three times the size of hers, with a large closet and even a window seat. She looked at his clothes on the floor and hanging in the closet. So much black, but it suited him.

A lot of band T-shirts, denim, and leather. Heavy metal posters dominated his cream-colored walls. Jamie immediately recognized the mummy guy Lucio had painted in the various Iron Maiden posters throughout the room. She spotted the exact one he'd copied. *The Trooper.*

Lucio plopped down on the top half of his queen-size bed and patted the bottom half for her to sit. "Have you ever listened to any Iron Maiden?"

Jamie shook her head, smiling at his boyish enthusiasm.

He went to a big boombox that stood on the end table next to his bed. "I'll play 'The Trooper' since you liked that painting. It's about the Crimean War. It's so epic and passionate, makes you feel like you're in battle."

The song was everything Lucio promised. Furious guitars played a galloping melody as the singer's powerful voice put her into the suspenseful story he told.

As Jamie listened to the operatic singing about battle and blood accompanied by the epic guitars, her imagination soared. Even after the song stopped, she remained in a bit of a trance, her mind grasping for more. She'd never heard anything like this band before. How had this powerful, passionate music shaped Lucio?

"What do you think?" His voice broke into her trance.

"They're incredible," she breathed. "I love that guy's voice."

"What kind of music do you like?"

Jamie plucked at one of the ties on his quilt. The blanket looked old, but well made, with a beautiful patchwork design of varying shades of blue.

Music was something she had little time for, but valued highly for its ability to make her forget the crappiness of housework, a shitty day at school, or dealing with assholes at work. She didn't have the time or money to keep up with the newest records and bands, so most of her collection was of older stuff, but when she heard something she liked on the radio, she saved her pennies and bought it.

She had to be careful though. Sometimes, the song she'd liked on the radio was the only good one on the album. "I like the older stuff by Heart and Fleetwood Mac, The Eurythmics, Pat Benatar, Blondie, and a lot of others."

"Okay, a little rock in there, so there's hope for you." He grinned at her, still keeping a respectable distance from her on the bed. "So why don't you want to be prom queen?"

Jamie stiffened at the sudden reemergence of a topic she'd hoped had passed. "You won't give up, will you?"

"I've always been a persistent person."

She sighed. "For one, I think your idea is insane. Also, the last thing I want is more visibility in our hellhole of a school. I want to keep my head down, graduate, get a scholarship, and go to college."

His head cocked to the side, making his dark curls sweep against his sharp cheekbones. "What do you want to study?"

"Business."

He frowned in disappointment. "Sounds boring."

She nodded, unable to deny that truth. "Yeah, but a business degree could land me a good job."

"Doing what?"

"I'll figure that out eventually." Jamie reluctantly brought back the subject of prom queen. "What would you do if I agreed to your insane plan anyway? I don't see how you can convince our classmates to vote for me as prom queen."

His broad grin radiated triumph, like he'd already won. "Well, first off, we'll get you a new wardrobe—that I'll pay for since this scheme is mine," he added quickly when she opened her mouth to protest. "Then we'll work on getting you more socialized with our classmates, you know, show them how cool you really are."

She raises an eyebrow. "You think I'm cool?"

"I do," he said emphatically. "You're smart, you can carry on a conversation, plus you're really pretty, and when you leave off the chip on your shoulder, you're a genuinely nice person. It doesn't take much to want to be your friend."

Jamie couldn't hold back a skeptical scoff. "If that was true, why have I been a pariah all my life?"

He tucked a lock of hair behind his ear and answered, matter of fact, "Because this is a small town and their first impressions of you from grade school stuck, partially because of Brittney's bitchery, and partly because you haven't gotten the opportunity to make another impression. I've never seen you at any of the parties, or out at Topper Too, or the Denny's, or the drive-in, or the mall."

"Because I've never been invited to go with anyone to any of those places."

"Easily fixed." He waved his hand dismissively. "We have more than a few trips to the mall ahead of us, and you can come with me to a party at Drew Creed's house next Saturday."

Jamie hesitated. She was slightly acquainted with Drew, a guy with rich parents who were never home. He'd never been mean to her, but he'd never been exactly kind either. "I work on Saturdays."

Lucio was undaunted. "The video store closes at ten on weekends. We'll be fashionably late."

Temptation coiled around her heart like vines at the prospect of new clothes, going to parties, and all the other things that almost every other girl her age got to enjoy. She still didn't think she had an icicle's chance in hell at being voted prom queen. However, maybe Lucio's *Pygmalion* scheme could make her more liked or, at the least, less reviled.

Even more enticing was the prospect of spending more time with Lucio.

She lowered her head, letting her hair fall down to conceal the budding excitement in her eyes. "Okay, fine. I'll do it."

Chapter Eight

Brittney scrubbed the lamb's blood off her hands and looked at the shadowy form in the mirror. "I hope this sacrifice was satisfactory because it sure was messy."

When she'd brought the demon the goat last week, Scar had devoured it and thanked her for making a payment for her debt. He'd still been annoyed about the situation with the dog. Then he'd left before she could make her request, much less banish him herself.

This time, she'd gotten a lamb that had wandered too far away from a farm in Sinchlep. Scar came quicker to this summoning than for the goat. She found a secluded grove of trees to make her pentagram so that she wouldn't have to haul the creature to her house. The goat had been a painful lesson. Not only did she have a bruise from its horns butting her, but she also had to clean goat shit out of her car. *Never again.* She'd kill the sacrifices where they were.

"I have a wish for you, Scar," she'd said after slitting the lamb's throat. The blood that spurted from the wound warmed her chilled hands.

The demon had chuckled, a low and ugly sound. "Patience, pretty one."

After he fed, Scar stepped over the lamb's corpse to face her. "You are cold. Let me accompany you to the warmth and safety of your home and I will listen to your desires."

Brittney paused. He'd never given two shits about her comfort before. Then again, she'd been warming her hands by the steam that rose off the lamb's corpse. Maybe he felt sorry for her, or perhaps remorseful at not giving her anything after she'd killed a goddamn goat for him.

Then she thought of something. "But the sage…" She needed to be able to banish him.

"You can light your little herb bundle any time you please. It does not have to be here in this frigid climate."

Relieved, she nodded. "Will you help me get rid of the remains? If someone catches me killing farm animals, your meal ticket is over."

Scar inclined his head. "I suppose I could lend my aid."

Brittney stepped back from the pentagram she'd scraped in the snow. "Great. I'll grab the tarp and—"

The lamb vanished, leaving only crimson stains in the snow.

Brittney's jaw dropped. "Could you *always* do that?" Because if he'd been letting her clean up the messes from his feedings this whole time when he could make them vanish…

"No. The larger sacrifices have given me more power."

"Okay then." For a moment she considered asking if he could transport her back to the car so she didn't have to hike through the snow with already numb toes, but decided she shouldn't press him. Not when she hadn't gotten to her real wishes.

Scarlionapskhis flickered in and out of view during her trek back to the car and the drive home. That was unnerving, though she was glad to get out of the cold.

Now home safe in her private bathroom, she eyed the demon in the mirror. "I wish to remove Heather Price's chances of being prom queen and I wish for Chet Morgan to fall in love with me."

Scar laughed. The sound was like metal grinding on broken glass. "I can't make anyone fall in love. Love is the antithesis of what I'm made of."

Brittney almost sneered at him admitting a weakness, then thought better of it. It was never a good idea to piss off a demon. "What about lust?"

"I can invoke that most of the time. Though if your intended victim is already in love with someone else, he would sadly be immune."

If Chet were in love with Heather, that meant Brittney would have to get rid of her. A whisper of grief blew over her heart. Heather was her best friend.

But Heather was also her biggest rival for prom queen. Not only because she was dating the quarterback, but also because of her beauty. She had strawberry-blonde hair, eyes the color of emeralds, and perfect, pale skin with invisible pores. More than once Brittney had seethed with envy at Heather's silken-soft skin.

But what if she ruined Heather's beauty? That would remove her friend as prom queen and would probably cause Chet to lose interest. Boys never loved ugly girls.

Then, after Heather was disfigured, Brittney could have Scar work a spell of lust over Chet and bam! Brittney would have her prom king.

"All right, we'll focus on Chet later." Brittney dried her clean hands and turned to face the demon. "I want to ruin Heather's face."

"We can do that," Scar said agreeably. "But you will help me."

"Me?" Brittney gaped at him, outraged. "You've always granted my wishes by yourself."

"But I know you wish to be there to see her hurt." A wicked smile spread across the demon's shadowy, shifting face. His sharp, pointed teeth glinted in the lamplight. "Consider it to be part of the sacrifice required for me to drown her lover in lust for you."

"All right."

The demon had a point. It would be glorious to see Heather's beauty ruined forever. Her mind ran over multiple possible ways to disfigure Heather. It would have to look like an accident. There were few things they did together that could easily result in an injury. Cheer practice was out. The padded mats on the floor prevented all but a sprained ankle. The party at Drew Creed's house? No. She didn't want to wait that long.

Then she thought of something.

Brittney picked up her phone and dialed her friend's number, hoping Heather wasn't out with Chet.

Fortune was on her side. Heather's sultry voice came on the line. "Hello?"

"Hey, do you want to go roller skating?" she forced a cheerful, cajoling tone. "We used to do it all the time, and it's been so long since we had a night where it was just us."

Heather sighed before she answered, sounding reluctant. "I don't know. I have a lot of homework and we both have to be up early for cheer practice."

"Come on," Brittney shifted her tone to pleading, "I miss you so much. You spend so much time with Chet and I was just as bad when I was dating Lucio. I'm scared that we're drifting apart. Come to Skate-O-Rama with me. Let's see if we can still do heel spins and the grapevine."

Silence hung in the air for the longest time before Heather sighed again. "Okay, but only for a little while. I'll meet you there so I can leave at a decent hour. I know how you can be a bad influence, keeping me out late."

Brittney bit back a wicked laugh. *You have no idea.* "Great. I'll be there in an hour."

Showering and getting prettied up with a demon hanging around her bedroom was unnerving, but not nearly as disturbing as when he surrounded her like a shroud of darkness before flowing into her.

I am with you now, Scar's voice slid through her head like cold kisses.

When she entered the Skate-O-Rama, Brittney grimaced. Instead of the handful of bored children and die-hard professional skaters that she'd expected on a Thursday night, the roller rink was packed. If she was going to trip Heather, she had to do it at the right time. Make sure no one saw, which would be difficult.

Heather waved at her from the line to turn in shoes. Her Day-Glo green skates were tucked under her arm. Brittney liked her pink rhinestone skates better.

Once their shoes were turned in, their hands stamped, and skates donned, Heather linked hands with Brittney and the girls made their way to the floor.

As if he'd been waiting for them, the DJ dimmed the lights and turned on the disco ball. Abba's "Dancing Queen" trilled through the surround speakers, accompanied by mixed cheers and groans.

Heather pulled Brittney into the flow of people, her skates gliding across the polished wood floor, grinning as she made disco moves to the song. "You were so right, Brit. I needed this."

Brittney grinned back. *Enjoy it while it lasts because after tonight, you won't want to show your face in public again.*

Heather continued talking as she managed to effortlessly skate and dance. "I'm sorry if I wasn't there for you enough after your breakup with Lucio. If you want to talk about it, you can."

An ache formed in Brittney's chest before she quashed it by focusing on how graceful Heather looked. She forced a sugary tone. "Don't be silly. You were there for me. We had that shopping spree and a sleepover, remember? And I'm totally over Lucio. He doesn't have any class, you know?"

"Well, you wanted to know what the bad boy was like," Heather chided gently. "Now you're back from the dark side. Who will be the lucky guy to take you out next?"

Chet. "I don't know."

She scanned the skating rink for shadowy corners and other good places to trip Heather. Maybe the stairs to the food and beverage area? No. The carpet would cushion the blow.

"The Hokey Pokey" came on and Brittney groaned in dread. She hated doing the hokey pokey. Especially on skates. But Heather giggled and rolled her way to the big circle the skaters formed.

As everyone lifted their left skate toward the circle, then moved their foot back, Brittney wobbled. Balancing on one skate was hard. She was out of practice. Heather, she noted bitterly, had no trouble. Then when the time came to "shake it all about," Brittney slipped and fell on her ass.

Brittney's face flamed as she heard a few snorts and snickers. Heather grabbed her hand to help her up, and for a moment Brittney was tempted to shove her away. But now was not the time for the push.

Scar's voice whispered in her mind. *Gotta keep doing the hokey pokey.*

She accepted Heather's help and allowed her to pull her back to her feet.

"Let's go closer to the back wall," Heather said, and guided her that way.

Brittney knew why. So that if she fell again, fewer people would see.

Fewer people would see, Scar's voice echoed.

A smile spread across her face, and she must have bared too many teeth because Heather frowned with concern. "Are you all right? You didn't hurt your tailbone, did you?"

"I'm fine," Brittney almost sang. "Let's go by the mirror. I want to check my mascara."

One part of the wall of the skating rink was taken up by a floor-to-ceiling mirror to make the area look bigger, and so skaters could admire their looks and form. Brittney skated up to the mirror and made a show of fixing her eye makeup. Then she looked at Heather and frowned. "Oh no. Your lipstick is a little smeared and there's something in your hair."

"My hair?" Heather echoed with a note of alarm. She'd gotten lice back in third grade and was paranoid about her perfect strawberry blonde waves ever since.

As she leaned forward to examine her hair, Brittney skated behind her. "I think it's…" she trailed off, pretending to examine her friend's hair while glancing behind to make sure everyone else was still occupied with the hokey pokey.

The skaters continued the stupid dance, singing along to the record. "You put your right foot in…"

Brittney lined up for her blow and silently called to her demon. *Scar, give me the strength to break her face and knock her out.*

Her skin prickled before his essence filled her with what felt like a roar of flame. Her eyes glowed yellow in the mirror and power surged through her as she shoved Heather's face into the mirror.

Heather crashed into the reflective glass with a dull thud. The sound wasn't particularly satisfying.

But the force of the demon went *through* Heather's body and into the mirror. A juddering sound surfaced beneath the music and the floor picked up a different vibration than that of the skaters.

The mirror was tilting forward.

"You do the hokey pokey and you turn yourself around…"

Brittney skated back and heard Heather moan with pain. Her nose bent to one side of her cheek and looked crushed. Blood gushed from her pixie-like chin.

"Ughhhh," Heather groaned and looked in the mirror. "Buuurrrriii—" she warbled in a pleading tone, meeting Brittney's eyes, which still glowed yellow.

The skaters continued to sing, oblivious to Heather's plight. *"That's what it's all about!"*

Heather's plea was replaced by her ear-piercing scream.

The mirror fell.

The sound of shattering glass echoed through the skating rink. The music cut off, only to be replaced with screams. One shard of glass the size of a car door tumbled down and severed Heather's head.

Brittney cried out as the demon's essence left her. The heat that flooded her body was replaced with cold.

"I only wanted to break her face," she whispered, staring at the ruined mess on the floor that used to be her best friend. "I didn't want this to happen."

Blood gushed from Heather's severed neck, pooling beneath her corpse. The puddle rapidly spread, reaching the toe of Brittney's skates. She scooted back farther and shrieked as her back hit a solid form.

"It's okay," a man's voice rumbled in her ear. "I got you. They're calling nine-one-one."

Brittney turned and allowed him to enfold her in his arms. She was shaking uncontrollably, but more from the aftershock of the demon's power than grief.

Sure, she'd miss Heather, but it would be more useful to have her completely out of the way. And safer. What if Heather hadn't believed that the push was an accident? What if someone had backed Heather up, regardless if they'd seen anything? If Heather had been disfigured, her usual aura of vulnerability that made people want to protect her would be astronomic. That trait, which Brittney had never managed to fully replicate, would spoil her plans.

She tried her best now to portray the grieving best friend. Even managing a few choking sobs. "It's all my fault. I bumped into her and she fell into the mirror." She raised her voice, so the gathering lookie-loos heard, in case someone had seen her push Heather.

There were a lot of people surrounding Heather's gory remains, staring like mindless idiots.

"And then the mirror tipped over. How could this have happened?" Brittney shot an accusatory glare toward the gawking staff members. "I thought the mirror was secure."

A siren warbled off in the distance. For a moment, Brittney stiffened, worried about what she'd say to the cops, but as more people made sympathetic sounds around her, the tension eased. She allowed her would-be rescuer to guide her away from the throng and off the skating floor.

Minutes later, Brittney was settled into one of the comfortable booths above the floor where people had pizza and burgers, and where birthday parties were often held. A cup of hot chocolate sat on the table in front of her. She wondered where it had come from. Hot chocolate wasn't even on the menu.

The floor of the skating rink had been evacuated and cordoned off with police tape. All the witnesses were crowded on the benches in the area where people put on their skates. One by one, they were pulled away by an officer and quickly questioned before they were able to leave.

Brittney may have lacked Heather's natural vulnerability, but the cops totally ate up her act of traumatized girl who lost her best friend to a tragic accident. She sipped her cocoa and basked in the attention she received. Especially when one officer told her how brave she was to hold herself together and tell them what happened.

Eventually, she grew bored with the cops, preferring instead to watch the emergency medical crews argue with the police on whether they could move or examine the body. The tension and barely checked anger radiated from them so thickly that it felt like she could breathe it in. Then Heather's parents arrived, bringing the drama to a rolling boil.

Delicious.

Brittney frowned.

Was that her thought, or Scar's?

Chapter Nine

One week later

Lucio watched Jamie turn around in front of the three-way mirror at Maurice's, admiring the way the dark blue crushed velvet dress fit her slender body. Honestly, she looked amazing in every outfit she'd tried on, even the ones they rejected. He was grateful he was *supposed* to be looking at her as she modeled the clothes because he was incapable of looking away. The pure, unadulterated joy in her face made his breath catch. She was absolutely radiant.

The blue of the dress complemented the golden tint of her eyes and the obsidian sheen to her hair. The garment was too formal for school, but she could wear it to a party or on a date with her candidate for prom king.

He frowned, not wanting to think about that unpleasant, albeit necessary, aspect of his plan. Instead, he tallied the other items in their growing collection of shopping bags from their first venture at the Silver Mountain Mall.

He'd bought her a pair of Guess jeans, since all the popular girls wore them, a new pair of fashionable snow boots because she needed them, an off-the-shoulder sweater, miscellaneous hair accessories and bangle bracelets from Claire's. And, of course, a Swatch. He'd also spent an ungodly amount of money on cosmetics, hairspray, and one of those crimper things that were becoming trendy.

The money for this investment ate a huge chunk of his savings account, and he'd have to wait tables a few more hours a week at Bava's, but seeing Jamie's delight in every new garment and little trinket made the expense more than worth it.

They went to the mall's food court, and each had a hot dog and an Orange Julius. Lucio couldn't help smiling at the look of pure bliss on Jamie's face with every bite of the simple food. He'd have to take her to Bava's sometime so she could have some really good food. And not something common like lasagna or spaghetti that she'd already had reheated at his house. Something like *osso buco* or *cioppino*, or…

Jamie broke into his thoughts of his family recipes. "You know, I'll have to come up with an explanation for my new wardrobe and stuff."

"Say your great-aunt died and you inherited some cash." Lucio felt foolish for not considering how people would react to a transformation that clearly cost money. "Everyone loves a good tale of a surprise inheritance."

"Won't I look stupid for wasting it on clothes?"

"No. You're a girl." Her furious glare made him chuckle. "Sorry, but stereotypes run strong."

"Hey, Lucio," a voice called, and he turned to see Tom Gallagher and Jason Shaye approaching. Both guys blinked in surprise at the sight of Jamie, but gave her polite nods. Tom eyed the mountain of shopping bags at Jamie's feet. "What're you guys up to?"

"Not much." Lucio scooted a little closer to Jamie, in case one of them decided to try to give her any shit. "I ran into Jamie, and we decided to grab a quick lunch. You know Jamie, right? She's my English tutor."

Jason nodded and smiled at Jamie. "Yeah. We had P.E. together last semester. Nice seeing you again."

"You too," Jamie whispered shyly.

"Are you guys going to Drew Creed's party on Saturday?" Lucio asked.

"I wouldn't miss it for the world." Tom leaned over the table between Lucio and Jamie and whispered loud, "I heard that he got a bottle of Everclear from Montana. That stuff is outlawed in Idaho because it's a hundred-eighty proof."

"Cool. We'll see you there." Lucio hid a smile at the new appraising look that Tom and Jason swept over Jamie at the casual announcement that she'd be at the party. From this one little encounter, Lucio knew her status on the social ladder had gone up a few rungs.

Tom's dad was a surgeon, and Jason was the son of the owner of Wild Bill's Auto Sales, the biggest dealership in Amteep. Neither were in the country club set Brittney associated with, but they were both well-liked at school.

Each clapped Lucio on the shoulder and gave Jamie respectful nods before heading off to the arcade.

"That went well." Lucio took a deep breath and broached the topic of phase two of his plan. "And Jason Shaye might be a good candidate to be your king. He's pretty popular."

"Don't go playing matchmaker yet," Jamie said quickly. "I am so not ready for that."

"Okay." Lucio was only too happy to agree. He wasn't ready either. He wanted Jamie to himself a little longer.

He loved how she marveled at every little thing, from the music he showed her, the food he cooked her on their study nights, and now her new clothes. How many things he'd taken for granted had she been deprived of experiencing?

Her help with his reading had been incredible. When their work schedules and efforts with Operation Prom Queen had gotten them behind on reading, Jamie had introduced Lucio to the wonder of books on tape. Though he'd been aware of their existence, he'd never tried one before. The tapes of *To Kill a Mockingbird* helped immensely, allowing him to follow along with the reading, even though the narrator had nothing on Jamie's soothing voice, something needed for this deep and powerful story.

The worksheets he turned in garnered him better grades than he'd ever gotten in English. So much that his overall grade had climbed from a D- to a C+. Mrs. Marsh pulled him aside, suspicious that he'd been cheating. She'd eased off when he told her about Jamie tutoring him.

Jamie had also found some newer books on dyslexia with helpful advice that his previous therapists and special ed teachers hadn't shown him, like using a transparent, colored ruler to hold over the lines he was reading.

With all of Jamie's help, he might actually pass all his classes and get his diploma after all. For that, he'd owe her the world.

He wished he knew more about her interests, hopes, and dreams so he could better repay her. Unfortunately, she was still cagey about herself and changed the subject when he tried to pry into her home life. Hell, she still wouldn't let him see her home. At least she'd finally ditched the separate vehicles thing and let him take her to the mall in his car.

"Oh no," Jamie's horrified whisper broke off his thoughts. "It's your ex."

Lucio turned to follow the direction of her gaze to see Brittney and Jennifer Armstrong walking past the food court, their arms laden with twice the shopping bags he and Jamie had.

Even though her best friend had died in front of her in a tragic freak accident, Brittney looked radiant and cheerful. Brit had taken a week off to grieve, but she didn't look like she was mourning at all.

Lucio tried to tell himself that he shouldn't judge her too harshly, that everyone processed loss differently, but the sound of her shrill laughter carrying through the mall made him doubt Brittney missed Heather at all.

Probably relieved that her biggest competition for prom queen was eliminated, he thought bitterly.

He turned back to see Jamie hunched down in her seat, trying to hide from Brittney. Lucio hated seeing her cringe like that. "Don't worry, Brit never comes to the food court. She only eats expensive shit."

Jamie wasn't soothed. "I think we should go."

Lucio sighed and took one last sip of his Orange Julius. "Okay. Now that you mention it, I don't feel like running into her either."

On their way back to his house, with Accept's newest album playing at low volume on the tape deck, Jamie brought up Brittney's apparent lack of grief.

"I don't get it. She and Heather were inseparable since fifth grade." Her frown deepened. "Maybe what happened was so terrible that she can't process it. It wasn't in the news, but Brian Matheson was there and he said a piece of the mirror took Heather's head clean off. I still can't believe that mirror fell."

Lucio nodded. That *was* messed up. "The building's old. Been around since the sixties, I think. The supports for the mirror probably rusted away, or rotted if they were rubber. And with the vibrations of the music, and the people skating…" he trailed off and shook his head. "No matter the cause, that was a fucked-up thing to happen. Heather and I didn't like each other, but nobody deserves to go out like that."

"So terrible." Jamie sighed and drew a circle in the fog on her window. "I wonder if the roller rink will close because of it. I hope not. I only got to go a few times, but I always had fun there. Then again, if they reopen, I hope it won't be haunted."

"A week ago, I would have thought a haunted roller rink would be badass." Lucio laughed. "But not one haunted by the ghost of Heather Price. She'd probably trip people if she didn't like their outfits."

Jamie's shoulders shook with repressed laughter. "Are we jerks to be making fun of the dead like this?"

"I don't think so. She wasn't nice to either of us. I'll take you skating in a couple weeks and we'll see if she's still hanging around." Lucio wanted to change the subject. "Which outfit do you want to wear to the party?"

"I don't know. Probably something casual. I don't want to draw too much attention to myself." Jamie's voice went soft and serious. "Lucio? You'll get me out of there if...if people aren't welcoming, right?"

Lucio wanted to kick himself for not thinking that the party could go sideways and result in her being rejected and bullied for daring to show her face. "Of course."

Back at his house, Jamie moved her shopping bags from his car to hers. "I have to head to work, but if you want to come by around eight, we can work on our English homework."

"Sounds good."

Before he could say anything else, she threw her arms around him. "Thank you so much—*for everything*. These boots don't leak and...thanks."

She started to release him, but Lucio held her tight for a moment longer. Her body felt warm and yielding against his, and seemed to fit against him perfectly.

The scent of her hair, lightly floral, teased his senses.

Letting her go was difficult.

***

The next day they had a snow day—no school. Lucio dressed and showered with enthusiasm at the prospect of spending more time with Jamie. He liked her. Aside from her being the critical aspect of his revenge plot and the best tutor he'd ever had, he was also beginning to see her as a friend. Thinking of how good she'd felt in in arms last night, his heart wrenched and his body stirred. Unfortunately, he was also thinking of her as something more: a dangerous direction to go. He couldn't let his heart overcome his will. If any of the prospective prom kings thought that Lucio had the slightest claim on Jamie, they wouldn't dare approach her.

He shook his head. That's what he got for working so hard on making his peers fear him so they wouldn't mock him for his dyslexia or for being held back.

Although Jamie was off-limits to him in the romantic sense, that didn't mean that he couldn't enjoy her friendship. And on that note, he needed to come up with an excuse to see her earlier than scheduled.

First he needed to clear the damn driveway so he could get to her. Oh, and so Dad could get to the restaurant. If Lucio was lucky, he'd get a couple bucks for shoveling the snow.

Now that he was nineteen, his father was hit or miss on whether Lucio would be paid for helping out around the house, which was fair, but he still appreciated the times when he was given a few bucks. Yesterday's shopping spree had cleaned out his wallet.

As he shoveled heaps of snow, a light bulb lit up in his mind. He took a quick shower, accepted ten bucks from his father, and then picked up the phone and dialed Jamie's number.

"Want me to help you clear your driveway?"

"Mom and I can handle it," she said stubbornly.

"I can't risk you slipping and hurting yourself," he countered smoothly. "Or risk you catching a cold. Come on, you don't have to be so tough all the time. Let me help you. It's the least I can do for you helping me in English."

Lucio heard a voice in the background. "Who are you talking to? And what are we supposed to be handling?"

Jamie's sigh echoed over the line. He shivered, wondering how her warm breath would feel against his ear. "Hold on." The line muffled, sounding like she put her hand over her phone's mouthpiece. A few seconds later, she came back on. "We accept your kind offer. I have chicken and rice soup in the crockpot too, if you want to stay for lunch. You got a pen so I can give you my address?"

"Yeah." Lucio frowned as her voice cracked with what sounded like fear as she told him where she lived. Was she really that afraid that he'd judge her?

When he pulled into Springwood Trailer Park, he saw that the answer was yes.

Jamie, who was standing outside waiting for him, looked so flustered when he pulled up near her trailer. It was an older model, single-wide, with chipped blue paint on its metal siding. He quickly noted that the flat roof would need to be shoveled too if the snow kept up.

Her face was pink as a sunrise as her gaze darted back and forth from him to her small house. "Th-thank you for coming to help."

"I told you, it's no big deal." He tried to convey that he wasn't only talking about shoveling.

Jamie's mom came outside but remained on the little porch. "Hi, I'm Leigh. Jamie tells me she's been tutoring you in English." Her blue eyes burned with curiosity and wariness that all parents had when he was near their daughters.

Lucio got his shovel out of the trunk and made his way down the little path that Jamie had already cleared. She hadn't listened to him about letting him do it all. "I'm Lucio Argento. It's a pleasure to meet you. Your daughter is keeping me from failing that class and may be instrumental to me getting my diploma."

Jamie's blush deepened to a cherry red while Leigh beamed with pride. "My daughter is a smart and kind person. And sometimes too humble. She was foolish to try to turn down help with this white mess out here. Thirteen inches in one night, can you believe it? My back is too sore from the last time, and Jamie is likely to hurt herself if she tried to tackle it alone. There'll be hot cocoa and soup waiting when you're done." The last line was delivered with a touch of reluctance.

When Lucio glanced at Jamie, he saw that she was blushing again.

"Thank you." Lucio watched Leigh rub her lower back as she made her way back inside the trailer's rickety steps. He turned to Jamie, but she had already grabbed a shovel and was working on widening her path. "Hey, I said I'd do it."

"You don't have to be so tough," she threw back at him. "If there's two of us, we can have it knocked out in twenty minutes. Besides, I gotta move the cars back as we go along."

"Okay." He honestly couldn't say that he wouldn't like her at his side.

They worked companionably, talking about their school assignments and what Jamie had told her mom about the clothes.

"I told her that I bought the boots with my savings, and got this outfit from Goodwill. The rest I hid and will gradually introduce them as more thrift shop scores." Neither of them wanted her mom, or anyone really, to know that he was the one responsible for her new wardrobe.

Lucio admired her rosy cheeks and the flex of her cute butt as she heaved loads of snow into the pile. Two women came out onto the porch of another trailer; the one who looked like she was Jamie's age held a baby in her arms.

Jamie waved at them, but also gave them a pointed shake of her head that made them go back inside. He wondered what that was all about. Had Jamie talked to one of them about him?

Fifteen minutes later, the driveway was cleared, with Leigh's car parked behind Jamie's so she could drive to work. Lucio did not like the look of Leigh's snow tires. The tread was worn and half the studs were gone. Jamie's weren't looking so hot either. But at least she had bags of traction sand in the back. Lucio knew he couldn't bring up the condition of their tires any more than he could talk about why Jamie didn't have good snow boots until yesterday.

As he followed her into the trailer, he frowned at the mushy feel of one of the steps. As if reading his mind, Jamie looked over her shoulder. "I'm going to scavenge a board for that step as soon as I can."

He gaped at her in awe. She could do house repairs too? She paused at the dented aluminum door and Lucio could read her reluctance to let him inside. Then she lifted her chin and opened the door.

The smell of hot soup warmed him almost as much as the actual heat of the trailer. Jamie took off her coat and hung it over the back of one of the chairs at the little dining table. Lucio placed his over the chair across from hers since there wasn't a coat rack.

He tried to hide his curiosity as he looked around. The small home was cozy, but cluttered. The brown carpet was stained and worn, and the wood-paneled walls scarred. The green couch in the narrow living room looked comfortable, adorned with a beautiful knitted blue and violet afghan, and velveteen throw pillows.

A small TV sat on a scratched wood cabinet, nestled between two mismatched bookcases. One held videocassettes, and the other held books. The other corner of the living room had an old stereo and a collection of records and cassette tapes. A short narrow hall led to the bedrooms and bathroom. Lucio burned with curiosity at what Jamie's room looked like. He doubted she'd have him in there with her mom here.

A few paintings hung on the walls, mostly cats and wildflowers. There were a few photographs of a younger Jamie and her mom, and Lucio wanted to look at them closer, but Jamie beckoned for him to sit at the green Formica table in the little dining nook.

One corner of the kitchen counter held a rotary phone, a jar full of pencils and pens, miscellaneous bills, and a big, worn-out purse that must be Leigh's.

Lucio caught a glimpse of the edge of a food stamp booklet and his heart tugged. He hadn't seen those since he was nine, after Mom died and before the money from the accidental death insurance came in.

Jamie's mom cleared her throat behind him and his face warmed as he stopped snooping.

Jamie got three mismatched bowls out of the cupboard in the tiny kitchen, set them next to the crockpot, and removed the lid. The heavenly smell of the soup thickened in the air while she ladled it into the bowls.

"Um, we're out of crackers, but I can make you some toast if you want." There was that nervous look again. Fear that he'd judge her.

Lucio gave her a smile that he hoped was reassuring. "I prefer most soups on their own so I can savor their flavor."

And it was worth savoring. Lucio tasted the garlic, onion, celery, and the herbs she'd used to season the soup. "This is delicious. Is there rosemary in there?"

Jamie nodded. "I have a little bush in the kitchen window. Keeping it alive through the sheer force of my will."

Lucio marveled. He wanted to ask her how she pulled this off, but then Leigh took her bowl and supplied that information in that same tone of fierce pride that she'd had when talking about her daughter's intelligence and kindness. That tone that clearly said: *You're not good enough for my daughter.*

"Jamie is an excellent cook and quite resourceful. Last year, she figured out where a lot of the expensive herbs and spices could be found cheaper. And when we can get a whole chicken on sale, she'll slow roast it, then freeze the leftover meat, and make stock from the carcass. Then we get to have soup, potpie, or a casserole."

"My father does that too," Lucio said, happy to find common ground. "He uses homemade stock in his restaurant instead of canned broth."

"Your father owns a restaurant?" Leigh's gaze whipped to her daughter and she almost looked embarrassed. "Jamie, why didn't you tell me? Which restaurant?"

He spoke before Jamie could answer. "He owns Bava's. I'd be happy to take you both sometime. My dad's an excellent cook, like Jamie."

"I'm not nearly as good as Mr. Argento." Jamie's cheeks pinkened again. "The leftovers you've shared with me make me feel like I've died and gone to heaven."

Leigh shook her head, and that prideful tone returned, though with warmth she hadn't given before. "I bet if you had ingredients to work with, you could create gourmet masterpieces." She leaned toward Lucio and confided with more gentleness, "She has at least thirty different ways to make Top Ramen."

His heart wrenched as he thought of how tough it would be to have to make freeze-dried ramen noodles fresh and interesting because you didn't have anything else to eat.

He wanted to know where Jamie's father was, and if he was alive, why he didn't help out. Lucio wondered how much Leigh made as a waitress at a bar. His father paid the waitresses at Bava's more than minimum wage, and they made generous tips most nights. Maybe he could talk to Dad and see if he needed any more help at the restaurant.

He shook his head. When he'd first approached Jamie, all he could think about was how he wanted her to help him.

Now he couldn't stop thinking of all the ways he wanted to help her.

Chapter Ten

Jamie wiped her sweating hands on her new black corduroy pants and rose from the couch when she saw the glow of headlights through the window of her trailer. Lucio was here, picking her up for a party at a rich guy's house. In sophomore year, she would have killed for this. Now the idea terrified her. Jamie was simultaneously relieved that Mom was working tonight, at the same time wishing she were home to give Jamie advice and words of comfort.

"Hey," Lucio said when she let him in. "You look amazing."

Her stomach fluttered at the blatant admiration in his eyes. Despite her casual outfit of the black pants, blue sweater, and matching blue hairband, she'd put extra effort into everything from the neck up, crimping her hair and spraying it until it had twice its usual volume.

Shiny blue eye shadow adorned her lids, and mascara doubled the thickness and length of her lashes. The cherry red lipstick she'd gotten at the mall yesterday might be her new favorite shade. Silver hoop earrings and bangle bracelets completed her look. She'd also borrowed some of her mom's precious Giorgio perfume. One of the regulars at the bar had gifted Mom a bottle after he stole it from his wife during a messy divorce.

Lucio looked even more gorgeous than usual tonight, with his long hair caressing the shoulders of his leather jacket, a black button-up shirt visible above the zipper. Crisp black jeans hugged his narrow hips and accentuated his muscular legs. His motorcycle boots didn't look practical for the snow and ice outside, but they were sexy as hell.

"Hi," she managed weakly.

"Hey." His voice was husky. Was it her imagination, or was he checking her out?

For the first part of the drive, Jamie fidgeted, trying to figure out what to say to break up the tension.

Lucio read her like a book. "Are you nervous?"

"Yeah," she confessed in the safety of the dark interior of the car. "I haven't really gone to many parties, or out anywhere, really."

"I remember you saying you weren't invited to many parties, but what's stopped you from going to other public places and events?" Then, Lucio fixed her with an intent look. "Why haven't you dated anyone? I've seen a few guys in shop class show interest."

"I did have a boyfriend, briefly in sophomore year," she answered. "Now, I don't want my plans for the future derailed, like what happened to my friend Arlene. She's one of my neighbors and a good friend."

"What happened to her?"

"She got pregnant. The father turned out to be a married man who already had children. He ran back to them as soon as Arlene told him she was going to have a baby."

Even in the darkness, she saw his mouth twist with scorn. "Christ, what an asshole."

Jamie nodded. "And then there's the Rusks, who dropped out in junior year and got married. They're constantly screaming at each other and the cops are there at least once a month. I mean, most of my neighbors are good people trying to get by, but I know when people learn where I live, they're picturing pregnant teenagers, alcoholics, and those mythical welfare queens that the president is always yammering about.

"I've had guys approach me thinking that because I live in a trailer park, I must be easy. And I've had girls laugh at me if I expressed interest in a guy whose parents are in a higher tax bracket than mine. So I've tried to keep a low profile."

"I admire you, you know," Lucio said quietly, returning his eyes to the road. "You have to put up with so much shit, and you overcome so much every day."

Heat flushed through her, from the top of her head to her toes. "Thanks," she squeaked. Grateful she didn't have to say more because they'd reached their destination, she took a deep breath to try to center herself.

Drew Creed lived in a house off Lakeview Drive. Technically, it wasn't a lake house, but it had a view of Lake Skeetshue from the large deck, which was full of people despite the late January cold.

The beat of the music and cheerful voices could be heard from outside.

Lucio helped her out of the car. "Watch the ice, and remember to clarify that we're just friends."

Jamie's heart writhed in frustration at his words, especially with the warm, firm feel of his hand gripping her arm in case she slipped. "Are you embarrassed at the idea that someone would think we're something more?"

He looked down at her, his dark silk curls hanging in his face. "*You* sure seemed to be when I first approached you."

"I thought you were pulling a prank on me, you know that." *Oh shit.* She'd implied that she'd be okay with being…more.

His lips quirked in a wicked smile as he led her up the stairs to the house. Despite all the people smoking outside, the air inside was also thick with cigarette smoke. Jamie followed Lucio's advice and lifted her chin, walking in like going to huge parties was a normal thing.

People stared and she resisted the urge to huddle into her coat. Instead, she focused on classmates she barely knew and people she didn't know and smiled at them like they were customers at the video store asking her for help.

Drew Creed nudged people away, a highball glass in one hand. "Lucio!" he bellowed jovially. "I didn't think you were gonna show."

Lucio shrugged, as if the fact that he was several hours late didn't matter. "I told you I'd come. Some of us have jobs, you know." He put a hand on Jamie's shoulder. "You've met Jamie Blair, right?"

Drew's face lit up with sincere interest as he turned to Jamie and offered his hand. "Yeah, I think you were in a couple of my classes over the years. But my brother, Hans, knows you really well. He says you're the best one at Prime Time Video to help him find things, and that you've often done special orders for him."

"Hans Creed is your brother?" Jamie adored that guy. He came in every other weekend like clockwork, asking about new releases, looking for new recommendations. She was far from the obsessive film buff that Hans was, but she loved movies and especially loved talking with him about them because she always learned fascinating details about her favorites.

And he was good-looking too. Unfortunately, he was also way too old for her, and *very* happily married to a woman who looked like Lily Munster. Jamie liked Angela Creed, but also seethed in envy at the woman's beautiful macabre style. Unfortunately, even with her newfound ability to buy clothes, she knew Lucio wouldn't allow her to wear anything unique. Only the latest trends would make her prom queen worthy.

Jamie scolded herself for thinking about Lucio again and focused back on Drew. "Is your brother here?"

Drew laughed and shook his head, though there was something guarded in his hazel eyes. "No, he doesn't come to many parties because people always pester him about what happened back in the summer of seventy-eight."

"Of course they would," Jamie said, inwardly kicking herself. The massacre at Camp Natty remained an avid legend at school. Twenty people, mostly high school seniors, were murdered by a psychopath. Hans and Angela were among the survivors. Jamie often forgot because she'd never presumed to bring it up.

"Anyway, I'm here, and though I'm not as interesting as my illustrious brother, I like movies too." Drew regarded her with a teasing smile. "So, if you get bored with mingling, I can entertain you."

"I'd like that," Jamie said sincerely. Drew was almost as handsome as his brother, with a lot more openness in his face. Understandable after what Hans had been through. And a guy without demons would be easier to handle anyway.

And yet, as well as she was hitting it off with Drew, Jamie's blood only heated for Lucio. The one guy she couldn't date now.

Lucio's deep voice rumbled beside her. "We should mingle." He didn't sound as happy as he should.

"Want a beer, cocktail, or something stronger?" Drew inserted himself between them. "Hans made sure I had a respectable selection."

"I'll have one beer, but that's it," Lucio said. "I'm Jamie's ride for the night."

As they headed for the open coolers full of various beverages, Brittney leapt between them and threw herself in Lucio's arms.

"Oh, Lucio, I'm so glad you're here." Her voice slurred and she looked up at him with a lopsided smile. "I'm still so torn apart over losing Heather. I miss her so much. You know how close we were."

A red haze filtered over Jamie's vision at the possessive way Brittney gripped Lucio's bicep. Then Brittney turned to face her with a saccharine smile. "Oh, hi, trailer trash. I didn't expect to see you here. Are you comforting Lucio in his grief over losing me?"

"Don't call her that again," Lucio growled through clenched teeth. "Her name is Jamie and she's my friend."

Jamie's heart stuttered at the utter fury in his voice, even if the clarification on their relationship deflated her a little.

Brittney laughed drunkenly but released her grip. "I don't even know why I wasted so much time with a loser like you in the first place."

Then she flounced off to Chet Morgan's side. Jamie was surprised to see Heather Price's boyfriend out at a party so soon after losing his girlfriend to a tragic accident. Then again, maybe he and Brittney were comforting each other, and plenty of people drowned their sorrows in booze.

Hell, she wanted to drown her irritation with Brittney in booze. But not too much since she had to work tomorrow afternoon. She took a bottle of champagne from the cooler and poured herself a glass.

Her nose wrinkled as she sipped. *This* was what all the fancy rich people rhapsodized about? The champagne was okay, but she'd had cheap wine coolers that tasted better. Still, the novelty was enjoyable and the bubbles felt nice on her tongue.

Jamie spent the rest of the evening "socializing." After the second glass of champagne, the lie about inheriting money from a distant aunt fell easily from her tongue. Girls who'd never before deigned to talk to her asked her for hair care tips. Boys who'd either ignored her or stood and laughed while she was being bullied asked her to dance.

She felt warm and fuzzy and for once in her life her peers were being kind to her. Whether it was her new look, or them seeing that Drew and Lucio had accepted her, or if it was simply cheer induced from the drugs and alcohol they'd consumed, Jamie didn't care. She basked in being liked.

Best of all, Brittney left clinging to Chet's hand like they were going steady.

With Jamie's third glass of champagne, she settled in a comfy corner with Drew and had a fascinating conversation about Giallo films. Lucio chimed in once in a while to correct them on their pronunciation of the actor's names and other Italian terms. Jamie felt comforted at his presence. Like he was a guardian angel there to sweep her away if things became unpleasant.

Someone else settled on the couch next to Drew. "Did you hear that another mutilated animal was found? It was a calf out at the Carver farms. The police are trying to figure out whether it's the same psycho who's been killing animals in town, or if it was a hate crime."

"Hate crime?" someone else asked.

"Yeah," Lucio said. He set down his bottle of Coke. True to his word, he'd only had one beer. "The Carvers are Black. Some people don't like that. And Dexter Carver's wife is Chinese. Her mom is Principal Cho." Anger darkened his features. "My father buys produce from them for his restaurant. They're good people. They don't deserve to lose any of their livestock. They don't even have that many cows to begin with."

Jamie shook her head and frowned as the room spun a little. "I think it's the same crazy guy. When the hate group is on a mission, they like to leave some ugly calling card so everyone knows it was them. Like shortly after Dexter and Lily's wedding, they covered the Carvers' greenhouse in spray-painted slurs. My mom overheard who did it, so those assholes got a visit from the cops, *and* the bikers."

Drew leaned forward. "Whoa, the bikers went after the hate group? I thought some of them were members."

"Some are. But not the ones at my mom's—" She broke off, not wanting to bring up that her mom was a waitress. "The ones my mom knows. Anyway, the Carvers and the Chos doubled up on security at their farm and business, and no one's messed with them since."

"That's good to hear," Lucio said. "How many livestock animals have been killed so far?"

"Three," Mandy Summers said. "The goat, then a lamb, and now the cow. I hope they don't kill a horse next. Horses are my favorite."

"Maybe it's aliens," someone else said.

The conversation veered to even more ridiculous speculations before people realized it was two in the morning and either wandered off to find somewhere to lie down, or grabbed their keys and headed out the door.

Jamie yawned and set down her empty champagne glass. She turned to Lucio and for a moment was so taken with his masculine beauty that she forgot what she was going to say.

Damn, she hadn't meant to get drunk tonight. "I think we should call it a night."

"Me too."

Drew reached over and patted each of their shoulders. "Hey, you guys can spend the night. It's icy out there and there's either aliens, or Satanists, or a killer on the loose."

Jamie looked over at the people who were passed out on the floor. "That's really generous of you, but my mom will kill me if I'm not in my own bed by morning."

"And I'm her ride," Lucio added, suddenly looking grumpy. He rose from the couch and stretched. His Slayer shirt rode up, exposing a fascinating line of golden skin and a flat stomach.

Jamie licked her lips and got up too. She swayed a little, and Lucio steadied her. He helped her with her coat, and she closed her eyes at the feel of his hand through the thick fabric. Outside, he gripped her shoulders, carefully guiding her down the stairs and down the icy path in the driveway to his car.

"You had too much to drink." His velvety voice made her senses tingle.

"Yeah." And normally, she'd be kicking herself because one of the most important things she'd learned from other girls' mistakes was to never let yourself be caught drunk and alone with a guy. But Lucio was safe. Not only because he wasn't interested in her in *that* way, but also because he was a genuinely good person, despite his rough edges.

"I don't want to drop you off at home like this. Why don't we go to Denny's for some coffee and a preemptive greasy hangover breakfast?"

Her stomach rumbled at the thought of hash browns and eggs. Ooh, and *bacon*. "That's why I'm so tipsy. I was in such a hurry after work that I forgot to eat something."

"Son of a bitch," Lucio growled under his breath in a tone that sounded like he blamed himself for her forgetfulness.

He had her stay in the running car while he scraped the ice off the windshield. Jamie burrowed in her coat, more than grateful. She *hated* that winter ritual with a passion. Spring could not come soon enough.

Lucio handled the icy roads like a pro, getting them safely to the twenty-four-hour diner. Jamie hid a smirk, wondering how many of her mom's clientele were here sobering up after a rowdy night. She spotted a few that she recognized. Crazy-eye Bill sat at the counter, nursing a coffee. A bit had dripped into his unkempt beard. He tipped her a nod and a wink.

A waitress guided her and Lucio to a booth in the back, giving them a knowing smirk.

"You're a bad influence," Jamie said after they were left alone with their menus. "If not for you, I wouldn't be out past two in the morning trying to sober up."

"Hey, I didn't tell you to drink."

"Yeah, but drinking did help. You have no idea how terrified I was. And that encounter with Brittney—" She shuddered. *I'm afraid of her. I don't know when that happened, but it's true, stupid as it sounds.*

Lucio nodded as if he'd read her mind. "She's been acting really creepy lately. But I don't want to talk about her. I think you did well tonight. People seemed to really like you. And some of them are people whose opinions carry a lot of weight."

"How did you get to know about everyone's social status?"

"I said I didn't want to talk about her." Lucio winked.

The server came back to take their orders and soon Jamie was devouring a Grand Slam with more butter and syrup than was sane. With that and two cups of coffee, she was feeling almost sober. But now she was sleepy, despite the caffeine.

Lucio gave her a studying look as she scraped the last bite off her plate. Her cheeks heated with embarrassment. "I'm so sorry. I ate like a pig."

"Don't say that," he said softly. "You skipped dinner tonight. You had to have been starving. Are you feeling better?"

"Yeah." It wasn't fair. Why couldn't she be with this gorgeous guy who treated her so well?

He paid for the meal and they left. The car still held a scant trace of warmth from the drive from Drew's lake house. Jamie's eyelids felt lined with lead as she rested her head on the seat.

She wondered about Lucio's naked torso. Her eyes drifted closed as she tried to imagine what that would look like. "I wanna have a sex dream about you."

Lucio's startled chuckle woke her up. "Excuse me?"

Oh shit. Did she say that out loud? "Um, nothing."

The drive to the trailer park didn't take long. A mixed blessing and tragedy, since she wanted him to forget what she'd mumbled, but she also didn't want her time with him to end.

When he parked, she unbuckled her seatbelt and put her hand over his. "I want to thank you."

"For what?"

"For everything. The new clothes, helping me make new friends, keeping me safe at the party, driving carefully, feeding me... Thank you for being so kind to me." To her humiliation, her voice broke off in a choked sob and tears streamed from her tired eyes.

"Hey," he said softly, then his strong arms were around her, pulling her into the driver's seat, practically on his lap. "It's okay. Even though you already know my motives, don't think that you don't deserve kindness. Honestly, I should have talked to you before noticing you'd be perfect to help me get back at Brittney."

Jamie rested her head on the crook of his neck and shoulder, feeling the heat radiating from his skin. The subtle, spicy cologne he wore smelled wonderful. The feeling of their bodies being so close together made her lower half stir with arousal.

"You don't have to feel bad for that. You had a girlfriend and other friends. And it's not like you were mean to me or anything. You stick up for me in shop class."

Lucio's strong hands caressed her back a moment before he drew her back. She bit back a moan of protest at being separated from his solid heat. "Your problem is that you lack confidence. Once you get some and go after what you want, you'll be unstoppable."

"What if I want you?" she whispered, aching with need.

"Oh hell," Lucio growled, before slanting his mouth over hers.

His lips were soft and molten hot. The kiss was firm, but not overly forceful like some guys liked to do. One of his hands splayed across her lower back, pulling her against his chest, the other tangled in her hair.

The steering wheel dug into her ribs, but she didn't mind. Lucio's lips caressed hers first in hard, hungry motions then alternated to a light, playful teasing that made her melt in his arms.

When his tongue slid across hers, Jamie jolted like she'd been struck by lightning.

Lucio stiffened and broke the kiss. Gently, he pushed her away. "Damn it. That shouldn't have happened."

"Why not?" She hated the pleading note in her voice even more than she hated the barely checked urge to throw herself back in his arms and resume the kiss that had turned her body to liquid.

"Because you're supposed to be with a guy who has a shot at being prom king." Lucio stared at the windshield, avoiding her gaze. But the heat in that stare still burned.

"But you said I didn't actually have to date that guy, only that we have to find one to escort me at the big night."

He opened his mouth, closed it, then shook his head. "Look. This can never happen again, okay? Valentine's Day is in two weeks. You need to find a date immediately."

Jamie flinched at the cold ultimatum, then lifted her chin, resolved to not let his rejection hurt her. "Fine. I will then."

She got out of the car, ignoring his offer to help her walk across the ice. It was all she could do not to slam the trailer door and wake her mom.

But despite her determination to forget about Lucio's kiss, she couldn't stop dreaming about it the moment she fell into bed.

Chapter Eleven

Valentine's Day

Lucio cursed as he hung back in a dark corner of the gym watching Jamie and Drew dance. He didn't know why he was in such a bad mood. Things were going exactly as planned. Jamie had made several new friends in the last two weeks, often cutting into her time with him to go shopping or have coffee with a group of girls...or have coffee with Drew. And she had done exactly what he'd asked: she'd found a date for the Valentine's Day dance.

She and Drew looked good together. There was no denying it. He cleaned up well in a matching dark sport coat and slacks, and a button-up shirt, even if he was growing out a mullet. In a tux, he'd be even more classy.

Jamie wore a long dark red dress of crushed velvet. It wasn't one he'd bought her, but several people had complimented her on it. Her raven hair was swept up elegantly, and was held in place with a shiny silver clip that was crusted with fake rubies.

Lucio had to admit to himself that he was jealous. Agonizingly jealous. He wished he was the one holding her in his arms on that dance floor. Even if the music wasn't great.

Despite his insistence two weeks ago that they could never do it again, Lucio couldn't stop thinking about the kiss they'd shared. Her lips had been so soft beneath his, her mouth sweet tasting, and the heat of her body pressed against his had felt like paradise. The memory continued to give him shivers, an echo of the waves of pleasure that had cascaded over him during that kiss.

Before he gave in to temptation and charged out to that dance floor to cut in and take Jamie into his arms, Lucio forced himself to turn away and instead looked at Brittney swaying in Chet Morgan's embrace. Not even three weeks since Heather Price was buried in the cold ground and Brittney had Chet wrapped around her finger.

Lucio didn't buy the bullshit excuse that they were comforting each other. Brittney wanted Chet because he was the quarterback and she was captain of the cheerleading squad. That made them ideal for prom king and queen.

Such cold human manipulation made Lucio even more determined to stop Brittney from getting the crown she coveted so much.

Drew's voice interrupted his reverie. "Hey, man, are you sure you're okay with me taking Jamie to the dance tonight?"

"Yeah. Why wouldn't I be?" The lie tasted like dust.

"Because you looked like you wanted to murder me the whole time I was dancing with her."

Shit. Was he that obvious? "I told you, we're just friends. I'm...protective of her. She's helped me a lot in class and stuff."

"Whatever you say, man." Drew's light chuckle made Lucio's hands ball into fists at his sides.

"Okay, there is one thing," Lucio spoke through gritted teeth. "If you hurt her in any way, I'll kick your ass."

Drew held up his hands. "Whoa, man. I thought you knew me better than that."

Jamie's voice broke in. "Did I miss something?"

"No," Lucio said. "We were discussing how Chet's been acting really weird lately."

Drew's eyes widened. "I thought I was the only who noticed that. The other day I asked him how he was holding up after losing Heather and all, and for a minute, he seemed to have forgotten her."

Jamie gave them both a long, assessing look like she didn't believe them. Then she sighed and went along with Lucio's suggested topic. "Maybe he didn't really care about Heather as much as everyone was led to believe. Guys usually only care about themselves and their wants anyway."

"That's not true," Lucio argued, stung by her words. "Some of us care a lot about important people in our lives."

"Well, they have a strange way of showing it."

Drew stepped between them. "Um, this is getting awkward. I'm gonna take off and get a shake from Topper Too. You wanna come, Jamie?"

Jamie flashed one last glare at Lucio before favoring Drew with a brilliant smile. "I'd love a milkshake, Drew."

Lucio cursed himself while watching them leave. Then he asked Jamie's friend, Allison Winthrop, to dance, wondering if it was to get any hints as to whether Jamie and Drew would get serious, or to make Jamie jealous.

Allison shut down both notions before either could be fully formed in his mind. "I'm only dancing with you so I can have a chance to tell you that you're a moron."

"Why is that?" he asked warily.

"You've got it bad for Jamie, but you're gonna lose any chance with her if you keep making her date other guys in your ridiculous mission to make her prom queen."

"She *told* you about that?"

Allison blew a bubble with her gum and popped it. "Duh. I'm her best friend. She tells me everything." Her green eyes narrowed. "And I tell her everything, so don't even think about trying to use me to make her jealous or anything that would hurt her."

"Don't worry, I don't want to do anything to hurt her," he said emphatically.

Allison snorted, and snapped her gum. "Too late there."

Lucio's heart clenched. He never should have pushed Jamie away after the kiss. Never should have given her the demand to date someone. "Can I make it better?"

"I dunno." Allison shrugged. "But you're gonna have to figure out which is more important. Her, or revenge."

Chapter Twelve

Brittney strolled into Topper Too with Chet on her arm. Whatever enchantment Scar had laid upon the quarterback was almost too powerful. Chet waited for her outside of every class like a pathetic puppy, eager to carry her books.

He agreed with everything she said, and did anything she asked him to. Such devotion was a lot more boring and dissatisfying than she'd expected.

May could not come fast enough.

The diner was packed with people from the dance eating burgers and fries in their finery. She spotted Jamie Blair and Drew Creed in a corner booth, drinking milkshakes. Her eyes narrowed. First, she'd seen Jamie at Drew's party last month, now he'd taken her to the Valentine's Day dance.

Drew was one of the most popular guys in school. Not by virtue of athletic prowess, like most of Amteep High's elite, but because he threw the best parties. Why Drew was bothering with Jamie boggled the mind.

Maybe he was still on the rebound. Drew had been dating Jane Carpenter for all of junior year. They'd split up over the summer for some unknown reason that even the most determined gossipmongers hadn't been able to uncover. But everyone could tell that Drew had been pining all of senior year. Sure, Jane was a major nerd like Jamie, only with more money and style. She was guaranteed to be valedictorian. So Jamie was a major step down.

Maybe Drew didn't know how big a step down. Brittney had heard all about Jamie's little inheritance that allowed her to get a new wardrobe, but maybe the stupid girl was trying to buy a new identity too. After all, she'd always been the most imaginative during the games of make-believe they'd played as children. Well,

Brittney wouldn't let a friend, or even an acquaintance like Drew, be taken in by an imposter. That wouldn't be right.

She sauntered over to the corner booth, putting an extra sway in her hips so every man in the diner had something to admire. She slapped both palms down on Drew's table, leaning over to display her cleavage.

"Hi, Drew."

Drew gave her an indifferent look that was a far cry from the admiration she deserved. "Um. Hi, Brittney."

"Did you know that Jamie lives in the Springwood Trailer Park? It would be a shame if she was trying to pretend to be something she's not."

"I know where she lives," Drew said in an icy tone. "What's your point?"

"Yeah," a voice behind her chimed in. "What is your point?"

Brittney turned to see Stacey Johnson standing behind her, hands on her hips. "What's your problem, Brittney? You've been a complete bitch to Jamie since sixth grade, and she hasn't done a damn thing to you. And now that she's coming out of her shell and some of us want to hang out with her, you got an issue with it?"

For a moment, Brittney was speechless. How dare Stacey speak against her? They'd never been friends, but still, Brittney assumed there'd be some class loyalty there because of their equal social standing.

She recovered her voice. "We live in a society, Stacey. If someone forgets their place and steps out of the natural pecking order, then that society falls in danger of collapse. What's next? Inviting one of the AV Club geeks to sit at our lunch table?"

Stacey blinked at her, then laughed. "You're crazy, Brittney."

Chet spoke up. "Don't call her names."

Good dog, Brittney nearly said aloud. Instead, she rolled her eyes at Stacey, Drew, and Jamie. "Whatever. Come on, Chet. Let's go to Bava's. We can do with some more class."

"Okay," Chet said obediently.

Despite her voluntarily leaving for someplace better, Brittney had the odd feeling that she was slinking away. She seethed all through dinner and during Chet's pathetic efforts at making love to her in the back of his Mercedes. It felt like he was trying to jackhammer her into the leather seats. How had Heather said he was good? Her dearly departed friend had to have been lying to make herself look better, unless she was truly too dumb to know better.

Lucio had been a much better lover. Too bad he was a loser. Still, maybe after she won prom queen, she could give him a consolation fuck. At least he wasn't slumming with Jamie Blair like she'd feared when she'd seen them together at Drew's party.

Thinking of Jamie made her remember Stacey's betrayal all over again. "Fuck," she growled just as Chet finished.

"Glad it was good for you, babe," he said in the dazed voice that had become usual for him.

"Yeah." Brittney rolled her eyes. "Take me home, Chet."

"Sure, babe."

When she got home, Scar was waiting for her in her bedroom. "I didn't summon you," she snapped. "And I'm too tired to deal with you right now."

The demon's form expanded, towering up to the ceiling. He loomed over her with flickering yellow eyes and roared, "Who do you think you are to speak to me with such insolence?"

Brittney shrank back. "I'm sorry, Scarlionapskhis." She used his full name to remind him and her that she hadn't forgotten who he was. "I misspoke in my exhaustion."

"You had better not forget yourself again. I made you and I can unmake you." Scar shrank back to a man's height and the air became easier to breathe again. "I am hungry."

"I know. I shall feed you again tomorrow."

"Feed me now."

Brittney bit back a protest and dug her car keys out of her pocket. "Very well. Do you want cow or sheep?"

"I want another human." Scar's voice was implacable. "Your friend's blood was so sweet and her death gave me such power. It is past time I have another such feast."

He wanted her to kill someone again? And this time on purpose. Brittney opened her mouth to carefully object, then closed it. "As a matter of fact, I have the perfect sacrifice in mind, but unfortunately, I can't get to her tonight. She is an enemy, not a friend, so I can't convince her to meet me somewhere, and if I don't take her alone, people will get suspicious and I could be arrested. But I can get to her soon. I know most of the places she goes."

"If you do not deliver her in seven days' time, I will devour you." Scar licked his fangs. "For now, I would like another cow."

Chapter Thirteen

March

Jamie sighed and watched rain trickle down the windshield of Drew's Volvo. "I can't do this anymore."

She wished she didn't have to say it. Drew was super nice and handsome, though she didn't really like his hairstyle, which was short in the front and longer in the back. It wasn't quite a full-on mullet, like a lot of the country music fans wore, but it was close enough to make her want to suggest that he either trim the back or grow it all out...like Lucio's hair.

Damn Lucio. It was all his fault that she was somehow not enjoying dating a cute, smart, rich, popular guy, whose parties were famous in town, and responsible for the new positive regard of her peers. Sure, Drew had a good shot at prom king, like Lucio had wanted, but he was also a decent guy.

She wished she had feelings for him, but she could only manage to think of him as a friend. Hell, she couldn't even muster a stirring of attraction. The first time he'd kissed her, it was everything she could do to kiss him back because she felt numb in his arms. Nothing like the storm of pleasure and excitement that had roared through her the night Lucio had kissed her.

Now no other guy would do.

Still, Jamie had really tried to make things work with Drew. Not to please Lucio, but to punish him. To show him to be careful what he wished for. Because she knew he'd felt something too when he'd kissed her. It had been evident in the fire in his eyes and his ragged breath when he'd pushed her away. But something had stopped him. When he'd pitched his original plan to her, he'd reassured her that she wouldn't have to actually date any guy as long as she could get one to take her to prom. Then, after the kiss, he'd suddenly changed his mind and had given her the ridiculous ultimatum to find some other guy to date.

Drew broke the awkward silence, bringing her back to the present. "I'm so relieved."

"What?" Jamie's jaw dropped. She hadn't expected him to be heartbroken or anything, since they'd only been going out a little over three weeks, and with only a few dates in that time, but relieved?

"Yeah." Drew ran a hand through his brown short-long hair. "I don't know what's going on between you and Lucio, but you two clearly have it bad for each other. And there's something else. Jane and I got to talking the other night, and, well...I think I asked you out to make her jealous."

Laughter burst from Jamie's lips. Drew and Jane Carpenter had been a major item last year. But because they were both siblings of survivors of the Summer Camp Massacre, they were pressured from the notoriety. No one really knew why the two had broken up, but Jamie suspected the constant attention from being associated with a tragedy had something to do with it.

Jamie liked Jane. The willowy blonde was sweet to everyone and super-smart and, most importantly, kind. They'd been lab partners in biology and had the best grades in the class. It didn't surprise Jamie in the slightest that Drew still carried a torch for Jane.

Drew's brows drew together with bemusement. "That...was not the reaction I'd expected."

"Revenge on an ex seems to be a theme at our school." She shook her head at the ridiculous coincidence.

"Because you're trying to get revenge on Lucio?"

"Only because *he's* using *me* to get revenge on Brittney Shaw," Jamie countered.

Drew gaped at her in astonishment. "Was that why you two stopped being so chummy? Did you think he started spending time with you to make her jealous? Because I think he really likes you."

Jamie bit back the urge to ask Drew what made him so convinced about Lucio's feelings. Instead, after careful consideration, she told him the truth, because after being drawn into hers and Lucio's problems, he deserved to know. "No, he wants me to become prom queen, but doesn't think he has a shot at prom king. That's why Brittney dumped him."

Drew's eyes widened. "Whoa. Brittney's even more mental than I thought. And wait, Lucio thinks *I* could be voted prom king?"

"Please don't tell him I told you." Shit, maybe she shouldn't have told him.

"I won't." But the promise did not sound at all sincere. "But I see the quandary. He's trying to put his mission over his feelings for you. Makes me tempted to keep dating you just to make him sweat."

Jamie nodded. That had been her mindset for the past two weeks. "That was my idea too, but I didn't want to keep using you. I *do* like you, but only as a friend."

"Well, *I* was using *you* back, to be fair." Drew shrugged. "So, we're even. I'd like to offer to take you to prom if you need me to, but if Jane takes me back..."

"You'll want to take her, of course," Jamie said quickly. "And I'm not even sure I want to keep being part of Lucio's plan. I mean, part of me does since Brittney's so horrible, and I'd love to see her taken down a peg or two, but..."

"You want to sort things out with Lucio first."

"Yeah."

Had he pushed her away because his feelings for her scared him in some way, or because he thought he was too good for her? Or could there be a chance that he wasn't over Brittney?

She wished she had the courage to ask him, but in the long run, it didn't matter. His rejection had hurt, but she didn't want him to know how much.

Drew turned on his windshield wipers and pulled his car back onto the road. "Well, I know that he usually hangs out at the Cove Bowl on Thursday nights, but then again, he's been putting in extra hours at Bava's."

Bava's. Where he said he'd take me and my mom any time we asked. Jamie ached with sudden longing to see Lucio right now. "Well, would you mind checking out the Cove Bowl to see if he's there?"

"Love to." Drew turned right onto Sherman Avenue. "Jane likes to hang out there too. She's a terrible bowler, but she loves their arcade and dart board."

94

The Cove Bowl was an old smoky bowling alley, and the closest thing to a bar where teens could hang out. Most of them didn't bowl though, much to the relief of the middle-aged adults who took their bowling leagues seriously.

Instead, people grouped together at the tables to eat, or they huddled around the arcade games and pinball table, and some monopolized the dartboards and pool table. Jane was nowhere in sight, but Lucio was at the pinball table. Jamie spotted other classmates. Stacey Johnson was playing foosball with Jennifer Armstrong. Shane Lowry was at a table with some guys on the football team, and Jason Shaye and Pete Nance were at the little arcade, intent on a game of *Karate Champ*.

And Brittney Shaw was at a darkened table in the corner by the pool tables. For once, Chet Morgan was not at her side. Nor were any of her loyal followers. Seeing one of the most popular girls in school sitting alone was unnerving on some level. Was it because people had finally decided that Brittney's cruelty had gone too far and that she should be shunned? Somehow, Jamie doubted it, especially looking at Brittney's expression, which was more calculating than petulant.

Protectiveness welled up in her heart. Brittney had better not be planning to mess with Lucio. Jamie kept an eye on the wicked cheerleader of the west and made her way to the guy who had seized her heart and invaded her dreams.

Lucio tensed as if he sensed her and Drew behind him and let his ball fall into the hole as he turned around. "Jamie. Drew. What's up?"

"We broke up," Jamie said.

"Um… Sorry to hear that." But to Jamie's amusement and relief, he didn't look sorry.

Drew chuckled. "Yeah, yeah. Keep telling yourself that. Anyway, I brought your study partner here because she wants to talk to you privately. She'll need a ride home too, because I'm heading over to that payphone to call Jane, since I don't see her here, and beg for her to take me back. You kids drive safe now."

He tipped an imaginary hat and left.

"Hi." Jamie's voice was barely above a whisper. This was a mistake. What if he laughed at her? What if he left her here stranded and she'd have to use the few bills in her wallet to call a cab?

Lucio's dark eyes stared at her so intently that part of her longed to run. "Hey. If you want to talk privately, my car's outside. I can't believe Drew just left you here though. What if I was a jerk and didn't want to give you a ride home?"

Exactly what she'd feared, but his tone assured her. "You're not though, are you?"

He sighed. "No. I'm not."

On their way out, Brittney thrust her foot out, making Jamie pitch forward.

"Oops." Brittney's white teeth flashed in a smarmy smile.

Jamie's fist balled up at her side and she almost brought it up to Brittney's chin, but then she saw a burly man in a Cove Bowl uniform watching them. Brittney had probably seen him before her stunt and orchestrated it accordingly.

Lucio opened his mouth, but Jamie spoke before he could. "You're lucky I don't want to get banned from this place, but one of these days, I might be more like you and forget to think about the consequences of my actions."

Brittney hugged her arms and pretended to shake while she laughed. "Ooh, I'm soooo scared."

Jamie and Lucio flipped her the bird before walking out. Jamie half expected Brittney to follow them with more taunts, but when she paused at the door to look back over her shoulder, Brittney had swiveled around in her seat to watch Stacey and Jennifer playing Foosball.

Lucio opened the passenger door of his Trans Am as he always did. Jamie had gotten in and he was settled in the driver's seat when he said, "Listen, I was wrong about pushing you away and pressuring you to date someone else because they'd make a good prom king. I'm not going to do that again. And if you want to quit the plan to be prom queen—"

"Oh no." Jamie laughed and clenched her fists in her lap, still wishing she'd punched Brittney in the face. "I'm still on board for the prom queen part. I am so sick of Brittney's shit. That bitch is going down."

"Okay, but only if that's what you want." He started the car and turned down the heater as cold air blasted through the vents. "As for me, while I'd still like to see her pay, not so much for dumping me, but for how she treats everyone she sees as beneath her, I don't want to make you do anything you don't want to do. And I don't really like the idea of you dating another guy. I never liked it to begin with to be honest."

"Then why were you so insistent that I do it?" Was the car's heater warming up, or did his words warm her that much? "Is it because I'm not good enough for you?"

"If we're going there, you're *too* good for me." Lucio leaned over and brushed a lock of her hair behind her ear. Pleasant shivers raced down her spine at his gentle touch.

"First, I wanted to ignore my attraction to you because I figured it would mess up my plan. Then, I was afraid of having feelings for someone so soon after being with someone else for so many months and having them throw me away like garbage. I don't want to be hurt like that again."

Jamie put her hand over his, reveling in the heat of his skin beneath her palm. "I understand. My last boyfriend hurt me so bad that I didn't want to think about being with anyone for over a year. And even after I'd gotten over that, I've been too scared to get involved with anyone because of all those fears about my future that I told you about."

"Have you changed your mind?" Lucio asked. His thumb brushed across her wrist.

Jamie's heart pounded against her ribs. "Yes. Have you?"

"I have." Lucio lowered his head so they were face-to-face. "I really like spending time with you, especially before I ruined things and made shit awkward. And I'd like to spend time with you as *more* than friends."

Jamie restrained herself from burying her hands in his long, soft curls and pulling him forward for a kiss. She needed to stay cool. "Okay, but no one can know because of the plan."

Lucio nodded. "The plan. Right. Can we forget about it for tonight? I missed you so much."

His words melted her attempt to stay cool. Jamie closed inches between them, covering his mouth with hers.

As hot bliss curled her toes, Jamie felt an alarming surge of fear and excitement.

This relationship would be more cataclysmic than any she'd ever had.

For better or for worse.

Chapter Fourteen

Brittney watched Stacey and Jennifer put on their coats and throw away their garbage left over from the bowling alley junk they'd eaten. Quickly, Brittney headed out of the bowling alley and ducked into her car. If Jennifer and Stacey had driven together, her plan would fail—again. She didn't know how much longer she could placate Scar and keep delaying the sacrifice she owed him. And Stacey was beginning to piss her off even more. First, for daring to mouth off to her and defend the trailer trash, but also because it looked like Stacey was trying to steal Jennifer's friendship away from Brittney.

Speaking of Jennifer. *She might have to pay too,* Scar's voice whispered hungrily.

As if conjured by the thought, Stacey and Jennifer appeared. The two hugged—to Brittney's everlasting irritation—before separating and heading off to separate cars.

Perfect.

Brittney closed her eyes as she waited for Stacey to pull out of the parking lot. "Scar, are you still with me?"

The reply came from inside her, eager and bloodthirsty. *Yes.*

Jennifer drove away first in her stupid Datsun 240Z. That's why Brittney hadn't seen her car. The damn thing was too tiny. She always hit her head riding in it with Jennifer.

Stacey's car was much more practical. A brand-new Pontiac Sunbird convertible. Even though Brittney loved her Porsche, she'd seethed with envy when Stacey had driven up in it after Christmas break. Its cherry red paint gleamed under the streetlights, making it easy to see in the foggy night when Stacey pulled out of the parking lot.

Maybe it was time to trade in for a convertible herself.

Brittney started her Porsche and followed Stacey at a safe distance, praying that the bitch was going home and not somewhere else. Stacey lived in one of the old-money lake houses around Bela Bay. A *real* lake house, and not a lakeview wannabe like Drew's. She ground her teeth, thinking of Drew disrespecting her as well.

But Stacey's house was another thing to envy, since Brittney lived in one of the newer neighborhoods of lake houses above Regan's Point. Where they had to go down a long, precarious staircase built into the tall cliff to be able to access their dock. Some of the old-money houses were like that too. Some even had their beach property separated by the road, but not Stacey's. She could walk out her back door, cross her lawn, and put her toes in the sand.

"It's too bad you're not the one who throws the parties, Stacey," Brittney murmured. "Then it would be you that I'd have to spare."

As Stacey's car left the downtown area and headed up Lakeview Drive, Brittney allowed herself to follow closer. The fog and lack of streetlights made her only able to see a faint red glow of taillights.

After they passed the marina and the first cluster of lake houses, the fog and darkness enclosed the two cars, making Brittney edge nearer. The farther apart the houses grew, the closer Brittney's car drew to Stacey's back bumper. But she couldn't let Stacey get too close to home. Not where she could scream for help.

Stacey's car accelerated suddenly, bringing an unwelcome distance. She must have figured out that she was being tailed.

"Oh no you don't, bitch." Brittney floored her accelerator, taking pleasure in the muted rumble of her Porsche's engine.

Stacey's little Pontiac was no match. Especially when the road began to wind around sharp curves. Brittney saw the Sunbird swerve and she cackled, keeping up the chase. The fog and treacherous path made Brittney a little nervous, but she knew that Scar would keep her safe.

Finally, they reached a section of road where there were no houses, except for the abandoned Raimi house that loomed on the cliff above them farther up. For a moment, Brittney was tempted to swerve her car and cut Stacey off and try to force her to head up the driveway to the town's most infamous haunted house.

But even she wouldn't dare go near there.

Scar's voice roared in her head. *Pay attention!*

Suddenly, a dark form appeared in the road in front of Stacey's car. Stacey slammed on the brakes and tried to swerve to avoid hitting the yellow-eyed figure. Brittney carefully hit her brakes and pulled to the opposite side, watching with delight as Stacey lost control of her vehicle.

The Pontiac spun and slid off the side of the road and down the embankment. Brittney turned off her ignition and got out of her car, listening to the wonderful sound of the car rolling down the steep hill and crashing down onto the beach below.

She quickly ran across the road to the embankment to see the crushed and dented Pontiac lying sideways on the sand. A low moan came from the smashed windshield. *Shit.* She'd have to finish this. The headlights of the Pontiac illuminated the ancient wood steps down to the beach, where the Raimi family could access their dock.

Brittney rushed down them, grimacing as overgrown branches scratched her face and tore at her coat. She reached the beach just as Stacey wriggled free of the wreckage of her car.

"Brittney," Stacey moaned. "Help me."

"Help you?" Brittney laughed. "I'm here to kill you."

"It was *you* who ran me off the road?" The pitiful look in Stacey's eyes made Brittney snort with derision.

She leaned over and grinned at her prey. "You should have showed me proper respect."

"What the—" Stacey broke off as her eyes shifted to something behind Brittney and widened with horror. A scream ripped the air, making Brittney wince.

Scar laughed. "Don't worry. This area has a certain protection."

Stacey ran, but the pumps she wore slowed her down, kicking up more sand than propelling her. Brittney had worn the old gym shoes she saved for dirty jobs like this, and caught up to Stacey easily.

She was about to snatch the collar of Stacey's oversize sweatshirt, but suddenly, Stacey tripped and went tumbling down onto the sand. Brittney stalked forward, listening to Stacey sob and watching her crawl across the sand. If she kept it up, she'd end up in the lake.

Stacey realized this at almost the last minute and crawled toward the rotting dock. She started to pull herself by grasping one of the pilings, and shrieked when the wood splintered and broke off into a large shard.

So delicious, Scar's voice purred. *Her fear and pain season my feast.*

Brittney laughed and stepped on Stacey's calves, keeping her on the ground. She grabbed a huge handful of Stacey's hair. She pulled Stacey's head back and pointed Stacey's face toward the largest jagged splinter sticking out of the piling. Her other hand kept Stacey's shoulder pinned.

"No," Stacey whimpered as Brittney pushed her head toward the splinter. "No, no..."

The pleas turned to a piercing scream as the tip of the wood pierced her eyeball. Beneath Stacey's agonized howls, Brittney could hear the eye rupture, a wet, squelching sound, like a giant zit that had been popped.

Blood and other fluids squirted onto the dock piling as Brittney kept pressing Stacey's head forward. Scar's primeval strength helped her keep her enemy immobile as she slowly drove the splinter into Stacey's brain. A part of the demon was inside her. She felt its chaotic glee at the brutality of the kill.

She then felt the life seep from Stacey's body a moment later before it went limp beneath her. Leaving the head impaled on the splinter, she released the body and stepped back, watching Scar feast. During the killings and feedings, the demon's omniscient composure vanished, transforming him into a feral beast.

A pang of fear knotted Brittney's stomach at the realization of the danger of having such a dangerous being working with her. She shrugged away the fear. *I'm the one who summoned him. I'm the one who he depends on for meals. I hold the power.*

After Scar finished dining, Brittney slid what was left of the body into the water under the dock. The car she left, since there was nothing she could do about it. It would likely be awhile before someone spotted it.

Chapter Fifteen

Tuesday morning, Drew cornered Lucio in the school parking lot. "You should have told me about the plan to make Brittney lose prom queen to the girl she likes to bully most. I would have been in from day one."

"Jamie told you?" Lucio wanted to be angry with her, but he knew that having help from someone as well-connected as Drew would be a good thing.

"Yeah. And she told me not to tell you she told, but I can't help it. I want to help."

"How?"

"Well, I can make sure Jamie is at all the right parties for starters. Not only mine, and I can help you two recruit the right prom king." Drew's eyes had flickered with enthusiasm. "One that will only be there for the big night. Unfortunately, it can't be me since Jane and I are back together, but I'm sure we can find a suitable candidate who will play his role and keep his hands to himself."

"Okay, fine." Lucio shook Drew's hand. "You're in."

Not even five minutes after the first period bell rang, Lucio found himself wondering if he should have told Drew no and shut the whole thing down because Stacey Johnson was reported missing.

When the announcement had been read over the school intercom, it took every bit of Lucio's will not to leave government class and find Jamie. His protective instincts were in overdrive, and he had to remind himself that he'd seen Jamie's car in the student lot this morning, not far from where he'd parked.

Maybe it was time to suggest riding to school together.

The moment they met up in the cafeteria for lunch, Lucio and Jamie started talking about Stacey. Allison, Drew, Jane, and Jason

Shaye were seated at the table around them, looking equally concerned.

"I wonder if the animal mutilator has taken their first victim," Lucio said grimly when he turned to Jamie. "I think you should let me give you rides to school and back. Then I'll know you're safe."

Jamie shook her head. "We live on opposite sides of town. That would be a waste of time and gas."

Allison interjected. "Wait, you guys think the crazy person who's been massacring all those farm animals is a budding serial killer? Everyone on the news seems to think it's a Satanic cult."

Drew heaved a melodramatic sigh. "That's because everything abnormal is automatically assumed to be Satanic these days. Also, the news people think every teenager in town is part of a cult. Especially guys like Lucio with their long hair, black clothes, and heavy metal shirts. Oh, and most of the A/V Club, since they play Dungeons and Dragons."

Jason made an exaggerating coughing sound. "Actually, the animal killer might really be a Satanist. A couple years ago, all of the occult books were taken from the library."

"They were?" Lucio did *not* feel optimistic about that news. "I don't remember hearing about that."

"I don't think it made the news or anything. I only know because I overheard my sister and her boyfriend—husband now—talking about it back when they were researching the history of her house. It's haunted, you know," Jason said the last nonchalantly, as if haunted houses were a normal thing. "Anyway, the librarian assumed that it was probably some overzealous church lady or protective parent who took them."

Jamie leaned forward, her beautiful face rapt with Jason's tale. "But what if it wasn't a concerned parent or religious nut who took those books? Remember, people's pets started going missing a little over a year ago. And now the pets seem to stop going missing and it's farm animals being mutilated."

"Are you saying you think someone was sacrificing them?" Lucio shuddered at the thought. He turned back to Jason. "And when did those books go missing from the library?"

"Back in eighty-one…three years ago," Jason replied after taking a bite of a carrot stick.

Allison turned to Drew with a smug look. "See? It totally could be a cult."

"Wait," Drew said. "Stacey was only reported missing. What makes you guys think she's dead? Let alone mutilated like the animals?"

Lucio paused. He *knew* Stacey was dead. He didn't know how he knew, but he did. He looked at Jamie, and from the look of resigned dread in her eyes, she sensed it too.

Jason looked around the lunch table. "When was the last time any of you saw her?"

"The night before last at the Cove Bowl." Lucio pushed aside his lunch tray. He had no desire to finish his sloppy joe. "She was hanging out with Jennifer Armstrong."

"And Brittney Shaw," Jamie added. "Wait, no. Brittney was sitting alone at a table far away from everyone."

She was right. Brittney hadn't been with her friends or her new conquest. Lucio realized that Chet hadn't been at the bowling alley that night. Since he was practically glued to Brittney's side these days, that had been a little weird.

The bell rang and they cleared their trays. As Lucio walked Jamie to class, he once more brought up the suggestion to let him give her rides to and from school. She wasn't having it. "Too wasteful."

"Okay, then what if we take turns?" Lucio suggested. "Then we'd be about even on time and gas."

"We can't," Jamie said quietly, giving him a pointed look. "Our relationship is supposed to be secret for now, remember?"

Suddenly, she looked past him, then she quickly grabbed his hand and shook it like they'd done a business deal before slipping into her classroom. Lucio was puzzled at her odd gesture until he turned and saw Brittney staring hot daggers into Jamie's back. Then she gave Lucio a smarmy smile that made him feel like she'd covered him in slime.

His revulsion had little to do with her petty reasons for dumping him. Now there was something else, and Lucio had the uncomfortable feeling that whatever was wrong with Brittney had been there all along. He'd been blind to it the whole time he'd been dating her.

Maybe Jamie was right to keep their relationship hidden from Brittney. At least until it was determined whether she had anything to do with Stacey's disappearance. But that didn't mean he wouldn't make sure that he and Jamie had time to enjoy being boyfriend and girlfriend.

After school, during their study session at his house, and between stealing kisses, he asked for a dinner date tomorrow.

"Can we go to Bava's?" Jamie asked with adorable eagerness as she bent to pick up his cat, Bruce.

"Sure, but I can take you to a different restaurant if you want," Lucio offered, in case she was trying to save him money. He reached down and petted Steve, who was winding around his chair legs. "I mean, you've already tried half the dishes here with all the leftovers my dad brings home."

"Are you kidding? For one thing, you and your dad keep telling me that the food is so much better fresh, even though the sauce in that leftover clam linguine haunts my dreams. But I want to try the Lobster Fra Diavolo that your dad was talking about the other day." She paused as if thinking something over. "Unless it costs too much."

"You can have whatever you want. I get a family discount. I guess Bava's will work great for our first official date. We're going to have to be sneaky when we try other places. Dad can be moody with some of his competition and fine with others." He rolled his eyes. "It's not like he doesn't understand that people want to eat more than one cuisine, but even after winning awards and turning a profit, his first few years made him insecure."

Jamie frowned. "You always sound grumpy when you talk about your dad. Why?"

Lucio's first instinct was to refuse to talk about his father, but something about her sympathetic tone coupled with her not having a father around made him want to talk to her about it.

"Mom died when I was nine. She was a maid at the resort and slipped when cleaning a bathroom and broke her neck on the bathtub. For the first year after, Dad ignored me to nurse his grief, as if I wasn't also suffering. Then he used the huge amount of insurance money he got to open his restaurant. He's put all his heart and time into Bava's ever since. I pretty much had to raise myself."

"I had no idea." Jamie's expression became sympathetic. "We can go somewhere else for our date."

"No," Lucio said quickly. "Don't get me wrong. I've honestly grown to love the restaurant and I have a lot of pride in learning to cook from my father and how to run the place. I'm also proud of him for getting to accomplish his dream. But I also carry a lot of resentment from the place taking up so much of my dad's attention when I needed him to be there for me."

"Is that why you got in so much trouble over the last couple years?"

Lucio sighed. "Yeah. Textbook acting out because 'Daddy didn't love me enough.' I'm kind of ashamed of that now."

When he and Jamie went downstairs, Lucio saw that his father was already home as if summoned by the talk he'd had with Jamie.

"You're home early." Lucio tried not to sound suspicious.

"Slow night." Mario grinned at Jamie. "Leaving so soon? We have homemade gelato in the freezer."

"Thanks, Mr. Argento, but I have to get going." She turned back to Lucio and tilted her face up for a kiss. "Pick me up at five-thirty tomorrow night?"

"Sounds perfect." He took her in his arms and kissed her good-bye.

After the door closed behind Jamie, Mario grinned at Lucio. "I am so happy you and that girl finally abandoned the pretense of being just friends. She seems very nice. I never liked that other girl."

Lucio smirked. "I know you didn't."

Mario raised one dark eyebrow. "Did you stay with her to spite me?"

"A few months ago, I would have said no. Now, I'm not so sure."

Until Jamie brought it up tonight, Lucio hadn't really thought all that much about the bitter anger he'd felt at his father's neglecting him after Mom died. Now that he was older, he understood that Dad had put all of his effort into his restaurant for the sake of making sure that Lucio had a good life, but when he was younger, he hadn't cared about having nice clothes and good food and health insurance. He'd wanted his father.

Only now was he beginning to grasp his father's side of the situation. He might even be starting to forgive him.

But he wasn't ready to talk about that. "I'm taking Jamie to Bava's tomorrow night."

Dad's face split in a wide grin. "That's wonderful. We'll make it the most romantic meal of her life. I'll ensure that the tablecloths are laundered, the candles replaced, and only the best cuts of meat will be on hand in the kitchen. Dinner will be on the house, and I'll serve you personally."

"Don't you dare," Lucio interrupted his dad's rapid-fire planning. He half feared that Mario would sing to him and Jamie like the chefs in *Lady and the Tramp* did. "*I'll* pay for dinner. I don't want to look cheap. And no offense, but I think having my dad hovering around me and my date will put a damper on the romantic mood. I mean, what if Grandpa had been your waiter when you took Mom out to dinner?"

"Okay, okay." Mario nodded vigorously. "But you'll still receive your discount and I will be in the kitchen, making sure Jamie receives the best."

***

The following night, Mario was true to his word. The food was unbelievable, and the service, care of Mike, the head waiter, was impeccable without being overbearing. Although Lucio ordered his usual favorite, manicotti, which he could make in his sleep, the cheese tasted somehow richer and there was something more savory than usual about the sauce. Jamie audibly moaned with almost every bite of her Lobster Fra Diavolo, and closed her eyes as if trying to turn off all her senses except for taste.

For the first time in years, he was proud to have a father who ran such a fantastic restaurant, and proud that he could bring his girlfriend here.

Contentment suffused him pleasantly. It was nice to be back where he'd been in January. Showing Jamie new experiences, feeding her, making her happy. If only there wasn't the niggling worry that she could be in danger because of his original idea to make her prom queen.

Lucio watched Jamie wipe up the rest of the sauce on her plate with the last breadstick. Then he saw his father peeking out from the kitchen, watching her as well. He gave him a subtle but firm shake of his head.

"What was that about?" Jamie asked.

"Just making sure Dad doesn't come out and embarrass us. How was your food?"

She heaved a blissful sigh. "This was the best thing I've eaten in my life. I guess I'm lucky to not be rich because I'd weigh five hundred pounds in record time. I'm sorry if I wasn't too talkative."

"Don't be. I was busy devouring the food too." Lucio settled back in his chair. "Though I do want to spend more time with you."

"About a possible prom king?" Jamie asked.

"I don't want to talk about that," Lucio said flatly. "And though part of me wishes you hadn't told Drew about it, at least he's probably better than me at finding possible candidates. He said he'd work on it, so let's not worry tonight and enjoy ourselves. Do you want to go to the movies? The drive-in reopened for the spring."

"That sounds lovely. But we should take my car."

"Why? Is it because mine's more recognizable?"

Her cheeks turned bright pink. "Because the backseat folds down."

"Ah." His body took note and he was rock-hard a moment later.

They went back to Springwood to switch cars and then headed to the drive-in. *Children of the Corn* was playing, but they didn't pay much attention since they were too busy kissing and cuddling.

Lucio marveled at how right she felt in his arms. Every hollow and curve of her body fit against his like they were made for each other. And although he could tell from some of her movements that she was likely a virgin, the passionate way in which she held him tightly and kissed him made this little make-out session more sensuous than anything he'd ever done with Brittney.

And when she grabbed his hand and shakily placed it over her breast, he went dizzy with arousal and tenderness at her welcoming his touch. Somehow, she made him feel like he earned each level they reached in physical intimacy.

By the time the movie was over, they were panting and the windows of Jamie's little Honda had fogged up. Lucio was so hard that he ached, but he forced himself to take deep breaths and tamp down his ardor.

This was only their first official date. There was no way he was going to try to go all the way with her so soon. He'd move slowly and keep to whatever pace she was most comfortable with.

But even the cold shower he took after he got home couldn't stop a torrent of erotic fantasies from haunting him all night.

***

The next day, Lucio vacillated between delight at seeing Jamie at school, and torment at not being able to kiss her or hold her hand. He didn't know how much longer he could take this pretense of being only friends.

Sitting next to her at lunch, and feeling the heat radiating from her leg pressed against his, he imagined how wonderful it would be to convince her to skip the rest of the school day and go to his place.

Then Allison shattered his daydream.

"You were right, Lucio. Stacey's dead. I saw it on the news this morning. Her car was found crashed on the beach off Bela's Point. The police say that it looks like she lost control and went off the road. They didn't find a body, but there was blood on the sand, so they think she went through the windshield and ended up in the lake. They're dragging the lake looking for the body, but it could have ended up in the St. John River by now since the current's so heavy from the thaw."

Lucio put down the rest of his sandwich. "Aren't those beaches private? I'd think someone would have noticed a wrecked car on their property a lot sooner."

Allison shrugged. "The lake thawed only a couple weeks ago, so I don't know how many people are taking their boats out or walking on the beach, for one thing. For another, it was the section of beach below the Raimi house where Stacey's car was found."

"Oh shit," Drew interjected. "That house is pure evil. Look up the history of that place, and you'll get nightmares. Go near it and—"

Jane chimed in, "You could die. Seriously. When my family moved here, I researched this town's history and have never seen anything like it. A lot of people think the Raimi House is haunted, like the Sazerac House, but I don't think it is. I think the very earth the place is built on is tainted. Hundreds of people have died there.

Including a property surveyor last fall." She paused and took a sip of chocolate milk. "That said, I've never heard of anyone dying on the beach part of the property. There's a road separating it from the house, and not only that, but the borders of the Indian burial ground don't go all the way to the water, for natural reasons."

"The Raimi House was built on Indian burial ground?"

Jane nodded. "A lot of downtown Amteep and parts of Sinchlep were. The soccer field on the Amteep Community College campus is on top of one as well. But the one that the Raimi House was built on was different."

Jamie leaned forward in rapt fascination. "How so?"

The bell rang before Jane could answer.

Lucio accompanied Jamie while they dumped their lunch trays. "I wonder if the Raimi House had something to do with Stacey's death."

"Possibly," Jamie said, though she looked doubtful. "I still think it's spooky that Brittney was around both times that someone ended up dead."

"You think she could have run Stacey off the road that night?"

"I don't know what I think. I know she and Stacey didn't get along." Jamie shook her head. "And that method would have kept her manicured hands clean."

"Stay away from her," Lucio said so sharply that she flinched. "And let's take turns giving each other rides to and from school."

"But people will catch on—"

"I don't care what people think," Lucio growled. "I don't want you alone until we learn whether these so-called accidents were accidents. I care about you too much to allow you to be in danger."

For a moment, Jamie looked like she was going to argue.

Then she sighed.

"Fine. You can take me to school and back tomorrow."

Chapter Sixteen

One week later

After her third date with Lucio, Jamie practically danced up the stairs to her trailer. He made her feel like she could accomplish anything with him at her side. And his kisses and caresses awakened feelings she'd never known existed within her. When she closed the door behind her, she leaned against it with a sigh. She was in love. She couldn't deny it. Though she was nowhere near ready to tell him that.

But she was ready to go all the way with him. Her eyes still closed, Jamie relived the feel of his lips on her neck, the way his kiss directed a hot flare of arousal to her core. And how his hardness had felt against her arousal. The layers of clothing separating them had been torture. She wanted more. *Needed* more.

"Ahem," Mom's voice interrupted Jamie's rapturous state.

"Mom." Jamie opened her eyes to see Leigh on the couch. "I didn't know you were home." She hadn't even looked to see if the Toyota was in the driveway when Lucio dropped her off.

"I wanted to talk to you, but it's hard to catch you these days, so I took off early." Leigh patted the spot on the couch beside her. "Come sit by me."

"Okay." She sat. Shadow immediately jumped on her lap. "Am I in trouble?"

"No." Leigh sighed. "Jamie, I know you're eighteen, almost a grown woman and capable of making your own decisions, but that's not going to stop me from worrying about you. First you get all those new clothes, and then you spend all that time with that handsome Italian boy. Then you date an equally handsome and even wealthier boy for two weeks and look miserable the entire time. Now you're seeing Lucio again."

"Uh-huh, that's correct." Jamie stroked her cat and didn't elaborate further.

Leigh crossed her arms over her chest and fixed her with a stern look. "And there's a million other things going on that you're not telling me about."

"Also correct."

"I hope you're being careful," Leigh's tone shifted from severe to soft. "And I hope you know that you can talk to me about anything."

Jamie didn't really want to bring up her and Lucio's increasing worry that there was a murderer on the loose, *or* that she was thinking of losing her virginity to Lucio. But she had to give Mom something, so with feigned reluctance, she admitted, "I'd been afraid that Lucio wasn't over his ex-girlfriend, so when Drew asked me out, I said yes. But it turned out that Drew was the one not over his ex. And I still had feelings for Lucio."

"Even though you insisted you were only friends." Leigh shook her head. "I don't know what prompted your sudden popularity, but for the most part, I'm happy you're finally getting out and having some fun. I'd thought you were going to take after me and be overwhelmed by social situations."

Oh, but I am, Jamie longed to say. While the parties and hanging out with new friends was exciting and validating, the novelty was beginning to wear off. Many nights she wished she and Lucio could hang out alone instead. But she couldn't talk to Mom about that without bringing up the prom queen scheme. Hell, she didn't know what she'd tell Mom when another guy showed up to take her to the prom.

Then Mom said something else that shocked her. "I'd also wondered if you were like me in that I'm not all that interested in men."

"You're a lesbian?" Jamie had wondered why Mom hadn't dated much. Though it was a relief that she didn't have to deal with her mother bringing home a new guy every few months like Allison's mom did, she'd worried about Mom being lonely. If she wanted to bring home a girlfriend, Jamie would be fine with it.

"No," Mom said gently, thankfully not sounding offended. "I'm not really interested in anyone in a…physical sense. That's why your father left."

Jamie's heart twisted at her mom blaming herself. "That's still not your fault. And that sure as hell didn't give him the right to abandon me and not pay you child support. But honestly, I'm better off without a selfish jerk. Lucio's mom died when he was young, so he knows what it's like to have only one parent. But the difference between us is that you spend more time with me than his dad did with him."

Mom looked sympathetic. "Well, running a restaurant would be demanding, I'd think. Either way, I hope Lucio treats you well. I hate to be pessimistic about the class differences, but…"

"He does treat me well, and he's hardly rich," Jamie said firmly before Mom could continue bringing up what scared her as well. "We're going to go roller skating tomorrow." She didn't mention the fact that she and Lucio had decided to check out Skate-O-Rama for any signs that Heather Price's death was suspicious. And then on Sunday, they'd check out the beach where Stacey's car had been found.

Her mom patted Jamie's leg, and she left the couch to soak in a bath, taking care of the fire that Lucio had ignited within her, then went to bed with Shadow curled up beside her. As soon as sleep took her under, Jamie was bombarded with nightmares about a faceless figure chasing her and stabbing her. Then the dream abruptly shifted to Lucio taking her in his arms and kissing her in a warm grotto in a tropical paradise.

***

Skate-O-Rama wasn't busy, which was understandable since not only was it a weeknight, but, someone had died tragically here only a month and a half ago.

When they made their way onto the polished hardwood rink, Jamie saw that the wall where the floor-length mirror had been now had a mural of the mountains over the lake beneath a night sky painted over it. It was honestly a nice piece, but she also noticed that the skaters veered away from it, warping the perfect circle of the track.

Jamie was a little out of practice and had to keep hold of Lucio's hand until she figured out how to keep her balance. They passed the spot where Heather died a few times, slowing down to see if anything looked...off.

The area was fairly clear to see when the lights turned all the way on between songs. The floor there had been cleaned, sanded, buffed, and coated with a fresh layer of varnish to eliminate not only the bloodstains, but also the chips and scars that the broken glass had to have made.

Jamie wondered if they'd slowly sand and varnish the rest of the floor so it blended in better. As it was now, this section was noticeably brighter. But between the mural, the floor repairs, and the huge payout that either the owner of Skate-O-Rama, or their insurance, would have made to Heather's parents, they probably wouldn't be able to afford to recondition the whole floor anytime soon.

Aside from the disturbingly lighter part of the floor that was only a little less obvious than police chalk lines, Jamie felt something *wrong* when she touched the mural where the mirror used to be. The air felt colder, even though there weren't any gaps in the wall to cause a draft, and the hair on the back of her neck stood on end, like the time she'd come across a cougar's den when picking huckleberries in the mountains.

Lucio felt it too. He put his hand on the mural and visibly shivered. "It's like the residue of something evil."

"Or we're being superstitious," Jamie tried to tell him, even though she couldn't convince herself of that.

He shook his head. "No. I definitely feel something. Maybe it's Heather's ghost, or maybe it's some sort of psychic energy from the terrible thing that happened to her. Either way, I get the sense that her death wasn't an accident." He pushed away from the wall and held out his hand. "I wanna get away from this spot like everyone else. I still want to skate with you, since I was an idiot and blew my chance to dance with you on Valentine's Day."

The lights went dark again and the disco ball came on as Dan Hill's "Sometimes When We Touch" began playing. Jamie took Lucio's hand and allowed him to slowly spin her a few times before he took her into his arms and they skated in slow circles, clinging to each other.

Jamie sighed as the warmth and strength of his body seeped into hers. She'd never felt so cherished and so safe with a guy before. Her heart felt close to bursting with the need to tell him she loved him.

Not yet, though.

They skated together for an hour before they got hot dogs and fries in the dining section. When their skating time was up, they removed their skates and laughed together at how weird and light their legs felt when they walked.

"This used to be my favorite part after going skating," Lucio told her.

"Me too. I always felt like I could jump really high after, but it never worked." Still, she tried an experimental hop and laughed.

When Lucio took her home, Jamie invited him in, relieved that Mom's car was not in the driveway. This time, she remembered to look.

"Want to see my room?" She gave him what she hoped was a coy smile.

"As scared as you were of me even seeing where your house is, I'd be honored."

Jamie's stomach dipped. Why did he have to remind her of that? Her room was pathetic compared to his.

But when he followed her into her small room and grinned at her Eurythmics and Fleetwood Mac posters, as well as the movie posters she'd taken from work, Jamie didn't feel ashamed.

He sat beside her on her little twin bed and ran his hand along the cat quilt her mom had made for her. "Are those cats painted?"

"Yeah. Mom uses Tri-Chem paints. I helped paint some of the squares too, but I can't sew at all, despite years of her struggling to teach me." Jamie threaded her fingers through his hair, never tired of feeling its soft texture. "My mom will be home in about an hour. Kiss me good night?"

Lucio gave her a devilish smile before covering her lips with his. In moments, his weight settled on top of her on the narrow bed. A low moan escaped her throat as his hardness ground against her arousal. Then he rolled them to the side and lifted her shirt to kiss the tops of her breasts. They kissed and explored each other for a blissful eternity, but Lucio never pressured her to go further, even though he had to be as out of his mind with lust as she was. The consideration made her love him even more.

When he left her panting and writhing with need, she decided that she'd tell him she was ready next week, before spring break started. Then they could figure out the perfect time and place for the... Jamie paused, not knowing how to phrase it. "Consummation of their love" sounded too cheesy, but "having sex" minimized the importance of the act.

She was still working that out in her mind when she picked Lucio up for school the next morning. She was starting to hate school. Now that she'd planned on making love—that was it, making love would work—with Lucio, pretending to be a mere friend and study partner was agony. Especially when girls passed him giving him admiring looks, some going so far as to drop a pencil and bend over in front of him to pick it up. By the end of the day, Jamie was gnashing her teeth in frustration. She'd also slipped and almost accidentally kissed him twice.

Maybe she *should* ditch the mission to become prom queen. The thought took a stronger hold as she watched Jane and Drew walk to Drew's car hand in hand. They'd look gorgeous together in their formal wear. Jamie would vote for them as king and queen and Brittney would still lose.

Brittney. Jamie's skin crawled at the thought of her. Was the head cheerleader really killing her rivals, or was Jamie merely thinking the worst of her? But could she really have imagined that eerie feeling she and Lucio got at the skating rink last night?

No. That feeling had been real. Whether Brittney had anything to do with whatever sinister force had knocked over the mirror was a different story though.

Would they feel anything similar at the beach where Stacey had been killed?

After school, Jamie pulled her Honda to the side of Lakeview Drive, below the Raimi property and above the dock. Black skid marks marred the pavement in front of her and Lucio, showing Stacey's path off the road. Jamie craned her neck, looking up the sharp basalt cliff to see if she could glimpse the infamous house. It must have been set back farther up the hillside because all she could see were a few precariously positioned trees sprouting out over the precipice.

While the tall cliffside looked spooky, even in the early spring sunshine, Jamie didn't feel anything evil from where she and Lucio stood.

They got fishing rods and tackle boxes out of the back hatch so they wouldn't look suspicious.

Trees lined the road, an odd mix of maple, willow, and pine, obscuring the view of the lake. A line of the trees and shrubs were cracked and broken from Stacey's car being winched up the hill and to the road so it could be towed off to wherever the authorities put vehicles involved in tragic deaths.

Beside the line of broken foliage, Jamie and Lucio found some old wooden steps embedded into the embankment, leading down to the beach. There was no handrail, so they made their way down as cautiously as young animals learning to walk.

Unlike the spot on the road where Jamie parked, the beach *did* feel a little creepy, though that might be as much from the tragedy that took place here as them skulking about looking for clues. The sand was trampled from multiple footprints, and there was a deep gouge in the earth where the car had fallen and then was hauled up the hillside.

The dock was ancient, rotted, and partially submerged, the dark water of the lake gently lapped over the gray surface. A thick splinter of wood stuck out from one of the pilings. Its paler shade made it apparent that the break happened recently.

"It's a shame that something so horrible happened here." Jamie stared out at the glittering expanse of Lake Skeetshue. The sky was clear and blue for once, and the sun lit up the beach and provided a first taste of spring warmth. "I bet this is an amazing fishing spot."

"You really fish?" The surprise in Lucio's tone was a little insulting.

Jamie whirled around and looked up at him in disbelief. "Duh. My mom taught me when I was five. Did you think I could afford to get this tackle only to use it as props?"

"I'm sorry." Lucio sounded sincerely regretful. "I didn't mean to sound shocked that a girl can fish or anything like that. My dad doesn't know how, so he never taught me. I think it's cool that you can."

"Oh." Sympathy squeezed her heart. How could someone live in this town of lakes and rivers and not learn to fish? It was so peaceful and then exciting, and then delicious. "I'm sorry I jumped to conclusions. Want to check out that damaged piling?"

Lucio and Jamie went closer to the dock and shivered in tandem.

"There it is," Lucio said. "That sense of wrongness. Do you feel it too?"

Jamie shifted her tackle box to the hand holding her fishing rod so she could rub the goosebumps on her arms. "Yeah. It's not as strong as what I felt at Skate-O-Rama, but it's there. Wait, is that blood?"

Cautiously, they approached the big splinter of piling and saw that it was a lot more than blood. A clear, gelatinous slime and curds of gray mush coated the jagged point of wood. Ants and maggots writhed in the sticky mess, feasting on what could be blood and guts from an animal, but probably weren't.

Jamie gagged and turned away.

Lucio rubbed her back. "From the direction of the gouges in the sand, I don't think Stacey could have landed on that splinter if she did in fact go through the windshield. I wish we'd been able to see this spot before the cops did their investigating. I mean, they're the experts, so they should have been able to figure out what happened..."

"But?"

"But that splinter looks new. Maybe a piece of the car went flying when the car came down, maybe not. I think whoever ran Stacey off the road killed her by the dock."

Jamie leaned against him, taking comfort from his solid presence beside her. "The killer would have had to have impaled her. Would Brittney even be strong enough to do that?"

Lucio looked back at the gore-encrusted splinter. "If she drove it into her eye, yeah."

"Can you see her doing something like that, though?" Jamie prodded. "I'm trying to be objective since I'm biased because of her bullying. She needed her friends to help her dump me into trashcans and dunk my head in the toilet. You got to know her as a person."

"I'm not so sure that I really did get to know her, though," Lucio said bitterly and shoved his hands in his pockets. "She was cold and often secretive. She never liked going outside or getting dirty, so that *does* point her away from being the culprit. But, like you said, she was the last person to see two of her biggest rivals before they ended up dead. Either way, we know there is a killer running loose in our town. It could be Brittney, or it could be someone else." He took her into his arms. "I don't want to let you out of my sight."

"I'm not helpless, you know." Though she had to admit, the fact that he cared so much warmed her to her toes. "And I'm not rich and popular, so I shouldn't be a target. Besides, one eerie accident and one unproved murder is not enough to establish a pattern." A big wave crashed on the beach, bringing back the chill she'd felt since coming down here. "Anyway, we should get going. I gotta be at work in an hour and a half."

Lucio's dark eyes still shone with worry. "Can you at least call me when you get to work and before you leave there so I know you're safe?"

More excuses to hear his voice when she was stuck rewinding tapes and missing him? Jamie feigned reluctance. "Okay."

"And one more thing. Can you teach me to fish?"

The boyish eagerness in his tone almost made her melt. "Only if you show me a new way to cook up our catch."

Speaking of catches, she'd certainly landed the best one of her life.

She prayed she'd get to keep him.

Chapter Seventeen

The next afternoon, Lucio and Jamie walked back up the embankment of a non-creepy part of the beach, each having one hand on the handle of a bucket of four trout and two bass sloshing in lake water to keep them fresh. Four fish in the catch were his. Triumph and delight surged through him that his first fishing lesson had gone so well. Jamie had taught him to tie the proper knots around the hooks, thread the weight at the correct distance for the bait to be able to float up past the seaweed. Then came the lesson of getting a mini marshmallow and half a nightcrawler onto a hook. That took him more tries since the damn things were slimy and wiggly.

Casting was an embarrassing trial and error, but Jamie's cheers when he made a good cast had him bursting with pride. And the thrill of his first bite? Oh man, he'd never experienced anything like it. Adrenaline raced as he fought to reel the fish in. It felt like a whopper.

The first trout was only twelve inches, but Jamie assured him that it was a good one, and would give them nice filets. He'd expected the rush to lessen with his other three catches, the second trout and the two bass, but nope, the thrill was equally as potent as the first time.

They went to his house to clean and filet the fish since there were better knives and herbs, and real butter. Lucio already knew how to filet, but he'd never gutted a fish before. Thankfully, it was easy...except when the bass started flopping around when he'd tried to cut its head off.

Jamie laughed when he'd jumped in horror. "Those do that a lot. They're almost as tough to kill as catfish."

They cooked up part of their catches with lots of butter and herbs and hummed in delight at the fresh flaky meat. Lucio sent Jamie home with the other half of the filets, knowing extra food was always welcome in her household.

The following morning, he practically danced with excitement when Jamie picked him up for school. "Can we go fishing again this afternoon?" he asked as soon as he got in the car.

"Not tonight because I work, but we can tomorrow."

Lucio's cheer died as soon as he and Jamie arrived at the school and heard the news that Stacey's body had been found.

The gruesome tale circulated through the school like an infection. Gretchen Lowell and Nick Peters had been swimming in Lake Skeetshue off Gretchen's parents' private dock. Gretchen had been floating on her back, or perfecting her breaststroke, depending on who was telling the story, when she felt something solid brush against her thigh. She'd thought it was a pike and had already shrieked. When she paddled away and glanced over her shoulder to see she'd been felt up by a waterlogged corpse, she'd screamed and fainted in the water. She would have drowned if Nick hadn't saved her.

Jason had shaken his head. "I doubt if this is true. It's only mid-March. The water has to still be freezing. They were probably necking on the dock and saw the corpse from there. Or maybe they tried to take a boat ride and fell out from shock."

"I believe it," Drew said. "Nick wears shorts all year, even in winter, so I know he's impervious to the cold. And Gretchen's one of those 'no pain, no gain' fitness junkies. She's won a few triathlons. Those two are totally the types to be swimming less than a month after the thaw."

Jamie broke in. "What about the body? Did it match up with a car accident?"

"Not at all," Allison said. "Even though the fish took plenty of bites out of Stacey, she was torn apart before she went into the water. And the injuries weren't consistent with the car wreck either. There was bruising and cuts from that, but she had some deep slashes and gouges like a large animal had been at her. She was also disemboweled. But the coroner thinks that what killed her was being stabbed in the eye with something made of wood. There were splinters in her brain."

Jason made a disgusted sound. "Do you guys have to be talking about this stuff during lunch? And how do you even know this stuff anyway?"

"Because my mom's the coroner's assistant." Allison took a bite of her spaghetti and smiled. "I want to be an investigative reporter."

Jamie laughed. "You're certainly nosy enough."

Jason smacked the table. "Enough about Stacey. It's giving me the creeps. What else is new lately?"

Jane Carpenter leaned over the table and spoke in a hushed tone. "My brother and sister-in-law lost one of their cows the other night. The poor thing was slashed up and also disemboweled. I hope the psycho animal killer isn't moving to people. Its eyes were intact, though. Linnea said the poor cow's throat was cut, probably before it was torn apart."

"Ugh." Jason's face screwed up in a repulsed expression. "Not *that* change of subject. I mean, I'm sorry about your family's livestock, but I can't handle any more death and gore. Talk about your spring break plans, or prom, or something normal."

Lucio saw Jamie blush and wondered if she was thinking about all the time they'd get to spend together over the break. Keeping their relationship secret was growing more agonizing every day.

Jane gave Jason an apologetic look and changed the subject. "The prom committee will be formed after the break. Drew and I will be signing up."

"Me too," Allison said. "I want to help decorate. Or maybe put together the ballots for king and queen." She gave Jamie a sideways smile that made Lucio's stomach sink. Who else was in on the plan?

The closer it came to prom, the more Lucio dreaded seeing Jamie on another guy's arm.

Jane interrupted his inner mourning. "We get to vote on the theme when we come back from break too. I'd love if it was 'Under the Sea.'"

Allison snorted. "That's because you can pull off a mermaid-style gown."

The conversation drifted to possible prom themes and dresses until the bell rang. Jamie took off with Allison, giving Lucio a slight shake of her head to indicate that she didn't want him walking her to class.

Drew clapped Lucio's shoulder. "Keep staring at her like that and the whole school's going to know that you two have a thing going on."

"Maybe they *should* know," Lucio said glumly as he shouldered his backpack and dumped his lunch tray.

"After all my hard work? I not only have her coming to my spring break party that everyone is going to be at, but I also managed to get you both invited to Shane Lowry's party at the end of the break. That one will raise her status another notch in time for the wave of prom preparations when we come back to school. Also, I have the perfect king in mind for her."

Lucio's fists clenched at his sides. "Who?"

"Alex Pugsley. He's class president, so he qualifies. In fact, his chances of being nominated prom king have gotten higher since Chet's popularity is waning. Not only because people think he was insensitive to hook up with Brittney so soon after Heather died, but also because he's been acting like he's on something, and he's been totally bombing football practice lately.

"Meanwhile, Alex is currently adored for already fulfilling one of his campaign promises by getting us pizza for lunch every week." Drew leaned closer to Lucio and lowered his voice. "But Alex is also gay, so that means he'll behave himself when escorting your fair maiden. I bet we could convince him to go along with our plan."

Lucio wanted to shut the whole thing down. Instead, he gave a noncommittal shrug. "We can talk about it when we come back from spring break. For now, I want to enjoy spending time with my girlfriend and not have to pretend she's not mine."

And Lucio began doing that as soon as school was over and they were alone in her bedroom. Even though Jamie had to go to work in an hour. He took her into his arms and couldn't stop kissing her. She was like a drug: intoxicating and addicting. And damn it, it wasn't fair that he had to keep her at arm's length when they were around their classmates.

He trailed kisses down her neck, loving the low moans pouring from her throat.

"Lucio?" Her voice sounded breathless, yet solemn.

"Yeah?" he inquired between kisses.

"I think I'm ready to…um…take things to the next level."

He stiffened and drew back to meet her wide brown eyes. "You mean?"

"I want to make love with you." She looked down shyly, like she actually feared that he'd reject her.

He tilted her chin up, forcing her to look at him. "I'd love to make love to you, but are you sure?"

"Yes, I'm sure. I mean, not tonight since I work and I want to be able to…um…dress nice and prepare. I hope that doesn't sound stupid."

"That doesn't sound stupid at all." It sounded oddly touching.

"And not here, though. I don't want to risk Mom coming home early. Or your dad, if we're at your house."

"Maybe a hotel room?" Lucio suggested, then paused, remembering something. "Wait. My dad is going out of town for the weekend: some conference for restaurant owners. I can make us a nice candlelit dinner, and then we can…have dessert."

"Could you show me how to cook something?"

"Yeah, we can cook together." Lucio couldn't hide his excitement at her suggestion. "That would be fun."

"Okay, it's a date." She looked down again and shifted nervously on the couch. Her cheeks pinkened. "Do you have protection?"

"Of course."

Her blush deepened to red. "Have you had…a lot of experience with sex?"

"Not as much as I've heard about people saying I have." He hoped that was the right answer.

"I'm a virgin." Her voice was barely above a whisper.

Lucio gave her a reassuring smile. "I kinda figured."

"How so?" She looked defensive.

"Because of how determined you've been about your future and all that. And because you're the first girl who's planned sex in advance." And he respected the hell out of her for both those things.

"Does my planning in advance bother you?" The vulnerability in her eyes wrenched his heart. "I know it ruins the spontaneity of it all."

"No. I mean, I'm a little nervous about hurting you, but I promise I'll be gentle and stop if you ask me to." She still didn't look reassured, so he took both her hands in his and did his best to convey the depth of his respect and caring for her. "If anything, I'm honored that you want me to be your first." *And I want to be your last,* his heart whispered.

Oh God, he'd fallen for her hard. When did that happen?

To keep from thinking about that revelation, Lucio kept talking in an attempt to reassure her that he wasn't bothered by her lack of experience. "My first time was…not good. It happened at a college house party. I was so drunk I barely knew what was happening. A girl dragged me into a room and pretty much had her way with me. I don't even remember if I liked it or not, only that the motion jostled my stomach so much that I threw up on the floor afterwards."

"Oh my God." Jamie squeezed his hands. "That sounds like rape. I'm so sorry."

"I might have said yes." Lucio shrugged. "I can't remember."

Jamie shook her head. "If you were that drunk, you wouldn't have been capable of reasoning the situation enough to say yes to something like that. Why do you think guys like to get girls drunk?"

She was right. His first sexual encounter was probably why, ever since, he never had sex with someone on a night where he'd had more than two beers or a glass of wine.

"Speaking of, I won't touch you if you've been drinking. I don't want anyone to experience what I did." Lucio softened his tone. "Also, I want to make sure that I give you a night to remember."

Jamie leaned forward and whispered against his lips. "I think I'll always remember every night with you."

Chapter Eighteen

After the bell rang on the last day of school before spring break, Brittney got into Chet's Mercedes, excited for Drew's party tomorrow night. Sure, he'd forgotten to invite her, but he'd hardly turn her and Chet away.

Chet didn't look nearly as excited at the prospect of a week free of school and full of parties. He stared straight ahead as he drove her home, not even bothering to ask her how her day went. He was probably still upset about how badly football practice was going. His coach had probably reamed him for his poor performance. Brittney let Chet stew, since he wasn't interesting to talk to anyway.

But when he pulled into her driveway and finally told her what was on his mind, Brittney reeled in shock.

She stared at Chet, willing herself to close her mouth and quit blinking at him like an idiot. "What did you say?"

"I said, I don't think our relationship is working," Chet repeated. For the first time since Scar put him under a spell, he sounded alert.

Although it was nice to hear him say something without the tone of a drugged dimwit that he'd had for the past two months, these were not the words she wanted to hear. "Why don't you think it's working?"

He looked down at his lap. "I think I went a little crazy from losing Heather, and instead of grieving properly, I used you for a distraction."

"Used *me*?" She bit back a laugh. He was such a pathetic fool. Temptation bubbled within her to tell him that she'd been using him as her tool, and if he was dumb enough to break up with her, his usefulness had come to an end.

"Yeah." Chet's voice was apologetic. "I'm sorry. My therapist says—"

"Oh God," Brittney groaned. He was *so* pathetic. "Shrinks are snake oil salesmen trying to trick you into thinking you're crazy so you hand over all your money."

"Well, I think he's helping me," Chet said in a surly tone.

Or the spell is wearing off. "I could help you, if you'd let me. You're not the only one grieving." Brittney forced a gentle tone. "And I really thought we were helping each other. What made you change your mind?"

"You're a little too weird for me," he continued on in a rush before she could contradict him. "You don't seem to miss Heather, and then you go off on your own and your parents don't know where you are. Hell, your friends don't even know what you're up to most nights." With each point, he wagged his finger at her like he was scolding a child. "You don't return my calls, and sometimes you act like a completely different person." His eyes narrowed on her at the last point. "Like at today's memorial assembly for Stacey? You *laughed.* I know you two didn't get along, but I didn't think you could be that heartless."

"I was crying, not laughing," Brittney lied. She honestly couldn't remember laughing. Actually…she couldn't remember the assembly. Like, any of it. She fought off a twinge of alarm at that. "Listen, can I call you later and we can have a good long talk about this? I promised I'd help my mom with…some stuff, and I don't want us to part on bad terms."

Chet remained belligerently silent for the longest time before he shrugged. "Okay. Call me tonight when you're done and we'll talk."

It took all her willpower not to slam his car door when she got out. How could he discard her like this? And call her weird and heartless? How dare he?

Brittney stormed into her room and pulled up her Oriental rug and drew a fresh pentagram in chalk. "Scarlionapskhis, I summon you forth. Heed my call."

Shadows trickled from between the floorboards flowing together in ink-black strands until Scar's form stood before her. "While I appreciate the formality, you still forgot to say please. I understand that is a required courtesy among your kind."

"Please," Brittney added, trying to conceal the impatience in her voice.

"What have you summoned me for this time? I hope you're ready to feed me. It is past time."

"Soon," Brittney quickly promised, hoping he wasn't too annoyed. "Your magic seems to be wearing off Chet. He wants to break up with me."

"I told you that love spells do not work. And even infatuation and lust enchantments run their course eventually." Scar didn't sound sympathetic at all. "If you provide me with a fresh sacrifice, I may be able to snare him with a fresh enchantment. Or you could rid yourself of him and find a new male to escort you to this dance. That Chet is a milksop. I've grown weary of him and I know you have as well. Let's kill him and bathe in his blood."

Brittney didn't know what a milksop was, but she got the gist. "Yeah, he is a lot lamer than I expected. But he's the quarterback, and most likely to be voted prom king, so I need him."

"Are you certain of that?" Scar's voice rang with doubt, and more than a hint of disappointment that she wasn't as eager as he was to kill Chet. "Are there no other males of prestige in your school? Because I have observed otherwise."

Those words chilled Brittney. How had he observed? Had he been with her when she hadn't invited him in? She'd definitely have to mull that over when he was gone. For now, she kept her eyes on the prize. Besides, Scar had a point. There were other popular guys, and Chet had grown tiresome. And now he thought he could dump her. Brittney had *never* been dumped.

Brittney rattled off stats from the rank book that she, Heather, and Jennifer kept to rate the statuses of their classmates. "Well, Drew Creed is pretty popular because of his parties, but he's back together with Jane Carpenter, who's a total nerd, so that made his status go down. Shane Lowry is even more popular for even more exclusive parties, and being a class clown, but he's only average-looking. Evan Legard has a new girlfriend every week and..." Brittney paused, remembering someone else. "Alex Pugsley is *extremely* good-looking. And he's class president. And I don't think he's dating anyone. He might do."

Scar nodded impatiently. "Choose one then, and give me the same type of sacrifice you performed in exchange for my last enchantment spell. This time, I will take care to moderate the magic so that it does not wear off so quickly."

Brittney nodded, understanding precisely what sort of sacrifice Scar wanted. A human. And exactly which human he wanted. Brittney was growing happier to oblige by the minute.

A few hours later, she called Chet and with the most pleading tone possible, asked him to meet her at Heather's grave. "That way, we can have some closure and say our good-byes to each other and to her. Or, if you decide to give me another chance, we can ask for her blessing."

"That sounds kinda morbid." Chet's voice dripped with reluctance, and he made it clear he would not change his mind and give her another chance.

"Please, Chet?" Brittney pleaded in the same cadence she used when she wanted Daddy to buy her something. "The first crocuses have bloomed in our garden and I want to put them on her grave. I also want to apologize to her for turning to you for comfort. I was selfish."

"Okay, that sounds understandable." Chet's voice softened. "And you weren't selfish, okay? We both lost someone we deeply cared about and turned to each other in an unhealthy way. It was perfectly natural. I'll see you at the cemetery in about twenty minutes. Then maybe we can go get a milkshake for old times' sake."

"That sounds lovely," she said breathily.

Twenty minutes later, Brittney stood in front of Heather's gravestone wearing her old gym shoes, black pants, and a black t-shirt under a dark brown coat that would hide bloodstains. The moon played hide-and-seek between a rolling mass of dark clouds. She hoped it wouldn't rain. Wet grass got slippery fast.

She turned to look at the grave, an elaborate statue of an angel atop a granite base that had flowers carved into the edges and some poem she couldn't read in the dark. One silver urn embedded in the base held a bouquet of dried roses that Chet placed there every month. The other urn held dying lilies from Heather's parents. They'd been here more recently.

Headlights illuminated the marble angel and Brittney's lips curved with satisfaction. Chet may have been a disappointment in almost every way, but at least he was punctual. His Mercedes pulled to the side of the path closest to the section of graves where Brittney waited.

Gripping her small bouquet of crocuses, she waved at him, making sure to keep her wrist limp. Her other hand remained in the pocket of the dark brown canvas trench coat.

Chet got out of the car and gave her a polite smile, his white teeth flashing in the moonlight. A shame. Few people in this town had such perfect teeth. He then leaned back into his car and pulled out a huge bouquet of roses to replace the dead ones in the urn. Brittney hated him then. For outdoing her simple offering of the first spring flowers from her home garden, and for the knowledge that if she died, he wouldn't bring expensive florist roses to her grave every month.

Chet walked up to the grave with the confident stride of a WASP who knew he'd be getting a football scholarship to countless universities of which he could take his pick. He wore his letterman jacket in the Amteep High colors of red and blue over a tennis shirt and pegged jeans. "I'm sorry I was so harsh earlier today. I shouldn't have accused you of not caring about Heather. I know you were her best friend. And I hope that even though we aren't going out anymore we can still be friends."

"Of course." Brittney gave him a sugary smile. She knelt and placed the crocuses on the granite base of the grave and then pulled the dead roses from the urn.

Chet's smile warmed as he bent down to put the fresh roses in.

Brittney reached into her pocket.

Then he paused and frowned, looking past the grave. "What is that painted on the grass?" He turned and crouched down again to look past Brittney. "It looks like a—"

Brittney slit his throat with the ceremonial blade she used for her animal sacrifices. Blood sprayed all over her new coat. At first, she felt a pang of annoyance at the prospect of having to wash out all the stains, but then bloodlust took over. Her lips peeled back to bare her teeth in a feral smile as she stabbed Chet again, this time in his eye. Ruining his perfect, Ken-doll face gave her inexplicable pleasure.

When she'd reduced his face to bloody shreds, she stabbed and slashed the rest of his body with savage abandon.

Blood splattered all over Heather's grave, painting the marble angel with crimson droplets, and yet Brittney could not make herself stop. The hunger for violence and chaos had overtaken her, and she wasn't sure if it was her hunger.

Then, a black cloud enveloped her, stars danced before her eyes until she surrendered and let the darkness swallow her.

When the blackness had dissipated, and Brittney regained her senses, she was straddling Chet in front of Heather's grave. His rib cage had been torn open, and his heart was missing from the glistening chest cavity.

Had she done that? Or had Scar come when she was... How long had she been out? Brittney scrambled up off the corpse and winced at her aching muscles. Her jaw was sore and she tasted blood in her mouth. She shuddered with revulsion, not wanting to know what she'd done.

She was reassured that at least she'd kept her sacrifice inside the pentagram she'd painted around the grave. That meant Scar had been kept contained.

She left Chet's corpse and his car where they were. The Satanic cult that the news was fretting about would get the blame as always. Because of that, she hadn't bothered to clean up her animal kills anymore. She opened the trunk of her car and cleaned up with the baby wipes she now always kept on hand, then put the bloody wipes in a little garbage sack to dispose of on the way home.

As Brittney drove away from the cemetery, she pouted in disappointment as she realized that since the body would be found right away, she wouldn't be able to go to Drew's party tomorrow. Instead, she'd have to play the tedious role of distraught and grieving girlfriend.

Damn it. She'd ruined at least half of her spring break. Maybe she should have waited.

Brittney shook her head. "No use crying over spilled blood."

She'd use this time to study her books to gain more power over Scar, cling to her friends for their sympathy, and remind them how much she deserved to be prom queen. And, of course, take a shopping trip to Spokane, or maybe even Seattle, to soothe her broken heart.

Then, after break, she would secure her prom king.

Chapter Nineteen

Jamie made her way up Lucio's walkway and wiped her sweating hands on the long billowy black skirt she'd chosen for the date. She'd found it at a yard sale with her mom two years ago, and since then it had been her lucky skirt. Usually she wore it with a long-sleeved peasant top and a shawl to look like Stevie Nicks, but since they'd be cooking together, she'd opted for a black shiny button-up blouse with short lacy sleeves. A little more Madonna than Stevie, but also fitting with "Like a Virgin" playing on the Top 40.

Dangly earrings made up of strands of tiny silver chains and a teardrop turquoise pendant on a long silver chain completed her ensemble. She'd curled and sprayed her hair, worked painstakingly on her violet and dark purple eye shadow, smoky eyeliner, and burgundy lipstick. She'd also "sampled" some Opium perfume at the mall on her way to Lucio's house.

She took a deep breath and willed her heart to stop pounding. Excitement coiled in her belly like a tight spring. This was it. The night she would engage in the ultimate intimacy with the man she loved. Jamie paused and rolled her eyes. Why did she have to be so melodramatic? It was just sex. The girls at school who'd done it acted like it was no big deal.

Her breath froze when she knocked on the door.

It was a *very* big deal.

Lucio answered the door, looking adorable in a long white apron and his mass of dark curls tied back. "You're early."

Heat flooded her cheeks. "I...couldn't wait." *Shit.* Now she sounded too eager.

"Nice suitcase." He grinned down at the canvas *Roadrunner and Wile E. Coyote Show* suitcase that she'd used for sleepovers ever since fourth or fifth grade. "I think I have my old *Jackson Five* one up in my bedroom closet somewhere."

"Well, you told me this would be a sleepover," Jamie said as she followed him into the house. Although they'd be doing a lot more than building blanket forts or making prank phone calls.

"It will be if you don't hog the covers." Lucio led her past the foyer and into the living room. "You can put your bag by the couch or take it upstairs. I was finishing prepping the kitchen for our cooking adventure."

Jamie set the bag down immediately. Although she was too nervous about losing her virginity to have much of an appetite, she was eager to cook something amazing with Lucio. "What are we making?"

"Lamb *osso buco*. The dish is usually made with veal, but Dad doesn't believe in eating baby animals."

Jamie agreed and was happy to not be eating a calf, but... "Aren't lambs babies?"

"Only spring lamb, which is tough to get in our area. The meat we get generally comes from sheep that are a little under a year old," Lucio assured her. "Dad had to pay more for lamb meat this month because the farm we buy it from upped their prices from losing two of their herd to the animal killer. It's probably going to happen with beef prices too, but we always buy local."

"Damn it. We can't go anywhere or do anything without being reminded of that monster." Jamie's fists clenched in bitterness.

"Yeah. I'm considering going to the farms we usually buy from and talking to them to see how many animals they've lost and how seriously the authorities are taking it. Granted, they may not be honest since farmers get a big check from the government if they can convince the authorities that their livestock was killed by a wolf or mountain lion." Lucio shook his head and headed into the kitchen. "But I don't want to think about that right now. I want to get this delicious food cooking."

Jamie followed him into the kitchen, where bundles of fresh herbs, tomatoes, cloves of garlic, and other ingredients waited beside a large cutting board on the island. A big cast-iron Dutch oven sat on the stove.

Lucio handed her an apron and they chopped up the vegetables together with sharp knives that Jamie would love to have at her place. Maybe that's what she'd suggest to Mom for a graduation present. Good knives.

As he showed her how to coat the cuts of lamb shank in flour and brown them in butter in the Dutch oven, he spoke to her with his usual friendly tone, and every movement of his gorgeous body radiated casualness.

Jamie wondered if it was because he wanted to put her at ease about their impending lovemaking, or if he was so experienced with sex that this wasn't a big deal. Although she wanted this to mean as much to him as it did to her, she was relieved that he wasn't acting weird or impatient to get in her pants like her last boyfriend, whose obsession with wanting to take her clothes off before she was ready was a big reason she dumped his ass.

After moving the browned meat to a plate and adding the vegetables to brown in the Dutch oven, Lucio finally brought up the real reason she was here. "I'm only showing you the main dish because I don't want us to spend all night cooking. So, I've got a salad tossed and garlic bread ready to roast and gelato for dessert."

Jamie met his knowing gaze and gave him what she hoped was a seductive smile. So he did care that they were going to make love. "I thought I was going to have *you* for dessert."

"We're adults. We can have more than one dessert," Lucio said before kissing her breathless. Then, frustrating her, he pulled away. "Now we need to add the tomato paste, caramelize it, then deglaze it with the wine."

Jamie swayed a little from the potency of his kiss. "Uh-huh."

Any other time, she'd be eager to learn the mysteries of caramelizing and deglazing, but now her belly fluttered and her lower body hummed in anticipation of him touching her again. Still, she followed his instructions and savored the delicious smells beginning to emanate from the Dutch oven even though she didn't think she'd be able to remember this part of the process in the future.

After they added chicken stock and herbs, they returned the lamb shanks to the Dutch oven, put the lid on, and placed the dish in the oven.

"And that's the first part," Lucio said as they washed their hands. "You're not really hungry right now, are you?"

"No," she confessed. "I'm too nervous…and excited."

134

"Me too." Lucio dried his hands and removed his apron before cupping her cheek with one large hand. His dimples flashed as he gave her a devastatingly sexy smile. "That's why I picked something that needs to cook for over two hours. We'll have to find something to do to occupy our time while we wait for dinner."

"Over *two hours*?" Jamie squeaked. From the talk she heard at school, most guys only lasted a few minutes.

It took a few tries to remove the tie on her apron.

"I want to make sure you're satisfied." He took her hand and led her up the stairs.

Lucio's bedroom was cleaner than she'd ever seen it. Candles and a vase of roses were arranged on his nightstand. Her heart turned over at the show of care. When he closed the door, her heartbeat sped up.

She stood in the middle of the room and watched as he lit the candles and turned off the overhead light, bathing the room in an intimate glow. "I thought about music, but I couldn't think of anything romantic. I'm not into Barry Manilow or anything like that."

Jamie smiled at his worried tone. He seemed to be as nervous as she was. She slipped her arms around his waist and looked up at him. "Everything's perfect. Now please kiss me before I go crazy."

He lowered his head and slanted his lips over hers. Jamie moaned and reached up under his shirt to caress his back. His skin felt smooth and hot under her fingertips. Lucio took her touch as a cue to remove his shirt.

The sight of his bare, bronze-tinged skin made her suck in a breath. His chest was smooth and muscled, his dark nipples erect. His flat stomach was toned, with an intriguing line of dark hair running from his bellybutton to disappear down the waistband of his black jeans.

Slowly, Jamie unbuttoned her blouse, shyly glancing up to see Lucio's hungry gaze on her. She hoped he found her attractive. She thanked the heavens that he'd bought her a new bra during their first shopping expedition so she didn't have to face him in one of her ratty old ones.

Lucio's dark eyes were full of worship as he pulled her tight against him. For a moment, he simply held her, the sensation of his bare skin against hers making her lightheaded with pleasure. Then he bent down and claimed her lips for another hungry kiss.

Still kissing her, he bent down and swept one arm under her legs and the other behind her back. Carefully, he lifted her and laid her on the bed.

She thought he'd take his pants off then, but he didn't. Instead, the weight of his body settled over hers and he resumed kissing her senseless. Jamie held him tight, gasping when the hard bulge in his jeans came in contact with the juncture between her legs. Lucio moved his hips, inflaming the sensations.

His lips moved from her mouth to her neck. First, he trailed whisper-soft kisses in a hot path down her neck to her shoulder, then his teeth gently nibbled at her skin, making electric frissons of pleasure jolt through her.

She undulated her hips against his, becoming more frustrated with the layers of clothing separating them.

When Lucio scooted down, she whimpered from the break in contact. Then she gasped with pleasure as he kissed the tops of her breasts and removed her bra after she nodded permission.

She'd never thought her chest had that much sensitivity until their make-out sessions had proved otherwise. His fingers were magic, teasing and caressing in all the right places. This time, he went farther. His tongue darted across her nipple, making her suck in a breath. Then, his mouth closed over her areola, and the gentle suction and circles of his tongue had her moaning and tangling her fingers in his hair.

Lucio went lower, kissing her belly before he tugged off her skirt and rested his head against her hip a moment. His breath was warm against the damp fabric of her panties. "Can I kiss you there?"

"Okay," she managed to reply in a broken squeak.

Her last scrap of clothing came off with a whisper. Jamie resisted the urge to cover herself, then bolted upright at the intensity of the sensation of Lucio's mouth on her. His palm rested on her hip and patted her softly as if to tell her to lie back and trust him.

When she did, magic ensued. His lips and tongue caressed and explored her in ways she'd never dared fantasize. She moaned and arched her hips, silently imploring him to keep going.

And he did. The tip of his tongue searched out every spot that made her writhe and moan. Then he focused on those points, teasing and testing different rhythms until her hands were buried in his hair and she was panting with need.

The pleasure he wrought climbed until her nerves sang and she cried out his name, quivering against his mouth, unable to take any more of the sweet torment.

Lucio raised his head and smiled at her, those dimples making her body go weak. Her head fell back on the pillow while she watched him slide off the bed to remove his pants. The sight of him naked made her jaw drop.

She spoke to recover her composure and to cover staring at him while he put on the condom. "You didn't have to...make me finish."

"Sure I did." He gave her another devastating smile and stretched out on the bed beside her. "I had to make sure that you got some pleasure out tonight in case I don't do well with the rest."

"Oh." Warmth unfurled in her heart at his consideration even as her pulse accelerated in anticipation of "the rest." "Do you want me to do anything with you before..."

Lucio shook his head and pulled her against him. "Not this time." One hand stroked her back while the other cupped her chin. "You're so beautiful that I keep thinking I'm dreaming."

He kept on like that, stroking her and whispering romantic nonsense until she pulled him on top of her. The weight of him felt so wonderful, so secure. She reached down and wrapped her fingers around the base of his hardness, intrigued at its heat and texture. She wished he'd let her explore him a little before he'd put on protection. Maybe next time.

A small smile teased the corners of her lips. They hadn't even started and she was already thinking of next time.

Then he rose up on his elbows and the tip of his erection stroked across her slick wetness, bringing a faint echo of the electric pleasure she'd experienced minutes before. He circled around her opening and rubbed across her sensitive place before slowly sliding into her. Barely an inch in and he withdrew.

Jamie didn't know whether to be frustrated or relieved.

Then he repeated the motion and she figured out what he was doing. Easing into her instead of shoving it in. Doing his best not to hurt her.

That was *not* how Allison's first time had gone. Or anyone else's that she'd heard about. Jamie worked with him, arching her hips to match his motions, noting that while there was a stretching pressure, so far, there was little pain. When he finally sank fully inside her, the pressure and sense of fullness bordered on discomfort.

Lucio lowered his full weight on her and remained still, kissing her with a slow sensuality that made her dizzy. Jamie stroked his back and moved beneath him, adjusting to the feel of him. The pressure didn't decrease so much as change to something more interesting. Lucio seemed to sense the shift and moved with her in slow shallow thrusts that gradually deepened.

His hands moved down and slid beneath her hips until he cupped her rear and thrust in even deeper. That made him reach a spot inside that surged with pleasure.

Jamie matched his rhythm to reach it again.

Time vanished as they moved together in a primal dance. Jamie alternated between closing her eyes and hearing Lucio's rapid heartbeat and heavy breathing to opening them to peer around his shoulder at the candlelight flickering over his muscled arms, broad back, and strong hips moving in tandem with hers. The sight of their joined bodies and his sounds of passion increased her spiraling arousal, flavored by the musky scent their joining made.

Her pleasure built and climbed again, deeper and more intense than his mouth had, or her fingers. The intensity tore a moan from her throat as she arched against him. The explosion took her off guard, making her contract and quake around him until she nearly sobbed from the power of the climax.

Lucio groaned and spasmed inside her, jolting her with aftershocks.

They clung to each other, catching their breath, riding the final waves.

When it was over, Lucio reluctantly withdrew from her to clean up in the small adjoining bathroom. He handed her a clean towel and she dabbed away the sweat. That part was true to what she'd heard. The rest? Had she gotten lucky, or was it this wonderful with many couples?

"How did you learn to be so good at this?" Jamie asked when Lucio returned to the bed and pulled her into his arms again. "I suppose it was a lot of practice."

"Not as much as you'd think," Lucio said, twirling a lock of her hair around his finger. "If I tell you how I learned, you gotta promise not to laugh."

That response ignited a fire of curiosity. "I promise."

His voice went stern. "I'm serious. I've never told anyone this story."

She reached for his free hand and squeezed it. "Okay."

"I read my mom's collection of romance novels." Lucio's cheeks appeared to darken in the candlelight. "I mean, I didn't do it specifically for tips on how to pleasure women, but I certainly kept that information in mind."

Jamie tried to conceal her surprise at a guy willingly reading those kinds of books. One time, Todd Banks, the guy who liked to pick on her in shop class, found a romance novel in her toolbox and mocked her mercilessly for a month.

"What made you pick them up?"

"For the longest time, Dad kept all of Mom's stuff in the guest room like a shrine to her memory. When I got to being lonely and missing her, I'd go in there and smell her perfume, look through her old photo albums, watch her favorite movies, and read the books from her collection so I could feel like she was still with me, and to get to know her better.

"With my dyslexia, it took a long time to get through each book, but that was kinda better anyway." Moisture glistened in his eyes before he blinked it away and forced a lighthearted tone. "I read sex scenes in those books long before I stumbled upon Dad's dirty magazines. And those books are where I learned to 'stroke the petals of your flower' and 'caress your tender bud,' as a few of the books like to say."

A faint beep sounded from downstairs.

"We need to move to the last step before we can eat." Lucio rolled out of bed and yanked his clothes on.

Only then did Jamie notice the rich smell of the food. Immediately, her mouth watered. "Oh my God, I'm starving."

As she dressed, he gave her a mournful look. "I'm sorry to tell you that it's going to take another hour."

Back in the kitchen, he took out a bowl full of chopped herbs. "This is *gremolada*. It's minced garlic, parsley, and lemon zest." He opened the oven door and used a potholder to remove the lid from the Dutch oven. The tantalizing smell of the cooking lamb made them both groan with hunger. Lucio spooned about half the gremolada onto the shank.

During the hour wait, they walked the dog, and then cuddled on the couch with the cats and watched *The Twilight Zone* until it was time to toast the garlic bread.

By the time the food was done, they burned their fingers getting the lamb shanks, scooped the salad onto their plates, and cut the bread, and devoured the food like ravenous animals. The cats and the dog begged pitifully, but got only one bite of lamb each.

After the meal, they took Fulci for a walk and then they ate their gelato and watched an old Dracula movie on TV. Jamie rested her head on Lucio's shoulder and sighed in pure bliss. "This might be the best night of my life. The best meal, the best lovemaking, the best dessert. I love—" she broke off, not wanting to scare him with the notorious L word. "I love everything about tonight."

"Me too." Lucio kissed the top of her head. "Definitely the most special date I've had in my life."

Almost her exact thoughts.

They talked during the movie, and the next, *The Horror of Party Beach*, aside from the times when they laughed at the ridiculous monster that looked like it had a mouthful of hot dogs.

Jamie's eyelids grew heavy halfway through the third movie and she fell asleep on his shoulder until he woke her up to feed the pets, then he led her upstairs.

He cuddled against her back, with his arm around her waist. Jamie thought it would be hard to sleep with a guy pressed up against her, but she drifted off feeling warm and secure.

They awoke to a loud pounding on the door. Lucio bolted out of his bed and peeked out the window. "What the hell? The cops are here."

All Jamie's grogginess evaporated. "What?"

They scrambled to get their clothes on and Lucio dashed down the stairs, Jamie following at a more cautious pace. Her heart ached with worry. Had something happened to his father? If so, would the cops have been notified and come in person? That didn't seem likely. Had something happened to her mom? Then why hadn't she called? Jamie had given her the Argentos' phone number.

As Lucio answered the door, she had a thought that was less terrifying than a hurt parent, but still ominous. What if someone had seen them trespassing on the Raimi beach the other day?

Her panicked thoughts ceased when one of the two officers spoke in a cold, stern voice. "Are you Lucio Argento?"

"Yes. How can I help you?"

"Where were you last night at eight-thirty p.m.?"

"I was here." A defensive edge crept into Lucio's voice. "What's this about?"

The cop ignored his question. "Can anyone vouch for you that you were here all night?"

Jamie spoke up, rushing to Lucio's side. "I can. I'm his girlfriend. I spent the night here with him."

Heat crept to her face as both cops leered at her from her bare toes, over the skirt she'd hastily put on, to the T-shirt she'd grabbed off Lucio's floor that did no favors in hiding that she wasn't wearing a bra. Their gazes lingered on her chest for an uncomfortably long time before shifting up to her face and narrowing with derision at her tousled hair and ruined makeup.

"I see," the second officer said to Lucio with a smirk. "How old are you, young lady?"

"Eighteen." Jamie edged closer to Lucio.

The cops exchanged glances and leered at Jamie again. Lucio reached out and pulled her against him protectively. "Yeah, I get it. Fornication is naughty. Now why are you here wondering where I was?"

The first cop recovered his stern tone. "Chet Morgan was murdered last night."

Chapter Twenty

Lucio's stomach turned to ice. "Chet is dead? And you think I killed him?"

The cop shrugged, unfazed by Lucio's horror and outrage. "From what we learned, he was dating your ex-girlfriend, Brittney Shaw. Jealousy is a common motive. But we see you've moved on."

"However, you *do* have a criminal record," the second officer chimed in with a smirk. Lucio recognized him then. Officer Felton, who'd arrested Lucio more than once in his delinquent years, and definitely held a grudge after he'd gotten suspended for roughing Lucio up the last time.

Lucio snorted. "Yeah, vandalism and other petty shit over a year ago. But murder? That's a leap. I get you guys thinking I could have been jealous about Chet being with my ex, but bringing up my juvenile record is ridiculous."

"That's our job," Felton said with a glare.

Your job is ridiculous. Lucio bit his cheeks to keep from smiling.

Jamie spoke from under Lucio's arm. "How was Chet killed?"

Both officers spoke at the same time.

"That's being kept private for now."

"Slashed and gutted in a cemetery in some kind of ri—" Felton shut up when his partner elbowed him.

Had he been about to say *ritual*?

Lucio wasn't Catholic, but he took advantage of the Italian stereotype and made a show of crossing himself. If the cops had suspected him first, and if they thought the killing looked ritualistic, the Slayer shirt he was wearing did *not* make him look innocent.

He forced a friendlier tone. "Do you want to come inside for some coffee? I'd be happy to answer any questions that could help you catch the monster."

Finally, there was a crack of warmth in the first cop's chilly exterior as he reached up to touch a chain around his neck that likely either held a cross or a saint's medallion. "Not at this time, though we will be back if we think of something that you might know."

After the police left, Lucio and Jamie collapsed on the couch. Lucio turned on the TV and switched to the local news station.

At first it seemed that they'd either missed the report, or it wasn't going to air until later. Then, after a story on areas where the Saint John River was still flooded, a pale wide-eyed anchorman appeared reporting breaking news that there had been a murder at the Forest Cemetery.

The station cut to a reporter at the cemetery, huddled under an umbrella, talking about how the caretaker found the body this morning. Police tape was wrapped around several graves, and police officers and other officials blocked most of the bloody grave.

"The body of high school senior and star quarterback Chet Morgan was found mutilated in front of the grave of Heather Price, his steady girlfriend until her tragic accidental death two months ago. Evidence indicates he'd come to place fresh flowers on her grave."

Jamie and Lucio squirmed on the couch, remarking that they wished they could see more behind the reporter and the milling officials. There were strange white markings on the grass that looked like spray paint.

"Are those like body chalk lines?" Jamie asked.

Lucio shook his head. "The parts I can see seem to be too spread out."

They saw paramedics loading a body bag onto a gurney, which made them both shiver. Lucio had a flashback of his mother's coffin being loaded into the hearse after her funeral and struggled to breathe.

The reporter continued, "The police are keeping certain details of the case quiet for now, but as more information is released, you can count on us to keep the public updated."

The anchor appeared on screen briefly to announce that they'd been in touch with Chet's family and friends.

Jamie and Lucio watched as the news camera alternated between shots of his crying parents and photos of Chet in his football uniform, one in his letterman jacket, and another with him and

Heather at junior prom. Another shot of his crying parents, then a big sweep of his football trophies.

The anchor came back on. "We now move to Chet's girlfriend, Brittney Shaw."

Lucio and Jamie watched in horror as Brittney sobbed for the camera about how much she loved him and how some monster had to have killed her precious Chet out of jealousy.

"His last girlfriend, Heather, was my best friend, and Chet and I grew close in our grief. I can't believe someone would kill him. We were supposed to go to prom together. It's what Heather would have wanted." She wiped her forced tears away with dainty care, barely marring her perfectly applied eye makeup. "Now they're together in heaven and I miss them both so much. I don't know who could hate Chet so much. I only know that I don't feel safe anymore."

The anchor reappeared and made some closing remarks. Not mentioning anything about how Heather had died or that Stacey had been killed a few weeks ago. Had the reporters not connected the dots, or had the police warned them to keep the patterns quiet?

Lucio turned off the TV. "Okay, Brittney is definitely responsible. She's probably the one who sent the cops to check me out and I don't think they'd believe us if we said she's a murderer. I don't know how she's doing it, but we've lost three classmates in the last three months and she's the common denominator with all of them. And to kill Chet on Heather's grave? That's pure sadism. Thank heavens you were with me all night."

Jamie nodded. "Heather and Stacey would have been likely candidates for prom queen, so it makes sense that Brittney'd take out her competition. And Chet must have done something to make her think her chances were in danger. I wonder if he was regretting getting together with her and realized that shock from Heather's death caused him to rebound or something. Or he was putting flowers on her grave and that was the only place Brittney could catch him alone. I mean, sadism is definitely her MO, but convenience could have been a factor too."

"Or maybe Chet stumbled upon a clue that she killed Stacey or Heather and had to be eliminated." Then the full extent of Jamie's words sank in. "Oh my god. I knew she was desperate to be prom queen, but I never imagined she'd kill people for that plastic crown."

"I wouldn't have thought *anyone* could sink to that, but here we are." Jamie's eyes widened. "I wonder if she's the one who's been mutilating animals too."

"If you'd asked me yesterday, I would have said she'd be too squeamish for that. Now, I'm not so sure."

If she could hack up a person, animals would be a piece of cake. And with Satanic ceremonies being connected to the animal mutilations and one of the cops started to say something about Chet's death, maybe that it had been a ritualistic killing, that meant that it had to be the same killer.

Lucio struggled to remember if there'd been any hint that Brittney was interested in the occult when he'd been dating her. Nothing came to mind. Maybe she had a friend who was into that stuff, though.

He leaned forward and met Jamie's gaze. "I think we should start following her and see what she's up to. If it's anything suspicious, maybe we'll be able to prove she had something to do with those deaths. Or at least save someone else from being killed."

"Okay, but I have to head to work in a little over an hour." Jamie rose from the couch and headed back upstairs to change into her work clothes. Lucio trailed behind and she talked to him over her shoulder. "I had the boss put me on the day shift for the break, not only for the extra hours, but to have more free nights with you. That means I'm off work at six instead of the usual nine or ten. If you want to tail her before that, please take Drew or Jason or Allison with you. I don't think it would be safe to follow her alone if she really is murdering people."

Lucio felt a warm pang in his heart that she worried about his safety. Honestly, he had no desire to follow his probably murderous ex-girlfriend by himself. Not that he was scared or anything—

Chet had been alone.

He would rather have Jamie with him, pure and simple. "I'll wait for you to get off work before playing private investigator."

As he watched Jamie take off his Anvil shirt, a fresh surge of lust roared through him. Last night had been incredible. When his father had given him the talk about the birds and the bees, he'd told Lucio to share his body only with someone he loved. Lucio hadn't listened, dismissing the advice as encouragement to keep it in his pants. Now he realized that there'd been truth to that. Then he realized that because of the stupid cops, he didn't have a chance to ask her how she felt about last night.

"How are you feeling?"

Jamie's head poked out of her uniform top. "Aside from being creeped out about Brittney and not in the mood to go to work, I'm fine. Why?"

"I meant, are you sore from last night or having any regrets?"

Roses bloomed in her cheeks again and the look she gave him sucked out his breath. "I'm a little tender, but I have no regrets at all." She crossed the small distance separating them and threaded her arms around his waist, resting her head against his heart. "Thank you for making my first time so perfect and magical."

"It was powerful for me too." *I love you.*

As he held her in his arms, he'd almost said the last part out loud. With aching reluctance, he released her. "So, um do you have time for breakfast? I can fry up some bacon, eggs, and hash browns."

Jamie's stomach growled as she nodded, and they both laughed.

The meal went too fast, and so did the kiss good-bye, as much as Lucio tried to make it long and lingering. The temptation to follow her to Prime Time Video and watch over her at work gnawed at him, but he knew that aside from the risk of making Jamie uncomfortable, he'd get busted by the manager for loitering, and he couldn't guard her every shift.

Instead, he occupied himself with cleaning up the kitchen, walking Fulci, and checking up on Bava's like he'd promised his father. Some supplies needed to be stocked and one of the servers was feeling unwell, so he ended up waiting tables until the dinner shift came in.

Still, he ended up at Prime Time Video an hour before Jamie's shift was over. She didn't mind, especially since he'd brought her a fresh calzone. Her coworker looked envious, so Lucio gave her the third one he was going to have later.

When Jamie was finally free, they argued over whose car to take.

"We should take my car," Jamie declared. "Your Trans Am is too conspicuous."

Lucio shook his head. "Your Honda may be smaller, but it's loud from the holes in the muffler, bright red, and sticks out like a sore thumb."

"Damn, you're right." Her lower lip stuck out in that adorable pout she got when something thwarted her. Then she brightened. "Wait, let's swing by the Shanty Bar and see if my mom will let me switch cars with her."

"That's brilliant. That brown Toyota will fade into the background. Especially at night." Lucio was relieved that she'd found a viable option. "But we'll need an excuse."

By the time they dropped Lucio's Trans Am at his house and made it to the bar where Jamie's mom worked, they had a plausible reason for wanting to swap cars—one even close to the truth.

That didn't make Lucio any less nervous when Leigh came out to greet them. He'd just taken her daughter's virginity and there was no way Leigh didn't know that.

Jamie rushed right up to her mom, but he stayed by the car. "We want to go to the drive-in and see *Children of the Corn* but we heard that Brittney might be going too and she'd recognize our cars, so I was wondering if I could borrow yours. I don't want her to ruin our evening."

Leigh stared at Lucio, seeming to not hear her daughter's question. He gave her a polite nod and that seemed to satisfy her and she addressed them both. "I can't believe that little monster is going to the movies when her latest boyfriend was found dead this morning. When I saw her on the news this morning, I knew those were crocodile tears." Then Leigh turned her blazing blue eyes on Lucio. "These deaths of your classmates have me terrified. You keep my daughter safe. She may be an adult now, but that doesn't make me worry any less. And if she doesn't come home or call by midnight, I'll be disappointed in you."

"Okay, Mom," Jamie said in a mortified voice before grabbing Lucio's hand and practically running to the brown Toyota Corolla parked two cars over.

"Why'd you tell her we were going to see *Children of the Corn*?" Lucio asked when Jamie pulled out of the Shanty's lot. "We already saw it."

"So, if she asks about the movie, I can tell her what happened."

"Brilliant."

They headed to Brittney's house, a modern mansion on a cliff overlooking Lake Skeetshue. Her yellow Porsche was in the driveway and her bedroom light was on. Jamie passed the mansion and continued on up the hill and to a darkened cul-de-sac up where empty lots awaited for new mansions that would soon be built.

"Maybe she *is* laying low for a little bit," Lucio said. Just in case, they continued the stakeout for a couple hours, talking about books and movies.

***

The next night, at Drew's party, they heard that Jennifer and Brittney had left for Seattle for a three-day shopping spree to heal her broken heart.

Lucio and Jamie breathed a sigh of relief at the reprieve. Although they wanted to find out for sure if Brittney was the murderer, and how she was getting away with the crimes, there were better things to do during spring break—like kissing, and cuddling, and making love.

They excused themselves from Drew's party early and made love in Lucio's bed the last night before his dad came home.

The night after that, they went to the drive-in and watched *This Is Spinal Tap*. The movie made them laugh until their sides ached. After they left the drive-in, they found a quiet place by the lake to park. The back of Jamie's Honda was a little cramped, but they made it work.

The fourth night, they used the "scared-of-Brittney" excuse to trade cars with Jamie's mom for the rest of the week. That stakeout led them outside of a boring country club party, but Lucio kept Jamie entertained with stories about the insane things he saw and heard in that club, like the mayor alternating between dining or dancing with his wife and mistress every forty-five minutes.

"You could set your watch by it." Lucio shook his head at the memory. "And then there was this super-rich lady, and I mean really rich, always wearing fur coats and dripping with jewels. She'd steal the appetizers. Pounds of mini quiches and shrimp cocktails and she'd wrap them in napkins and stash them in her purse."

The fifth night, when it looked like they'd be outside Brittney's house all night, they spotted her heading out a little after ten, dressed in a dark brown coat, dark pants, and work boots.

"She's going somewhere alone," Lucio said, and Jamie started the Toyota. "There's no way she'd be caught dead in public in a getup like that."

Jamie followed the Porsche from a distance, leaving the headlights off until they left Brittney's rich hilltop neighborhood and merged with the town traffic. They also remained two or three cars back from Brittney.

Lucio leaned forward, watching their progress north through Amteep and out of the city limits. "Looks like she's heading to Sinchlep."

"Where there are a lot of farms," Jamie said in an ominous tone.

Sure enough, Brittney passed the grocery stores, bars, and restaurants, went through the residential area and up the road where the houses on Sinchlep Lake were, and into the open country. Eventually, she steered her Porsche down Iowa Match Road, and turned off onto a little dirt road. A large sign was nailed to a tall white post: Ferguson Dairy Farm.

"Oh God," Jamie whispered. "She's going to massacre another cow."

"Only one way to find out," Lucio said. "Turn off your headlights and creep a little closer. When she stops, we gotta find somewhere to pull over and hide so she can't see us." Then he spotted a familiar sign indicating an upcoming forest service road. "I know this road. The farm must be between this one and the forest service road that Dad and I take when we go pick morels. Turn on the opposite fork she takes."

Brittney veered right, keeping on the road to the dairy farm. Jamie went left, wincing a little as the car rattled across a cattle guard. Thankfully, Brittney's Porsche didn't slow. Instead, she continued on to a large barn and turned into the dirt driveway leading to the structure. The path went around the barn, where a tractor and a large flatbed truck were parked. Brittney passed those and parked behind the barn.

Jamie tucked her mom's Toyota in a low ditch surrounded by honeysuckle bushes and under the boughs of a large white pine. Lucio prayed they'd be able to drive out of it.

They got out and carefully approached the field between the two roads. The moon cast a large shadow from the barn, and Jamie and Lucio did their best to stay sheltered in its darkness.

A herd of cattle stood sleeping in the field on the other side of the barn near a corral, and a human shape in this distance slowly crept toward the sleeping animals.

"I still can't believe this," Lucio whispered. "Brittney hated going outdoors. Now she's walking through cow pies in the dark?"

"Shhh," Jamie chided.

They made their way to the corral and huddled beneath the cattle chute for a concealed vantage point.

Keeping to the shadows, they watched Brittney edge closer to the herd. The lithe stalking pace of her steps made her resemble a hungry lioness closing in on a wildebeest. With frightening speed, the lioness pounced. Brittney seized a calf that stood farther from the rest and, with strength she shouldn't have had, put the poor animal into a chokehold and dragged it back away from the herd.

Lucio and Jamie watched her haul the calf across the field, then to the forest service road where Jamie had stashed the Toyota. Lucio held his breath, watching to see if Brittney spotted the car, but the evil cheerleader seemed occupied with dragging the calf. She brought her prey across the road and into the woods.

Jamie's eyes were wide and frightened. "She shouldn't be able to do that. Calves aren't light."

With shaky steps, Lucio and Jamie left their hiding place and followed Brittney. Their progress was almost too fast. The minute they made it across the road, they heard Brittney heaving and cursing only about ten feet away.

A twig snapped under Lucio's foot and he sucked in a breath, but Brittney was making so much noise hauling the poor calf that she didn't hear them.

They hid beneath the boughs of a large fir when Brittney stopped in a clearing. The calf slid limply from Brittney's grasp and fell to the ground, motionless. Its sides moved up and down, the only indicator that it was still alive.

Brittney reached in her coat pocket and pulled out a can of green spray paint. The rattle of the ball striking the aluminum as she shook the can was disconcerting in the silent forest. Lucio gripped Jamie's hand. The woods shouldn't be that quiet. Where were the owls, the bats? The nocturnal creatures that hunted in the darkness? Perhaps they sensed this predator, one who was unnatural and sinister.

The hiss of paint made him jump, even though it was a familiar sound. Brittney made a wide circle around the calf and then drew some odd symbols inside the circle. With a satisfied nod, she pocketed the paint can and withdrew a container of salt that she spread around the circle.

When the salt circle was complete, Brittney reached beneath her coat and pulled out a long, sharp knife. Moonlight glinted on the blade, revealing some intricate etching on the steel.

She straddled the calf and wrapped her free arm around its neck, lifting the creature's head skyward.

When she spoke rapidly in a different language, Jamie and Lucio drew closer together. Icy chills raced up his spine, prickling his skin until he wanted to run.

Brittney switched back to English. "Scarlionapskhis, I call you forth with this offering of innocent blood." With that, she slit the calf's throat in a practiced slash.

Blood sprayed across the clearing, bathing some of the spray-painted symbols on the ground and trickling into the salt circle. Lucio stared at Brittney in stunned horror. With her golden hair and perfect skin, she should have still been beautiful, but the feral curl of her upper lip, baring her teeth in a snarl, her blood-drenched hands and the greedy and hateful intensity of her eyes—eyes that glinted yellow like a flicker, but that had to be a trick of the light—Brittney Shaw looked monstrous.

The ground turned black in the circle in front of Brittney and the dead calf. Then the blackness rose up like smoke pouring and swirling into the shape of a twisted, horned monster.

Chapter Twenty-One

Jamie couldn't believe what they were seeing. The most beautiful, popular girl in school since middle school, the head cheerleader, and Jamie's most dreaded tormentor, had put a calf in a chokehold, made a circle containing a pentagram and arcane symbols, slit the calf's throat, and summoned a demon.

The demon didn't appear to be fully corporeal, as Jamie could kind of see through it in some places, but she didn't doubt that the thing could harm her and Lucio if it spotted them. She stared at its claws and twisted horns and the spikes protruding out of its back and pinched herself to make sure she wasn't dreaming.

The demon spoke in a voice that sounded like crushed bones and buzzing wasps. "I accept this sacrifice and..." The rest of the words went so fast that Jamie couldn't decipher them.

And she didn't want to. She met Lucio's terrified gaze and they communicated silently. They needed to get the hell out of here.

As the demon fell upon the calf and ripped into it with sharp claws, Lucio and Jamie used the noise to creep away from the horrific scene.

Her heart pounded in her throat with each step. She wanted to run, but knew they didn't dare risk the noise. The skin between her shoulder blades alternately prickled and burned in wait for Brittney or the creature she'd summoned to catch Jamie and Lucio.

By the time they made it back to the road, her skin was drenched in cold sweat. They walked faster to the car. When they reached the Toyota, Jamie paused, gripping the door handle. "Won't she hear us if we drive away now?"

Lucio looked back at the woods and then at her. "She might, but she won't recognize the car. Either way, I think we're better off driving away now instead of hiding down here and hoping she and that thing don't spot us."

Jamie nodded. The urge to drive away made her quiver and reach into her pocket for her mom's keys. "Hopefully that thing is confined to the circle she made."

They got into the car and closed their doors as quietly as possible. Jamie started the car and closed her eyes at the fairly quiet sound, thanking the heavens that Mom's Corolla had a little sewing machine engine instead of a turbo V8.

"Go straight instead of backing out of the cattle guard." Lucio's voice shook. "And drive casually. Don't go tearing out."

Jamie wanted to argue passing under the hill where Brittney was, but then she nodded. Her knuckles were white as she gripped the steering wheel. "As long as you can get us home from this road."

"I can." The confidence in his voice soothed the edges of her panic. "I know this road really well, and soon I'll take you back here to get morels so we can make a mushroom cream sauce that will take you to heaven. Right now, drive like we've been on the road for a while."

Jamie nodded and held his breath as she drove down the forest service road. Her heart seized as they passed the path up where Brittney had dragged the cow. She looked out the window and saw nothing but trees and darkness.

Her heartbeat resumed and she and Lucio both let out a breath even though they weren't out of the woods yet. She watched the rearview mirror in case Brittney had seen them and decided to chase them. Maybe run them off the road like Stacey. When they'd gone another mile, the tension in her shoulders eased up a bit. No headlights were behind them.

She went another mile before she dared to speak. "No one will believe us."

"You got that right." Lucio placed his hand on her leg, not in a lustful way, but like he needed to touch her for reassurance. "What the hell are we going to do?"

Jamie took comfort in his touch. "We have to stop her from killing again. That's the first priority."

Lucio's sigh radiated doubt. "But...she summoned a fucking demon. Where in the hell did she learn how to do that?"

Jamie was clueless about that at first. Then it clicked. "The occult books from the library that vanished three years ago. She was the one who took them. Three years of studying could amount to something."

"Okay, then that means that we'll need to find out from the library which books they were and get our own copies." Lucio sounded a little more confident. "If Brittney learned how to summon a demon, then we can learn how to banish it, or at least protect ourselves from it."

"Exactly."

Some of the tightness in Jamie's chest eased. Having a plan made her feel so much better after the monstrous nightmare they'd witnessed. She needed that small comfort to try to deal with the knowledge that the girl who'd tormented her for years was a cold-blooded murderer who could summon demons.

As soon as Lucio guided her back to one of Sinchlep's main roads, she took one hand from the wheel to grip Lucio's. His presence soothed her even more than making plans. "I don't want to be alone tonight."

"Me neither," Lucio said. "Will your mom flip if you stay the night at my place?"

Jamie recalled the palpable fear in her mother's eyes the day Chet's body was found when she'd cautioned Lucio to take care of her. "We already went over that the first time I slept with you. I'm an adult, so she can't do anything more than worry. But if she objects, I can say that some creep was hanging around outside my work, or that we saw something suspicious."

When they went to the Shanty to drop off the Toyota and get the keys to the Honda, no excuses were needed. Leigh gave both of them a stern look and said as long as they weren't going to give her early grandchildren, she didn't care where Jamie slept as long as she wasn't alone until the murderer was caught.

Activities that could make grandchildren were the last thing on Jamie's mind as she dropped by her trailer to pack an overnight bag. Especially when they arrived at Lucio's house to see Mario in the recliner watching some Italian horror films.

"Hello, *bella*, I see you're staying the night. You and Lucio should join me and watch some Giallo films. I made popcorn."

Lucio cleared his throat. "Um, Dad, in light of recent events, we're not really interested in seeing people get hacked up. Maybe another time?"

Mario's face reddened. "Of course." Then he gave them a knowing smile and wink. "You probably want some alone time, eh? I will remain down here to give you privacy, but Lucio?"

"Yes, Dad?" he replied cautiously.

"If you do not listen to my advice about safety, be prepared for a wedding."

Lucio's face turned tomato red and Jamie's face burned as they raced up the stairs.

With Lucio's dad down there, they weren't remotely in the mood for lovemaking. Instead, they changed into their pajamas and lay cuddled together in Lucio's bed, listening to Dio on the stereo at low volume. Jamie loved the singer's voice.

She dozed off in Lucio's arms, surrounded in a cocoon of contentment.

The next morning, after Mario cooked them a heavy breakfast of crepes, omelets, and sausage, Lucio and Jamie headed straight to the library.

Miss Hanlon, the head librarian, was immediately disturbed and suspicious as to why they wanted the full list of all the occult books that went missing from the library back in 1981.

Jamie came up with an excuse to mollify her. "We have a group of classmates who we're beginning to suspect might be part of the Satanic cult. They play Dungeons and Dragons and listen to heavy metal music." She wrinkled her nose in mock disgust. "But I don't want to accuse them if they're innocent. Lucio and I thought that if we could see what was in those books, maybe we could find out if they're exhibiting any behavior described in them. Or maybe even find one of those books in their backpacks."

Miss Hanlon nodded with visible relief. "I'll have to go in the back and look up our ledgers from that year. Feel free to browse while you're waiting." She smiled at Lucio. "We received more books on tape that might interest you."

An hour later, she came back with a list made up in her perfect librarian penmanship. Jamie wished she could write that neatly. Lucio checked out a book on tape of a Bradbury novel she'd spotted on his bookshelf.

They went to Paul Bunyan's Burgers for lunch while they perused the list.

Jamie read the titles to Lucio. "*Spellcraft for the Modern Witch*, by Claudette Bachman. Mystic Press, 1965." She giggled. "Not so modern now.

"*Hocus Pocus: Witchcraft for Beginners*, by Roberta McCammon. Mystic Orb Press, 1980.

"*Guide to New Age Magic*, by Sylvia Gilmour, Fancy Publishing, 1969.

"*Make Wishes Come True: Magic and Talismans*, by Ronette Blackmore, Fancy Publishing 1978.

"*Harness the Dark Side: A Complete Guide to the Pantheon of Demons and How to Use Them to Improve Your Life*." Jamie tapped on the worn cover. "Bingo."

It took the rest of spring break, trips to ten bookstores in Amteep, Sinchlep, and even Spokane, Washington, and one interlibrary loan to secure all the occult books from Miss Hanlon's list.

Studying the books took even longer. The demon book was dense and confusing, with all its footnotes and references and diagrams.

Jamie frowned at the complex text. "I almost feel guilty for calling Brittney a dumb blonde."

Her phone rang, and Drew's voice came on the line when she answered. "Are you guys still coming to Shane Lowry's party tonight? Because Alex is going to be there and we're thinking of giving him our pitch tonight."

Jane had agreed to be designated driver for the party, and she and Drew had offered to pick up Lucio and Jamie.

"I'm not sure." The last thing Jamie wanted to think about was the stupid prom. "My boss might make me work later. I'll call you and let you know soon, okay?"

After Jamie hung up the phone, she turned back to Lucio. "Should we cancel going to Shane's party tonight? I mean, I know we're supposed to be securing my date for the prom and working on me getting more popular and all, but—"

Lucio broke in. "That depends on your answer to this question."

"What?"

Alarmingly, he got down on one knee. "Jamie Blair, will you go to prom with me?" He got back up and took her hand. "Maybe I'm not prom king material, but I don't want to see you dancing in another guy's arms again. Watching you at the Valentine's Dance gutted me, especially when I'd brought that on myself."

Jamie's heart soared in elation. She didn't want to go with another guy. Still, she had to make certain he was sure. "What about your revenge against Brittney?"

Lucio blinked. Twice. "In light of recent events, I've discovered that I no longer care about punishing her for dumping me. I care about losing you. When beautiful girls from our school are dying, I care more about your safety than vengeance."

Neither of them needed to voice the certain knowledge that if Jamie was indeed crowned prom queen, Brittney would go after her.

Jamie leaned forward and kissed him. "I'd be honored to have you as my escort to the prom. And even if prom queen contenders weren't dropping like flies, I still have no interest in the stupid crown."

Lucio kissed her again, harder and deeper. They made love in Jamie's bed before she had to go to work.

"Oh crap," she said as she changed into her work clothes. "I forgot to call Drew back about the party. Should we decline?"

"Nah." Lucio shook his head. "Brittney's probably going to be there. We should keep an eye on her and see if we can determine who her next target is. Also, we need to make it clear to Drew and everyone else he blabbed to that Operation Carrie is cancelled."

"Operation Carrie?"

Lucio's cheeks reddened. "Drew came up with that code name for the plan because you were an outcast who's transformed into a beauty, not because of the horrors that happened afterward."

Jamie laughed. *Carrie* was honestly one of her favorite films. She cried every time Tommy Ross kissed Carrie White before everything went to shit. "There might be horrors on the big night, but not from me."

Getting off work at six instead of ten made going to a party much better. Not only did Jamie have more time to dress up and do her makeup, but she and Lucio were able to talk with people before they were drunk off their asses.

To Jamie's pleasant surprise, Allison was there. Her boisterous friend was nearly as big an outcast as Jamie was. It seemed Lucio's original mission to make her popular had reaped peripheral benefits since Allison had been sitting with Jamie and Lucio at one of the cooler tables. Jason also seemed to be taking an interest in Allison, despite him being frequently grossed out at her lunch table conversations.

On the downside, Brittney had indeed made an appearance. She purposefully bumped into Jamie and made her spill her drink, but otherwise left her alone. Still, Jamie's skin crawled with revulsion at being in the same room with a known killer whom she'd witnessed sacrificing an innocent calf to a demon only a few nights ago.

She and Lucio carried packets of herbs mentioned in some of the occult books that were associated with protection. Most were found in Mario's kitchen: basil for protection and purification, bay leaf for success and wisdom, and black pepper for exorcism and driving enemies away. Garlic seemed to be a cure-all for all evil, so they each kept a couple cloves in their pockets as well.

On their first venture into the woods to look for morels—which resulted in a wild ride on Lucio's motorcycle—Lucio had found some wormwood plants and dug up the roots because one book mentioned that it could protect you from car accidents if you hung it from your rearview mirror. Neither he nor Jamie were religious, but they considered stealing some holy water from one of the Catholic churches to see what would happen if they snuck some into Brittney's drink. But they'd never found the time.

Unfortunately, not only were Lucio and Jamie not able to tell their classmates that the head cheerleader was a murderer with occult powers, they also had little luck with telling Allison, Drew, and Jane that they were no longer interested in having Jamie win the vote for prom queen.

"Come on," Allison pleaded. "After all those years of Brittney being mean to you, she deserves to lose to you."

Jamie hated saying the next words because they were a twisted lie. "She lost her best friend and her boyfriend in a short time. Maybe it won't hurt to let her have it."

"A boyfriend who'd been going steady with said best friend. Then Brittney snagged him before Heather was cold in the ground." Allison's brown eyes were cold and remorseless. "I never really bought her grief for Heather or her feelings for Chet. She could be so callous."

That was too close to the truth to be comfortable. Jamie broke in while everyone else was nodding in agreement with Allison's assessment. "Besides, I don't want to go with another guy to prom. Not after Lucio asked me."

Drew didn't seem disappointed that Operation Carrie was off. "Oh, you two gave up on the secrecy?"

Lucio nodded. "It wasn't worth it to hide." His arm came around Jamie's shoulders and he tucked her firmly against him. "And I was sick of watching you get to be openly affectionate with Jane. I swear you were laying it on thick on purpose to rub it in my face that you could kiss your girl in the hallway and I couldn't."

Jane frowned at Drew. "I *hope* that's not what you were doing. I thought your affection was genuine."

"It *is* genuine, babe." Drew pulled Jane on his lap and shot Lucio a glare, and Jamie struggled not to laugh.

"Maybe we should nominate you two for prom king and queen," Jamie suggested. "Drew, you're plenty popular, and Jane, you're guaranteed to be our class valedictorian."

"Don't you dare." Jane turned to Jamie in wide-eyed horror. "I'd be mortified to be paraded up there in front of everyone like that."

Lucio reassured her. "Okay, we'll behave. It's safer that way. But I mean it. Jamie is out of the race. Being with me already disqualifies her, but we thought we should tell you first before we waste your time making any more plans."

Safer. Oh shit, Lucio was right. Even though Brittney would be most furious to lose to Jamie, she would still be hostile to anyone who took the crown that she'd already proven she was willing to kill for. Jamie felt like a moron for forgetting that.

Allison wasn't ready to drop the matter. She turned to Jamie with a determined look. "Who says Lucio isn't good enough to be prom king? He's handsome, people like him, and you two look so good together."

Jamie quietly agreed, and in any other circumstance, would have campaigned for Lucio to be prom king. Now that would be the best way to spite Brittney. She'd be proven wrong on her reasons for dumping him. But since she didn't want Brittney to kill her boyfriend, or even notice him for that matter, Jamie did her best to steer Allison and her new friends away from the idea.

"We don't exactly like the idea of prancing around on stage in dumb plastic crowns either. I'd rather we all show up in our finery, dance until our feet ache, and have the best time we can. And when prom queen is announced, we can all walk out in protest or something. It's a dumb tradition anyway. A useless popularity contest that's kinda sexist."

"Yeah." Drew looked intrigued at the idea of a good protest. "But even with you out of the running, Brittney might not win anyway. She hasn't exactly endeared herself to any of us lately." He paused and looked past Jamie and Lucio. "Oh my God. She's all over Alex Pugsley right now. Oddly enough, he seems to be kind of into it."

Jamie and Lucio turned to look at the scene that was unbelievable. Alex had his head bent toward Brittney, an adoring smile on his face as she said something and giggled.

Jamie remembered the way Chet had looked when he'd been with Brittney. Following her like a lost puppy. Staring at her with slavish devotion, though there had been an emptiness in his eyes, totally different from his animated affection when he and Heather had been together.

They're together in death now, Jamie realized with a shiver before turning her attention back to Brittney and Alex. Sure, Brittney was gorgeous and could be charming when she wanted to be, but something was off. Could she be bewitching Alex somehow?

After Drew and Jane drove them back to Jamie's house after the party, Lucio confirmed Jamie's suspicions. "When we were trying to find a guy to take you to prom, we'd picked Alex because Drew told me he's gay. If he is, Brittney can't make him straight. She must be using some of that weird dark magic on him. That could be why she sacrificed the calf the other night."

That made sense. The creature did her favors in exchange for the sacrifices. "Do you think we could find a way to break the spell?"

"Maybe, but should we?" Lucio bent down to pet Shadow. "I mean, if Alex suddenly decides not to take Brittney to prom, she could kill him like she killed Chet. Hell, that could be why she killed Chet in the first place. Maybe the enchantment or whatever wears off after a time."

He was right, but still. "It seems so wrong to leave someone under an evil person's thrall like that."

"I know. But I don't know what else we can do. The people who are in the most danger are the other popular girls in our school." Lucio picked up Jamie's cat and hugged him for a moment before settling him on his lap. "She's killing all of her rivals and entrapping the guys most likely to be prom king. I'd been glad she broke up with me before all this, but now I'm even more relieved."

Jamie reached over to scratch between Shadow's ears. "Wait, you were happy about her dumping you before you learned that she was a demon-summoning murderer? When did your feelings about that change?"

He set the cat down and brushed his knuckles across Jamie's cheek, whisper soft. "When I first kissed you."

Liquid warmth coursed through her, making her forget about Brittney.

"Kiss me again."

Chapter Twenty-Two

On the first day back from spring break, Brittney scowled as she saw the first prom poster hanging in the hall at school. "The Lilac Ball? Seriously? That's the best they could come up with? I knew I should have joined the stupid committee."

If she'd had her say, she would have come up with something classy and original, like "A Night in Paris," or something tropical themed, or maybe something invoking royalty.

If they had to do flowers, Brittney could have done better with that. Lilacs weren't even that special of a flower. They grew everywhere in town. Brittney would have chosen literally anything else. Orchids, lilies, cherry blossoms…hell, even roses were better.

Tickets went on sale Friday. She'd have Alex Pugsley ready to buy them by then. She'd had Scar work his magic a little more subtly so that the spell wouldn't wear off and leave her without a date this time. She'd also left off from working lust over him.

With Chet, Brittney had been curious as to Heather's long-lasting devotion to the guy and baffled at Chet's utter dismissal of her charms. Having him tumble into helpless desire for her had been a balm to her pride and exactly what he'd deserved.

But perhaps unleashing such potent magic had been too greedy. With Alex, Brittney only had Scar work the magic he'd used to make people like her in the first place, and only slightly stronger at that.

Though she had no desire to sleep with the class president, Brittney was mildly surprised that he didn't have a date lined up for prom in the first place. Maybe his occupation with student politics and multiple other extracurricular programs left him with little time for courtship. Or maybe, like Brittney, he had high standards.

He definitely had good taste in fashion. His blazers were always designer brands and he almost always wore polo shirts with a popped collar. When he didn't wear slacks, his jeans were acid-washed and pegged. He'd even recognized that Brittney's dress was a Laura Ashley at Shane's party the other night, and they'd had a fun conversation about fashion and their favorite actresses.

She couldn't recall enjoying talking to a guy as much as that evening with Alex. Lucio had irritated her with his indifference to all the things she'd cared about, like designer fashion, who was who in this town, and which celebrities were on the rise.

She'd also been disappointed when she'd learned that Lucio's criminal exploits had been so much tamer than the rumors made them out to be. And Chet? He'd been little more than a lapdog when under the enchantment, then as it had begun to wear off, all he'd ever wanted to talk about was football and how much he'd missed Heather.

But Alex? Talking with him had been a breath of fresh air, even with the knowledge that that the enchantment was the only reason he'd approached her in the first place.

As if summoned by the recollection, Alex appeared next to her in the hall and sneered at the prom poster. "Lilacs?" he snorted in disgust. "Those things are practically weeds."

Brittney was inordinately pleased that he agreed. God help her, she actually liked this guy. She decided to go in for the kill. "Are you going to go?"

"I've been going back and forth on it. On one hand, it would be amusing to see what hideous outfits people are going to be wearing. On the other, I'll have to *look* at those hideous outfits."

Brittney tempered her voice to that adoring cadence men almost always fell for. "You'd definitely be the best dressed there. I think you have a good shot at prom king. Another accolade in the yearbook."

Alex raised one eyebrow and smiled. "And I suppose you'd like to be my queen. You're attractive enough, and you've got the sympathy vote in hand for losing a best friend and a boyfriend, but your popularity is waning."

Brittney gasped. *How dare he!* But before she could lash out, she considered his words. She'd been so busy with feeding Scar and advancing her plans that she'd been neglecting to spend time with her friends.

When Heather had been alive, they'd all gotten together for sleepovers, shopping trips, roller skating, and countless parties. Aside from appearances at two parties and that brief shopping trip with Jennifer, she'd been making herself scarce.

"You're right," she told Alex, silently willing Scar's enchantment to work on him. "But I can easily fix that." Whether by having Scar work his magic, or by taking a less popular girl under her wing, she'd get back on the A-list in no time.

Alex's gaze raked over her in a blatant appraising stare, though without any heat. "Okay, but what are you going to wear?"

Brittney grinned, knowing she'd won. "I just got the latest Gunne Sax catalogue in the mail on Saturday. But if I don't find anything worthy in there, there's always Versace."

Alex nodded in approval. "Gunne Sax is *the* place to get a prom dress. Do you have the catalogue with you? We could look through it at lunch. And I have the latest Brooks Brothers catalogue."

"It's a date." Brittney winked at him and headed off as the bell rang.

During class, Brittney tried to focus since her grades were slipping. Something else she needed to work on. But she kept spacing out. The bell would ring when it had seemed only a few minutes had gone by. She'd look down at her worksheet and see that only part of it had been filled out.

At least her lunch date with Alex was successful. Neither decided on what they'd wear to the prom yet, dragging it out for the joy of taking time to shop longer. And by the time the bell rang, he'd promised to purchase tickets and start their campaign for king and queen. Brittney wished she'd chosen him first. If she had, Heather and Chet would still be alive.

A wave of grief settled on her like a shroud through government class. Not for Chet. She'd never cared about him except for his contribution to school pride with the football games he'd helped win for the Amteep Devils. But Heather... Brittney's heart tightened with how much she missed shopping with her, gossiping, and making fun of everyone who was below them in the school hierarchy.

But she couldn't bring Heather back from the dead... Well, maybe Scar could, but there was no way she wanted to find out. Brittney could only move forward, so she needed to reconnect with her old friends.

She started that mission during cheerleading practice. While Jennifer wasn't nearly as friendly as she used to be, she warmed up by the end when Brittney invited her, Vanessa Ernst, and Sue Norman—the new cheerleader who'd been brought into the ranks to take Heather's place—over to her house to look at catalogues and choose their prom dresses. Brittney hadn't remembered approving Sue's audition. Had the coach done it without her? That would be unlike the coach, and it bothered Brittney that she didn't remember.

With the four girls gathered in her bedroom after a light snack of cucumber sandwiches made by the housekeeper, Brittney turned on the charm and eagerly shared her catalogues, trying to bring back the cozy atmosphere and camaraderie that she'd long experienced with her fellow elites.

Even though she enjoyed talking with her friends about what they were going to wear to prom, and the guys who would be taking them, Brittney couldn't help but feel a little alienated from them. They lived peaceful lives consisting of homework, cheerleading, shopping, gossiping, and deciding whether to go all the way with their boyfriends.

Meanwhile, Brittney had the homework, cheerleading, and shopping parts, but she also had to study complex spells and rituals before she'd learned to summon Scar. And now she had to pay frequent visits to farms, hiking out in fields and getting filthy in the process of slitting their throats to feed the demon.

Regret pooled in her stomach. She wished she could go back to the simple life the others had. A memory of a birthday party in her old neighborhood back in fifth grade taunted her, one she'd tried to forget even before she'd discovered the powers of the occult.

She and Jennifer, Margaret Chelan, and Jamie Blair had spent the day playing games, eating cake, and pulling pranks on Margaret's little brothers. Later, they'd rolled out their sleeping bags in Margaret's tree house and stayed up all night making s'mores with a candle and talking about how cool and popular they'd be in middle school.

Scar's voice slashed the memory to ribbons. *You don't want to go back to that. You were lower middle class, you had stringy hair with bad skin, and you had to wear hand-me-down clothes from your cousin. The older country club girls laughed at you. You have no reason to covet the lives of these girls here. You may not have the simplicity of living that they have, but that means that you are more evolved than them.*

They haven't felt the glory of hot blood flowing across their fingers. They haven't experienced the power coursing through your veins. They haven't bent the world to their will. You are a lioness among lambs. You are honoring them by being in their presence and they don't know to appreciate it. And you're having to lower yourself to be amongst the lambs only for the sake of winning the crown that you deserve.

Brittney nodded. "You're right."

"Who's right?" Sue asked.

Brittney blinked and saw her three friends staring at her with confusion. How long had Scar been talking in her mind?

"Um, I was thinking about Vanessa's idea to get a dress that's like Cha Cha's from *Grease*, but have it red with black polka dots like Rizzo's. Sorry for my delay. It took me awhile to turn it around in my head and imagine how it would look on her."

Sue seemed to buy the excuse, but Jennifer's eyes remained narrowed in suspicion. Vanessa ignored both reactions and immediately began rattling off about how she'd seen the perfect fabric at the store and how her mom could get a pattern for it.

Brittney thought homemade clothes were tacky but didn't dare risk having anyone thinking she was stuck up. Even though Heather would have agreed with her. Besides, if Vanessa wore a homemade dress that was a mishmash of two dresses from a movie that came out last decade, that would lower Vanessa's chances of being voted prom queen.

Yes, Scar whispered. *They are all competition. While you do need them to like you, you can't forget that. And if they don't fall in line, we will kill them.*

Brittney was smart enough not to respond to him out loud. She frowned. Why was he here now anyway? She hadn't summoned him. He was showing up more often without her performing the ritual.

Maybe she needed to cool off on feeding him sacrifices. Her biggest rivals were dead, she had Alex Pugsley, the handsome, fashionable class president as her date, and he knew how to campaign better than anyone at Amteep High. And she was making headway reconnecting with her friends and recovering her popularity. The crown was practically guaranteed to be hers. She didn't need to kill anyone or have any more wishes granted for now.

After her friends left, she spent extra time in a hot bubble bath, pampering herself and enjoying a night off from sneaking onto farms and slaughtering livestock. When she finished her bath, she put on her most comfortable pair of pajamas and bundled up in bed. Brittney fell asleep with visions of pink satin and tulle parading through her head.

At four in the morning, she awoke downstairs on the living room couch. Her pajama bottoms were shredded, dirt caked her feet, and there was dried blood under her nails.

Brittney stared at her gore-encrusted hands in horror. "Where the hell was I?"

Quickly she ran upstairs and changed and then went back down to clean up the dirt before the housekeeper saw.

Her hands shook as she cleaned the dried blood. Scar had done this.

Once back in her room, she pulled out her box of spell implements and burned a bundle of sage in her room.

"This has got to stop, Scar," she said in case he was still around. "You can't take me places without my knowing. If I got caught and arrested, who would feed you?"

Even as she spoke, Brittney knew she'd been feeding the demon too much. She should have stuck with small animals.

Scar didn't respond. She sighed with relief and got one of her occult books out of her closet. There had to be a way to rein him in. And even if she couldn't find a ritual to bind the demon, maybe starving him would work.

The next day at school, Brittney seemed to be demon free. She didn't fade out in any of her classes and she amassed a nice group of admirers and sycophants at the lunch table with her with Alex sitting on one end, holding court like the king and queen they were going to be. By the time she went to cheerleading practice, Jennifer had warmed up to her enough to invite her to a sleepover at her house on Friday.

When Scar tried to whisper in her mind, she shut him down by silently singing that stupid YMCA song in her head. She was the one in control, damn it. Not him. She returned home, determined to not offer the demon any more sacrifices.

He appeared in her room and laughed. "Little girl, you think that now that you got everything you've asked of me that you can shirk your side of our bargain? You think you can stop giving me what I want? You're nothing without me. And I can make you nothing again."

Brittney threw a handful of salt, pepper, and crumbled dried rue at him. "Scarlionapskhis, I command you to leave me. Begone, demon."

Scar faded away like a smoke wisp from a dying campfire. Brittney's heart surged with victory. When she awoke in her own bed with her hands and pajamas still clean, her confidence grew. She would banish Scar and stop him from taking over her life.

The next few days went well with only minor intrusions from the demon trying to surface. Starving and ignoring him was working.

She chose the perfect Gunne Sax prom dress from the catalogue, and luckily when she called for it, there was a dress in her size in a formal wear store in Spokane. She called the family driver immediately.

When she arrived at Jennifer's house for the sleepover, Brittney was carrying her dress in a protective bag, eager to see her friends seethe with envy. None of them could have dresses as fantastic as hers. Especially not Vanessa with her silly *Grease* dress. Brittney rolled her eyes. She couldn't wait for this fifties trend to die.

To her shock, Vanessa's mom had finished the dress already. All the girls at the sleepover had brought their dresses. At first, Brittney felt a twinge of irritation at not being the first and only, but then she told herself that it would be fun to take turns trying on their dresses and showing them off to each other and then deciding on how to do their makeup and hair. No doubt in her mind, Brittney would still be the most beautiful of them all.

They ate a quick dinner and meticulously scrubbed their hands before going up to Jennifer's room to put on their prom dresses. Vanessa actually looked good in her Cha Cha/Rizzo dress, the rockabilly style flattering her curvy figure, and the red and black polka dots going well with her dark brown hair and olive-tinted skin. Sue went with a Gunne Sax dress too. A sleek, velvet knee-length shift that would have been a plain black tube hanging on her if not for the giant turquoise bow around her waist.

"The model in the catalogue had short slicked-back hair, but I think I'm going to curl my hair and wear it up," Sue said.

Brittney nodded even though she thought curls would look silly with Sue's angular face. Then it was Brittney's turn to display her dress. Jennifer was going last as a courtesy as hostess, but Brittney thought *she* should have been last since hers was the best. She went into Jennifer's bathroom and put on her prom dress.

When Brittney emerged, she was showered with sighs and oohs, and admiring comments about the beauty of her pink confection. The sweetheart bodice was satin, but covered in lace that reached to a point at the waist. The satin skirt was like that of a Southern belle, two layers with the top gathered up in darker pink bows. She wore a crinoline under to make the skirt bell out a little, but nothing extreme.

She took her seat next to Vanessa on the foot of Jennifer's bed and decided that it was best that Jennifer went last. It gave her wicked pleasure that she'd have to follow in an inferior gown. That's what she deserved for being cold to her for the past couple months. That's what she got for—

Brittney's jaw dropped when Jennifer emerged, resplendent in a metallic blue gown with short ruffled sleeves that melded with ruffles over her scooped-neck bodice. Like Brittney's dress, Jennifer's was full-skirted with a crinoline underneath to flare it out. Tiers of long metallic blue ruffles made up her overskirt, which were gathered by fabric roses instead of bows.

Brittney's stomach roiled in envy and her fists clenched in her lap. While Brittney's dress was the most stylish and in with the trends, pink being the color of the year, Jennifer's dress was most unique, and made her look like a princess.

Or a queen.

When the other girls' praising and cooing over Vanessa's dress faded, Brittney managed to speak. "It's incredible. Are you sure your date is going to be worthy?"

"Definitely," Jennifer said, all starry-eyed. "I showed Shane a fabric swatch that matches this dress, since I don't want him to see me in it, and he found a ruffled dress shirt in the same color. And my dress came with a spare rose that he can use as a boutonnière."

They'd look perfect together. A matching set that could spell competition. Brittney would have to get a fabric swatch so Alex could match her. Then the rest of Jennifer's words sank in. "Wait, you're going with Shane Lowry?"

"Yeah, I told you that the day before yesterday." Jennifer's eyes narrowed. "You acted like an airhead yesterday. And your face was so blank that it made me worry."

"Yeah." Brittney's laugh sounded brittle even to herself. *I could do worse to your head and face, Jennifer*, an inner voice sneered.

No, she couldn't let Scar call the shots. Jennifer was her friend. And Brittney needed friends, so she couldn't kill any more of them.

Instead, she settled on giving Jennifer and the others bad makeup advice. There were other ways to make sure Jennifer didn't win.

The next night when Brittney was home from the sleepover and getting ready for bed, Scar returned. "It is past time that you feed me."

"No." Brittney cursed herself for not having any herbs on hand. "You got too powerful and put me in danger. I am not letting you take me over again."

Scar laughed; the scornful sound felt like countless tiny cuts on her skin. "Silly chit. I've been inside you for days. I can have you whenever I choose. And if you don't feed me, I'll help myself. And if I have to help myself, I will have a feeding the likes of which this world hasn't seen in many years. But for now, I shall indulge in a little snack."

Blackness enclosed Brittney, darkening her vision before it was engulfed in a red haze.

She awoke in her bed. Her mother was shaking her shoulder.

"Your friend Jennifer was found dead this morning. Some maniac broke into her room and poured acid on her face and gutted her. I don't want you driving alone until that evil man is caught. Chalmers will drive you to school."

"What?" Brittney started to get out of bed, but when she lifted the covers, she saw that her hands and arms were covered with blood all the way down to her elbows. Luckily, her mom was looking out the window and muttering about having bars installed. Brittney jerked the covers back over her and clenched the fabric in a death grip. "I don't think I can handle going to school today." She forced a choked sob. "I don't think I can get out of bed."

"Of course, sweetheart. I'll call the school." Her mom bent down to kiss her on the forehead before backing away. "My poor angel. You've been through so much this year."

When her mom left and closed the door behind her, Brittney lurched out of bed and turned on the shower. As she huddled under the spray, Scar's voice echoed in her head. *"I told you I can have you whenever I choose."* His tone lightened. *"Look on the bright side, at least we've eliminated another competitor for the crown."*

A real sob built in Brittney's throat.

Scar tsked. *"Come now, you remember how you felt when she paraded in that beautiful gown and then blithely announced that she had a formidable escort as well. Your instincts were correct all along. She was a threat."*

Brittney almost argued, but sighed as she saw the truth of his words. Also, Jennifer had a tendency to be randomly bitchy toward her anyway. "Maybe you're right."

"Do you want that crown?" His voice became seductive and cajoling.

"Yes." She'd worked too hard not to have it. Done too many unspeakable things that she could not come back from to achieve this goal.

"Then do not try to shut me out or banish me again. Defy me again, and I will unleash a torrent of chaos and destruction that will take you down." Although she heard his voice in her mind, she felt his claws lightly caressing her bare shoulders. *"Give me what I want, and I will give you what you want. That was our bargain."*

But what would she do after being prom queen? Her original plan was to take a year off and then use her powers to get into an Ivy League university where maybe she'd get a fancy degree that could lead to her becoming a fashion executive, or becoming a trophy wife to a millionaire and getting a place on Park Avenue, or both. But she had no idea how she would do those things and keep making blood sacrifices to her demon.

"Do not worry about the future," Scar whispered. *"I will take care of you."*

Chapter Twenty-Three

Being back at school and having his relationship with Jamie public filled Lucio with bliss and fear. He loved being able to hold her hand and kiss her between classes, and yeah, make it clear to the other guys that she was his. But he also dreaded Brittney's reaction. Would she be angry that her ex-boyfriend was dating the girl she most loved to torment? Did she think that she still had a claim to him?

The news of Jennifer Armstrong's death hit the school hard. After Chet's death, a town hall meeting had been held, advising parents to make sure that their kids were always accompanied by a friend, echoing Jamie's mom's orders.

But now those precautions seemed useless, since Jennifer had been killed in her own bed. Brittney had poured some kind of acid on her face that had melted the flesh from her skull and then had proceeded to gut her like a trout.

Brittney, of course, hadn't been at school for the next two days after Jennifer's death. Jamie and Lucio longed to tell someone it was her, but couldn't risk Brittney learning that they were on to her, much less being laughed at by authorities.

The cops had an awful tendency to ignore anything the country club WASPs did, and almost all the teachers loved Brittney because despite her ditzy blonde cheerleader act, she was a good student. And the principal adored her school spirit and participation. As with the jocks, most of the cheerleaders could indeed get away with murder.

Lucio and Jamie momentarily considered asking the chemistry teacher if any of his supplies had gone missing, but worried that not only would Brittney hear about it, but also that the authorities would turn their suspicions to an unfortunate student who didn't deserve the scrutiny. Like one with a previous criminal record. Or another who was often bullied by the cheerleaders. Or one with darker skin tone than the majority of people in town.

Reluctantly, they decided not to say anything. They couldn't afford to risk drawing Brittney's attention to them. Not until they learned how to stop her.

At first, he and Jamie seemed to be lucky in that Brittney hadn't noticed them when she came back to school. She seemed too occupied with talking with her fellow cheerleaders, or working her evil charms on Alex. He wasn't acting quite as weird as Chet, but his eyes followed her everywhere, and he seemed to need to be touching her at all times. Jamie had been the one to spot that sign of attachment.

"And look at how her friends are acting around her," Jamie had whispered to him at lunch one day. "When she speaks, they all turn their heads like she's a queen bee communicating with her drones."

"That is terrifying," he whispered back. "What if she can hypnotize anyone she speaks to at will? We better keep our friends away from her too."

Thankfully, Drew had already gotten to the point where he couldn't stand Brittney. Jane had always disliked her, and so did Allison. And Allison was spending a lot of time with Jason lately, so that would keep him away from Brittney and her drones. Not that Jason hung around the cheerleaders much anyway.

The group that joined Lucio and Jamie at the lunch table remained fairly oblivious to Brittney, aside from when they brought up the ballots for prom king and queen. Allison, Drew, and Jane were all part of the committee and had to poll their fellow students to come up with a list of candidates.

"We are not options," Lucio had told Drew when he'd suggested Lucio and Jamie for the fourth time.

"Don't be so humble," Drew chided.

Eventually, he dropped the subject and let Allison talk about the plans they had for decorating the gym, and which bands they were considering auditioning. Lucio and Jamie didn't pay much attention since they had far bigger concerns.

Since they couldn't stop Brittney yet, they tried to focus on studying the occult books and continued to find joy in spending time with each other. They rode his motorcycle in the mountains, where he taught her to identify and search out morel mushrooms, a seasonal delicacy that was crucial to many of his favorite dishes.

She caught on quickly and ended up finding more of the weird-looking mushrooms than he did. Afterward, they took on the two-day endeavor of making a stuffed leg of lamb from the Julia Child cookbook.

Lucio also wanted to put Jamie's mom at ease about him dating her daughter, so he took Leigh and Jamie to Bava's as he'd promised when he'd helped Jamie shovel snow.

Leigh had enjoyed his father's restaurant more than he'd anticipated. Even Jamie acted like it was her first time at Bava's as she'd hummed in pleasure with every bite of her crab manicotti. Lucio relished their enjoyment more than he'd anticipated, and his father had been almost embarrassing in his delight, waiting upon them himself and then giving them a tour of the kitchen afterward.

During the kitchen tour Lucio felt his first flush of pride in the family restaurant. Jamie's eyes had sparkled with excitement as she'd asked him and his dad about every instrument and utensil. She'd begged his father to show her how to make alfredo sauce, and Dad's eyes had gotten misty as he showed her how to blend the cream, butter, cheese, and his until-now secret extras.

Cooking had made Jamie come alive in a way Lucio had seen only when they were intimate. Watching her joy brought back memories that he'd buried of happy times of learning to cook with his mom and dad before Mom died and Dad put his whole life into starting this restaurant.

Lucio had blinked away moisture in his eyes. Had his resentment over the restaurant carried over to take away his own enjoyment of cooking, and his father's accomplishment? Something to mull later. Instead, he focused on Jamie's delight when Dad had filled a bag with herbs, garlic, shallots, butter, olive oil, and a third of a bottle of the wine he preferred for cooking. Dad's warmth and kindness toward Jamie and her mom made Lucio see him in a better light.

"Practice, *passerotta*," Dad told Jamie. "I will need to hire another cook soon. Especially if Lucio decides to leave after graduation."

He hadn't missed the accusatory look his father had given him, and saw Jamie noticed the silent exchange as well.

Before she could ask about it, Lucio led her and Leigh out of the kitchen and took them home. Then he went back to the restaurant and had a talk with his father.

"I've decided that I'm not cut out for college, Dad," Lucio had announced. "Not only because even with a tutor my dyslexia will make some courses impossible, but also because I don't feel like it's the right path for me."

Mario's expression was unreadable, aside from mild surprise that Lucio wasn't going away. "Then what *do* you plan on doing after graduation?"

"Help you in the restaurant, of course." Lucio met his father's eyes and grinned. "I can cook all of the dishes, since I was taught by the best, and I am good at making sure we have the correct inventory." At his father's misty-eyed look, he almost faltered in bringing up his ulterior motive. "I want to visit the local farms where we purchase our ingredients. Actually, to talk with *all* of the farmers in our area. I will buy the meat and vegetables we need from some, and talk to the others to see if we can get better prices. I was thinking of starting on that tomorrow afternoon and—"

He was silenced as his father's arms came around him and held him tight. "I thought you hated our restaurant."

Lucio blinked at the word "our." He hugged his father back. "I thought I hated it too. I've been coming to realize I don't. I'm proud of what you built, Dad."

He wasn't ready to get into the complex, emotional baggage of those years of feeling abandoned. Instead, he and his dad shared glasses of wine and talked about Jamie. Dad only expressed how much he liked her, and also rhapsodized about how much he admired Jamie's hardworking attitude and her determination to learn how to cook complex dishes.

"I'm tempted to ask her to leave that video store and come work at Bava's as a prep cook, then she can graduate to chef. But I would not want to cause awkwardness for you two if you break up. How do you truly feel about her? Do you see this as long-term?"

"I *love* her." Admitting the truth aloud felt freeing and terrifying all at once. "I know it's too soon because we've only really known each other for five months, and have been dating for less than two months, but every time I'm with her, I feel this surge of...I don't know, something in my heart. I think she's the one."

Dad nodded as if he'd known all along. "Have you told her how you feel?"

"No. I don't want to frighten her off."

"Well, don't take too long either." His dad clapped him on the shoulder. "Taking too long could frighten her off too. I almost lost your mother with my slow pace."

While Jamie was at work, Lucio took the next few afternoons to visit every farm within thirty miles of the restaurant. Sometimes, the visits were legitimate shopping trips, and sometimes he checked the prices of meat and produce.

Each time, he'd asked the farmers about how many animals they'd lost and when. The amount was more than the news had reported, although some may have been in the back pages of the paper.

Lucio jotted down the animals and dates. The kills were more frequent over the winter and were smaller animals, like chickens and rabbits, then goats and lambs. The pigs and cattle were more spread out. One incident a week. Except when Heather died. Then there hadn't been a livestock death in three weeks.

When he picked up Jamie from work, they looked at the calendar and checked off all the dates of known livestock deaths against the deaths of Heather, Stacey, Chet, and Jennifer. He'd opened his math book and found the chapter on predictability and worked out a formula, and the answer indicated that a person was due to be killed sometime during prom week.

He and Jamie also studied the book about the demons and had started a list on which ones demanded death sacrifices rather than blood sacrifices that would allow the donor to live. It turned out that there were a lot of demons who fed on death. They still had to finish the list on which ones were willing to do the bidding of the person who summoned them.

Meanwhile, preparations for prom were gearing up. Lucio had already purchased his tickets and went shopping with Drew and Jason for his tux. He'd expected trying on tuxedos to be a tedious and possibly embarrassing experience, but instead it was sort of fun. Completely different than the times Brittney forced him to wear things she thought would be suitable for her precious country club. Instead, he had a choice and time to try on different options.

He turned and looked at this tux in the three-way mirror. Finally, he'd found the one that looked right. The others were either too ruffled, too tight around the shoulders, were weird pastel colors, or too grim and made him look like a pallbearer.

The one he wore now was ruffle-free with a stiff-collared white dress shirt with black buttons. The black dinner jacket had wide satin lapels, and a black waistcoat that was high enough to show underneath. Black trousers with satin stripes and a bowtie completed the look. He'd have to borrow dress shoes and cufflinks from his dad.

Drew arched one eyebrow as he looked at Lucio's outfit. "Did you purposefully copy Don Corleone's outfit from *The Godfather*?"

Lucio blinked and did a double take in the mirror. "No, but I'm Italian, so maybe it was instinct."

Jason laughed. "Who cares? It looks damn good."

Drew and Jason had chosen outfits that suited them well. Drew's was a pale blue ruffled ensemble that looked like an updated version of what Tommy Ross had worn in *Carrie*, while Jason had gone for a white suit that gave him a bit of a James Bond look.

Lucio was surprised that he was excited to take Jamie to prom. Before, he'd always thought the dance was something for the girls to get excited about, and the only thing a guy cared about was whether the girl would let him get a hotel room after.

He'd gotten one because Jamie had asked him to, and he was plenty excited about that, but he also anticipated dancing with her. Making up for the time he'd lost when she'd gone with Drew to the Valentine's dance. She'd looked so beautiful that night in that red crushed-velvet dress, and he couldn't wait to see what she'd wear to the prom. Jamie refused to tell him. All he knew was that Leigh would be making the dress, and that Jamie wanted a white corsage.

Despite his excitement, he was also scared. Brittney's campaign for prom queen was heating up, and more classmates had turned into drones when they were around her. He dreaded knowing that she was probably going to kill someone else soon. Although her next target was probably one of her fellow cheerleaders, or Alex, Lucio shuddered at the thought of having Brittney's notice fall on him.

A week before the prom, it did. Lucio had been kissing Jamie in the parking lot after school and Brittney walked by.

Lucio tightened his grip on his girl, doing his best to shield her. Unfortunately, Brittney didn't keep walking. She spun on the heels of her designer high tops and approached them with an exaggerated sway in her hips that made her seem serpentine.

"You're with the trailer trash now?" Brittney threw back her head and let a bout of mocking laughter pour out of her perfect lips. "After having me, this must be the downgrade of a lifetime."

Lucio's arms tightened around Jamie until she made a noise of protest. In murmured apology, he loosened his hold on her. Every fiber of his being burned with the urge to lash out as he'd vowed when he'd told Brittney not to call Jamie "trailer trash" again, but he didn't want either of them to be slaughtered by her pet demon.

Jamie spoke up. "Leave us alone, Brittney. Prom is coming up and a *good* prom queen is supposed to be gracious. Can't you be nice for once?"

To Lucio's surprise, Brittney seemed a little placated by Jamie's implying that she'd win the crown. She smiled, though it looked more like a sinister baring of teeth, then she stuck her nose in the air.

"Fine. I suppose I can be generous and say you two are a much more compatible couple in social status, even if Jamie is slightly beneath you, Lucio. Jamie, you're lucky to move up to dating someone higher class than you. Now if you'll excuse me, I've got to help my king-to-be pick out his tux."

When she walked away, Lucio and Jamie heaved huge sighs of relief.

He shook his head as he opened the passenger door for her. "I can't believe she can act like a stuck-up socialite by day and then massacre animals and people for a demon by night. Talk about split personalities."

"Yeah." An off note rang in Jamie's voice. "Do you think I'm beneath you, class-wise?"

The worry in her voice squeezed his heart. He took her hand and met her gaze. "No, I don't. If you'd had a father who hadn't abandoned you, your household would bring in twice the income. I don't think someone being dealt a shitty hand in life has much to do with some people's version of a class system. And why are you letting Brittney get to you anyway? I don't care about where you live, or how much money you and your mom make. I care about what kind of people you are."

"My neighbors in the trailer park have been making a big deal about us lately." Jamie's gaze fled from his as she looked down at her hands on her lap. "To hear some of them talk, I'm like Cinderella meeting Prince Charming...which is how I feel. But others are saying I'm reaching above my station and doomed to heartbreak."

Lucio tilted her chin back up. "You know how I feel? Like a mere mortal daring to reach for a goddess." Now was the time. He gathered his courage and leaned forward and whispered against her lips. "I love you, Jamie."

Silence engulfed the car. The space seemed to shrink, sucking away the oxygen. He found himself unable to take a breath.

She pulled her hand away. A lump formed in his throat. Then she put her arms around his neck and whispered back, "I love you too, Lucio."

They kissed for what seemed like an eternity. In some distant part of his consciousness, he heard car horns honk and some people shout, "Woooo." By the time they broke the kiss, most of the student parking lot was empty.

Lucio chuckled. "We better head out so we can work on our English paper on *Nineteen-Eighty-Four*."

But when they got to his house and went upstairs to his room, studying was delayed. She pulled him down on the bed and tugged at his clothes. He needed no further encouragement. They made long and lingering love.

After lying in each other's arms for a while, they dressed quickly and got some work done on the paper, then they dug out the occult books Brittney had used to become a monster.

Jamie read silently from the book on demons while Lucio carefully read the one on charms and talismans, looking for more things that could help protect them. He used a clear colored ruler to read each line and other techniques that she'd found to help with his dyslexia. Though reading wasn't as difficult as it used to be, he still read slowly.

"Hey," she said suddenly. "This says that if you learn a demon's name, you can gain some power over it." She took out the notebook on the list she'd made of the demons who granted wishes in exchange for death sacrifices.

"Nesamermewynight, Scarlionapskhis, Yejascojem, Deryanan —"

"The S one!" Lucio reached out and tapped the book. "Brittney said a name that started with that letter and it sounded like she'd said 'Scar-whatsis.'"

"I think I remember that now," Jamie said. "But we haven't finished reading about all the demons, so there could be others that fit the criteria and also start with S."

They studied further and did indeed find two more: Sejalems and Siffatgrosditelz. They wrote down the names and tried to make guesses on how to pronounce them.

Lucio tucked his list in the front pocket of his backpack. "I bet the reason why all their names are hard to say is because they don't want people to have power over them. This whole thing is so weird. I thought demons gained power over people." He leaned over Jamie's shoulder, enjoying the light floral scent of her hair mixed with the subtle musk of their lovemaking. "Have you read anything else in there about how we can get power over it or make it go away?"

She leaned back against him. "I'm still not all the way through the books, but I read that one can perform a banishing spell or call up another being to fight it, which sounds both dangerous and unlikely. Also, there is a lot in here about the demons gaining control of their summoners. If Brittney isn't careful, she's gonna get possessed."

Lucio shuddered as he remembered scenes from *The Exorcist* and imagined Brittney puking green slime and levitating...and having superhuman strength. "She might already be. Remember when we saw her subduing and hauling that calf across the field and up a hill?"

"Oh shit." Jamie looked up at him with wide eyes. "We need to figure out how to do an exorcism and get rid of the thing once it's outside of Brittney's body."

"Okay." He flipped the pages of the book. "Wait. Did you see this part?" He pointed to a picture of what looked like an angel. The first sentence beside the picture was so surprising that he had to reread it three times to make sure his dyslexia wasn't making him read it wrong. "This says you can call a light-bringer to extract a demon and change it to a physical form that can be killed."

Jamie blinked. "I skimmed it but didn't pay much mind. Anyway, I wasn't raised religious, but doesn't Lucifer's name mean 'light-bringer'? Does this book think we should call the demon's boss and tattle or something?"

"Possibly, but I don't think so." Lucio pointed at the picture. "This angel is clearly a woman. And Lucifer *was* an angel to begin with anyway."

They read the section with intent and saw that the method to call a light-bringer sounded incredibly simple. Neither believed it would work, but they jotted down the words and supplies needed to try it as a last resort.

The exorcism rituals they found were fairly simple too, though some of the plants and roots listed would be a little tough to get. That meant another trip to the international food market in Spokane.

"But how are we going to do an exorcism on Brittney? Do we follow her and kidnap her and throw her in the trunk and perform it in the woods somewhere?"

Jamie giggled and shook her head. "I figured we can do it during a moment when we're all together, like at the next big party."

"The next big party is after the prom at Shane Lowry's house," Lucio muttered while carefully listing the herbs they'd need to get. He looked up. "We could corner her in a bedroom and try it."

"Prom night it is."

Lucio stared at the pile of occult books in disbelief.

"Dancing, punch, and an exorcism afterward. Sounds like a night to remember."

Chapter Twenty-Four

Jamie stood on an upturned laundry soap bucket and stared in awe at her reflection in her small bathroom mirror. Her dress had turned out better than she could've hoped. Since pink and pale blue were trendy this year, she'd decided to be daring and go with white. She'd picked a sewing pattern that held some similarities to the dresses in the catalogues and *Seventeen Magazine,* but had other features she'd liked more. Yet, knowing the pattern didn't prepare her for how amazing the completed version looked.

The white taffeta gown was tea-length and had a strapless, heart-shaped lace- and bead-covered bodice that ended in a vee slightly below her waist, then giving way to the shiny taffeta skirting that flared out thanks to a starched petticoat that Mom had worn under her wedding gown and kept stored away.

Jamie also wore antique pearl teardrop earrings and a matching pearl necklace that had belonged to her great-grandmother. She'd used her meager savings for a pair of fake pearl-encrusted ballet flats, which were a little misnamed because there was a bit of a heel, though it was low and chunky.

Although she'd been tempted by some gorgeous T-strap heels at the mall, she knew the flats were a more practical choice. Not only for dancing, but also for the likelihood that she and Lucio may need to be able to run fast tonight. A pearlescent beaded handbag on a silver chain completed her look, and would be useful for holding the supplies she and Lucio would need for their upcoming exorcism attempt.

Holding a hand mirror, she carefully turned on the bucket to admire the full effect. She looked beautiful, and she hadn't put on her makeup yet. Mom was a miracle worker.

After stepping down from the bucket, Jamie ran out of the bathroom so fast she almost tripped and fell face-first into the fake wood-paneled wall. After recovering her balance, she flung herself into her mother's arms.

"It's so beautiful. Thank you so much." Tears leaked from the corners of her eyes.

"It turned out pretty good, didn't it?" Leigh squeezed her, and then gently released her. "Careful. Don't wrinkle the dress. Do you need help with your hair and makeup?"

Not really, but Jamie could see the eagerness to help in her mom's eyes. "Sure."

When they finished, it was still at least fifteen minutes before Lucio was due to come pick her up. Jamie paced in front of the living room window.

Suddenly, her mom blurted, "You're in love with him, aren't you?"

Jamie met her mother's blue eyes. "Yes. And he loves me too. He told me last week."

"Really?" Leigh laughed. "From the way he acts around you, I would have thought he'd have said the words a month ago or more." Her expression sobered. "I know I was nervous about him in the beginning, but I really do like him. Especially the way he treats you. I know most high school sweethearts don't end up staying together, but with you two, I think there's hope. But we *really* need to get his father to stop flirting with me."

When the clock struck six, the familiar rumble of Lucio's Trans Am's engine sounded outside. Jamie raced to the window, her heart thudding with anticipation.

"Sit down," Mom scolded. "Wait, no. Stand over there in front of the couch where the light's good. Let him see the full effect of your dress. And let *him* make an entrance."

And what an entrance he made.

Jamie's breath fled her body when Lucio came inside. He looked debonair in a black tux with satin lapels, a starched dress shirt with black buttons that peeked out beneath a black waistcoat. His black trousers had a thick black satin stripe on the sides of each leg. He wore a bowtie and his dress shoes were mirror-shiny. He even wore silver and pearl cufflinks and a fancy silver watch.

His dark curls hung loose and shining over his shoulders, and his chiseled face was clean-shaven. How could she be with a man this gorgeous?

Lucio spoke first, staring at her with heated admiration. "You look incredible."

Jamie recovered her breath. "So do you."

"I hope your corsage works."

The flower was perfect, a fully bloomed white rose. Lucio put it on her wrist and then Leigh made them pose for pictures. Jamie took her overnight suitcase for their planned stay at a hotel, and put it in Lucio's trunk next to his. They had to drive back to Lucio's house to do the whole picture thing. Mario was even more enthusiastic than Mom had been. He kissed Jamie's hand like an old-world gentleman and took at least twenty pictures.

When they finally escaped, Jamie opened her handbag. "I have the herbs, the basalt, and a paper with the ritual words to drive out the demon. I also have the words to call the angel if the other ritual doesn't work."

Lucio nodded. "I have both rituals written down in my pocket along with herbs too. Did you remember a precious stone as a gift for the angel? I got an amethyst."

"I got an Idaho star garnet." Jamie reached into her purse and pulled out a ring box that held the gorgeous polished stone that was so dark purple it was almost black. She'd need more light to be able to show him the asterism effect that made the star. "Star garnets are my favorite stones, and they're rare and unique. I hope that it's something an angel would appreciate."

Lucio nodded, though his beautiful lips were curved in a doubtful frown. "Do you really believe we can summon an angel?"

"If Brittney can summon a demon, why can't we get an angel?" Her voice trembled with false bravado. "But I am worried that it won't work. All we can do is hope."

When they arrived at school, Jamie was impressed at the work the committee had done to transform the gym.

Real lilacs were everywhere, filling the area with their heavenly scent. Silver streamers hung from the doorways, rafters, and basketball hoops like giant tinsel, interspersed with lavender and silver balloons. They'd even gotten a huge disco ball, which hung from the rafters and glittered in the tiny white Christmas lights threaded all around.

A small stage was set up, where the hired band played a cover of Madonna's "Material Girl." At the opposite corner, a photographer took photos of the happy couples in front of a lilac-framed backdrop of a starry sky.

Lucio squeezed her hand and looked down at her with a tender smile. "Do you want to dance, or do you want to find a table and sit?"

"Let's sit." Jamie spotted some of their friends at one of the round lavender-clothed tables opposite from the dance area. "I see Allison and Jason over there."

They joined their friends and took turns praising each other's outfits. Jamie admired Allison's gown, which was almost a complete replica of the one in *Footloose*. Jason looked dapper in a white tux that went well with his red hair.

Drew and Jane joined them. Drew wore a baby blue tux with a darker blue cummerbund and a ruffled dress shirt. His hair looked like it held a ton of mousse, the short part puffed up inches higher than normal. The long part in the back most definitely curled and teased to double volume to frame his neck. Jane had eschewed the flounces and flared skirts and instead wore a long dark blue dress of some sort of shimmering material with spaghetti straps that flattered her tall, slim figure. Like Jamie, she wore ballet flats.

She switched from talking about their clothes to the décor. "I love what you guys and the rest of the prom committee did with the place. How'd you get a disco ball?"

Allison's enthusiasm as she answered was endearing. "We fundraised to rent it. And that's not the only surprise we have in store."

"What else?" Lucio asked.

"You'll see." Allison's mischievous grin was contagious. Jamie wondered if there was going to be a second band or something.

For a while, Lucio and Jamie chatted with their friends and watched their classmates trickle into the quickly filling gym. Jamie saw from the stiff set of his jaw that Lucio was waiting as tensely as she was for a specific entrance.

And then she arrived.

A hush fell over the assembly as Brittney Shaw walked in on Alex Pugsley's arm. Brittney was breathtaking in her pink Gunne Sax gown.

Jamie noticed with some discomfort that their bodice styles were similar. Heart-shaped with lace over the satin. But the bottom half of Brittney's dress was completely different, being floor-length, with a gathered overskirt held up with bows.

The gym had fallen silent. Everyone had turned to look at Brittney. The band began playing Hall and Oates's "Maneater," which was eerily fitting.

Jamie leaned over and whispered to Lucio. "She's enchanting everyone. I can feel it."

Lucio nodded. "It's tough to look away from her, but I don't think we have it as bad as the others. Our herbs must be helping or something."

Then the spell broke with an almost audible pop. Like when pressure released from her ears when coming down from the mountains after going morel hunting with Lucio. Everyone shook themselves, looking confused.

"Do you want to dance?" Lucio asked. "We'll stay away from her for now. I want us to try to enjoy ourselves and let this be a normal, romantic experience before..." He trailed off, but Jamie knew what he couldn't bear to say. Before possibly being killed by Brittney and her demon.

Brittney had studied those books for years, having a chance to find out what worked and what didn't. Jamie and Lucio had only gone through them in a month. The salt, herbs, and stones they carried could be useless.

Then there'd be no going back from confronting Brittney.

She'd know that they'd found out she was behind the killings, and they'd be dead meat for her pet.

Lucio interrupted Jamie's thoughts. "Why do you look so gloomy? I didn't know you thought dancing was that bad."

Jamie shoved aside the dark cloud of impending doom. "Sorry, I got lost in thought. I'd love to dance."

Thankfully, the first song was a slow one: Cyndi Lauper's "Time After Time." It was one of those romantic pop songs that Jamie secretly liked. The singer of the hired band did a pretty good job with it too.

Jamie clung to Lucio and swayed to the music, allowing herself to forget about Brittney and the sense of impending doom.

"That felt nice," Lucio said when the song ended. "But I'm going to request something more up our alley."

He took her hand and they went to the band. The Judas Priest ballads Lucio wanted were declined, but he got a yes for AC/DC's "Touch Too Much."

Lucio managed to work his hips in a really sexy way to that one. After that, the band went back to the more current popular songs. They danced to Corey Hart's "Sunglasses at Night," Taco's "Puttin' on the Ritz," Eddie Grant's "Electric Avenue," and Men Without Hats' "Safety Dance."

Jamie was getting tired and almost asked for a break, but then they played Fleetwood Mac's "Rhiannon" and she nearly squealed with delight. Lucio matched her grin and she felt a flood of joy that her happiness made him happy. She hoped this night could stay normal. That they could dance and drink punch, and then go to Denny's for a late meal, and then make love in their hotel room.

She wasn't religious, but she prayed anyway for no deaths or destruction tonight.

When the band started up the B-52s "Rock Lobster" and almost every student got up to do the ridiculous dance, Lucio gave her a pleading look. "Punch break?"

"Definitely." Her feet ached, even with the flats, and she was a failure at that dance.

After "Rock Lobster," the band set down their instruments to take a break. Mrs. Cho, the principal, approached the microphone. Jamie and Lucio looked at each other with dread and held hands under the table. It was time for possible disaster.

"Thank you all for attending our forty-second annual senior prom. Please give applause and appreciation to the prom committee for their hard work in organizing and decorating our wonderful lilac ball."

Dutifully, everyone clapped.

"As I look down and see your lovely faces, all the handsome gentlemen and lovely ladies, and see the adults you are soon to become, words cannot express how proud I am of all of you." She smirked at the distracted mutters below her. "But I won't bore you with my sentimentality. Now is the time to vote for our prom king and queen. Volunteers from the committee will pass out ballots and they'll collect them in five minutes."

Music started up again, "Cruel Summer" by Bananarama, not from the band, but from a stereo hooked up behind the stage. Jamie recognized the DJ as Leland Curtis, the president of the AV club.

Jane rose from the table. "I'm on duty now."

When a different volunteer, Bridgit Case, handed Lucio and Jamie their ballots, they gasped in tandem. "Oh shit, we're on the ballot."

Lucio's furious glare swept over each person at their table who was on the prom committee. "I told you guys that we didn't want to be in the running!"

"And I told *you* that you were too humble," Drew countered. "If you and Jamie win, Brittney will blow her top."

"That's exactly what we're afraid of," Jamie said.

Drew's brows drew together in confusion. "Why?"

"Because she's the one who's been murdering our classmates," Lucio growled.

"What?" everyone at the table exclaimed. Jane returned to the table, looking between everyone with a baffled expression.

Jason, the only one who wasn't part of the committee, waved his hands as if asking for a truce. "Look, I've seen some crazy, unbelievable stuff in my life, but Heather's death was an accident with witnesses, and Stacey's could've also been an accident. As for Chet, not only would Brittney not have the strength to subdue him, but she also had no motive. He would have been the *perfect* prom king. The guy looked like a Ken Doll and was the quarterback for Christ's sake. And Jennifer...she and Brittney were close."

Jamie sighed and grabbed Lucio's hand. "I told you no one would believe us." Then she turned to the others. "You'll see. Hopefully, when it's not too late, but you'll see. And we all better pray to all that is holy that she gets the crown tonight."

Allison stared at her in slack-jawed horror. "You're voting for that bitch? Seriously?"

Drew shook his head. "Maybe the shock has given them temporary insanity."

Jamie looked at her friends' expressions and knew it was hopeless to try to convince them to vote for Brittney. The last thing she wanted to do was reward a murderess. Still, she took a pencil from the little can next to the lilac bouquet centerpiece and checked the box for Brittney and Alex. She really would have rather voted for Vanessa Ernst, because she liked her *Grease*-inspired dress so much, and because she had never been mean to anyone. Hell, even Sue Norman and Marie Gonzales weren't that bad either.

"At least it's unlikely we'll win," Lucio said, and he voted for Brittney as well. They'd both seen *Carrie* enough times to know better than to vote for themselves.

Jane took their ballots and placed them in the pretty decorated box she carried, and went back to the small table in the corner of the gym where the other volunteers waited to count the ballots. Drew and Allison followed to help.

Bananarama gave way to the Eurythmics' "Sweet Dreams," and then Pat Benatar's "Love is a Battlefield."

When the third song ended, the gym went quiet again as a spotlight focused on Jane and Drew and followed their ascent up to the decorated stage. Each carried a fancy folded paper tied with a ribbon.

Drew approached the mic first, and no one missed the grateful look that Jane cast him. Mrs. Cho must be making them announce the results of the vote since Jane was going to be valedictorian.

"Ladies and germs," Drew announced with his usual boisterousness. "It's the moment you've all been waiting for. Time to announce the prom king and queen." He gestured to the band, who'd reassembled behind him. "Drumroll please."

Jamie clung to Lucio as the staccato beat started. He held her just as tight.

Neither of them breathed.

Drew untied the ribbon holding his paper and unfolded it with dramatic flair. "The prom king for Amteep High's forty-second annual senior prom, the man to reign over us for the night, is our favorite rebel without a cause, Lucio Argento."

"Oh no," Jamie groaned as the gym roared with applause. "Should we run away?"

Lucio looked like he was considering it, but then the spotlight swiveled over to him and everyone cheered. He sighed in resignation. "Maybe we can escape after."

Jamie let her fingers slip from Lucio's grip as he slowly walked to the stage. They both looked up at the rafters in case there was a bucket of blood or something waiting.

Drew nudged Jane over to the mic. She didn't bother building up suspense. "And our lovely prom queen is Jamie Blair."

Thunderous applause filled the gym. Jamie blinked in surprise. She hadn't expected people to be *that* happy about her winning, and thought Drew and Allison rigged the ballots. Instead, her classmates were acting like they'd actually voted for her and Lucio.

Not daring to look back to see where Brittney was, Jamie clutched her purse full of herbs and protective stones and made her way to Lucio, focusing only on him. When she reached him, a measure of her fear fled.

Together, they were stronger.

Lucio bent as Drew placed an elaborate plastic crown on his head and handed him a gaudy scepter. Since Jane was so tall, Jamie didn't have to bend. Jane settled a silver tiara with fake purple jewels on Jamie's head and then handed her a bouquet of pink roses.

Her heart thudded as she looked out at the crowd. At first all she could see was a faceless mass. Then she spotted Brittney. She was over by the punch bowl, fists clenched at her sides, gaping at Jamie and Lucio in wide-eyed disbelief, her perfect lips parted in an O of surprise. But she wasn't moving forward and that was what counted. However, Jamie didn't like the sight of Brittney twitching, like she was fighting an inner battle.

Bright light blinded Jamie as the yearbook photographer took pictures. Jamie clung to Lucio's hands as he bent to kiss her.

Drew took the microphone. "Now the king and queen will share their first dance."

The beginning piano notes to "Total Eclipse of the Heart" trilled from the stereo. Jamie *loved* this song, though wild horses could not drag that confession from her—except for that one time she'd told Allison when they'd gotten drunk off 40s of MD2020.

Lucio's worried gaze met hers. He started to pull her to the back of the stage, so they could escape the gym, but Drew pushed him forward. Reluctantly, he led Jamie down the stairs as the crowd cleared a space for them to dance.

A bestial roar sounded behind them, echoing from the rafters.

Jamie and Lucio froze as Brittney charged toward them, her eyes glowing a flaming yellow and her fingers curled like claws.

"Oh shit." Jamie clung to Lucio's arm. "We're gonna die."

Chapter Twenty-Five

Lucio moved in front of Jamie, trying to shield her from Brittney's oncoming assault. He reached in his pocket for the packet of banishing salt and herbs.

"How dare you!" Brittney shrieked at Jamie. Her voice was hers, and yet...not. Her shrieking had an awful echoing edge to it, like the sound of breaking glass. "That crown is *mine*. I didn't work my ass off on mastering the dark arts and kill the most popular girls in school for that crown to go on your filthy, trailer trash head!"

More gasps and murmurs followed her glib confession. Lucio heard someone shout for the police to be called.

"Chet too," Jamie said with a calmness that Lucio couldn't believe.

"Yes," Brittney growled, still stalking forward. "I killed Chet. And now I'm going to kill you."

She ran toward them, but then Mr. Kramden, the P.E. coach, tackled her. A wolfish growl sounded before the coach went flying. He crashed into the edge of the stage, a sickening snap carrying over the music before he landed on the floor in a crumpled mess, his back and ribs broken. Blood trickled from his open mouth.

Pandemonium ensued. The band scrambled off the stage, leaving their equipment behind, and burst out the back door closest to them. Lucio saw Alex Pugsley, Jason, and Allison run out the other door before the demonic creature that was Brittney flung out her hand and slammed the door shut. The gathering masses tugged at the handles in vain. They were trapped inside.

So much for catching Brittney by surprise. Lucio pulled out a handful of salt and herbs and threw them at Brittney. "Scarlionapskhis, I banish you from this vessel and back to the place from whence you came."

Brittney flinched as the salt and herbs struck her; a monstrous shriek poured from her throat, hurting his ears. As she crumbled to her knees and writhed, Lucio took Jamie's hand and pulled her away. "The doors should work now."

"Shouldn't we try to make sure she's stopped?" Jamie protested as he dragged her away.

Lucio shook his head. "I only care about making sure you're safe. Besides, we might have gotten her." They reached the rear door the band and several others had escaped through and sure enough, the door gave. Three more people forced their way past them, nearly knocking them over. "She looked pretty bad. Maybe it worked."

Then they heard Brittney scream, "No, I *won't* do it!"

Another roar sounded, followed by an awful voice that sounded like metal gears grinding glass. *"I warned you not to defy me again. Now you shall pay the price, and I will feast like never before."*

Lucio and Jamie barely made it out before the doors slammed shut behind them. Lucio pulled on the handle, but it didn't budge. He heard the demon roar so loud the door handle vibrated under his palm.

Screams sounded next, along with various loud slams.

"Shit."

"She's killing more people, Lucio." Jamie pulled on his sleeve. "We have to help them and stop her. I think she was fighting the demon. Didn't you hear her protest? Maybe we can help exorcise it, like we originally planned."

"How?" Lucio couldn't hide his terror. "We're locked out, and now, with the demon in her, she's got telekinetic powers, super strength, and who knows what else."

"There's gotta be a way we can get up and through the windows, or maybe somehow break down the door."

Lucio wanted to argue that they should go somewhere safe instead. They'd just escaped and now Jamie wanted to go back in? That was insanity. But his conscience wouldn't let him refuse. "Wait. There are tools in the groundskeeper's shed on the other side of the field. I used to smoke back there."

"Excellent." Jamie lifted up on her tiptoes and kissed him quickly before running across the field.

He caught up with her, running at her side. They reached the shed and Lucio's lips twisted in an amused smirk. If the boards forming the shed weren't so old, they wouldn't be able to get inside. But Amteep High was known to cut all possible corners so they could give more money to their athletic programs.

Two solid kicks and the board holding the lock broke. His father's shoes were definitely ruined after that, but he didn't think his father would care after learning what happened.

After they carefully made their way into the dark shed, Jamie pulled a lighter from her purse and lit it. Sadly, most of the shed's equipment consisted of lawnmowers and other landscaping crap, but Lucio found a sledgehammer and Jamie found a chainsaw. Either would be useful.

Taking their weapons, they jogged, a little slower with their heavy burdens, back to the gym door. The chainsaw would be useless on the metal door, but Lucio made an effort with the sledgehammer.

At first, the metal doors didn't budge. Then Jamie held up a stone and said some words that he couldn't understand. The door swung open with such force that Jamie and Lucio fell on their butts.

"What did you do?" he asked as they scrambled to get to their feet and avoid being trampled by the horde of students trying to get out.

"It was a spell in one of the books." Jamie sounded awestruck. "I didn't expect it to work."

They fought against the flow of people that broke suddenly as the door slammed shut again from the demon's power. Jamie and Lucio used their weapons to gently move people out of the way and pressed themselves against the wall, carefully making their way to the folded-up bleachers where they could hide and plot their attack.

The sight before them was horrific. Brittney and her demon were launching a multiple attack from every direction. Mr. Davis, the government teacher, was being electrocuted by the microphone, then the PA systems exploded, pelting people with shrapnel before the stage caught on fire.

Todd Banks pulled out the fire hose to put out the blaze, but the hose came alive in his hands like an angry snake and coiled around Todd's neck, strangling him. Lucio didn't feel as bad for him since the guy was such a jerk to Jamie and many others.

Brittney was at the refreshment table, one hand twisting Vanessa Ernst's hands behind her back, the other hand forcing Vanessa's face into the punch bowl. Vanessa should have been able to struggle more but could only manage the most pitiful wiggling. Lucio again remembered how Brittney had subdued and carried a calf with no problems.

When Vanessa's struggles ceased, Brittney released her limp form to collapse on the floor. The punch bowl tumbled down onto her head and spilled blood-red liquid all over her and the waxed wood floor.

Brittney threw back her head and let out another ground-shaking roar. "You should have voted me as prom queen. Now you will all be punished for your mistake. Witness my power and kneel before me."

The disco ball came crashing down on Evan Legard and his date's heads, killing them instantly. Everyone else in a ten-foot radius was sliced with flying pieces of broken glass.

Drew charged Brittney, and she lifted him by his throat.

"I will eviscerate you," she hissed.

"Leave him alone," Jane Carpenter shrieked and shoved Brittney from behind, making her drop Drew.

Jamie squeezed Lucio's arm. "We gotta stop her now, before she kills Jane and Drew."

Jamie pulled the cord on her chainsaw, starting up the engine and killing their element of surprise. As Brittney reached for Jane, Lucio charged forward, swinging at Brittney with the sledgehammer. He struck her shoulder and knocked her down, but seemed to do minimal damage. Her shoulder should have been crushed, but instead, she seemed fine.

At least Drew and Jane got away.

The glowing yellow orbs of Brittney's eyes narrowed to slits and her lips curved into a wide, hungry grin. "Ah, Lucio. My bad boy lover. You won prom king. I can't believe I was so wrong about you." Suddenly, Brittney's smile faded and her eyes went back to blue. She spoke in her own voice. "To think that if I hadn't dumped you, we could have been up on that stage wearing our crowns, and my friends would still be alive. Help me, Lucio."

Lucio tried a gentle approach first. "You can stop killing people now. Let them go. Fight the demon inside you."

This time, the demon's voice poured out with foul laughter. "She can't fight me. I own her now. This sow happily handed me the power I needed for the sake of her own pitiful ambitions."

Lucio took the gloves off, trying to goad Brittney into surfacing. "I'm damn glad you dumped me, Brittney. Then I was able to find true love and happiness that you'll never be able to have because you're too selfish and ugly on the inside."

A furious snarl escaped from Brittney's curled lips, and her voice emerged. "How dare you call me ugly. You're just bitter because you'll never have anyone as good as me again. You're dreaming if you think anyone could love that trailer trash."

Her eyes flared yellow again and the demon's voice spoke. "I'll show you the folly of your insolence when I kill your pathetic love." She thrust her hand toward Jamie, attempting to force her forward like with Drew.

Jamie remained where she stood. Something in her herb and stone collection must be protecting her. Lucio wondered if he was protected too. Then Jamie moved forward of her own volition, swinging her chainsaw at Brittney.

The chainsaw should have severed Brittney's arm, but instead Jamie had only managed to give the cheerleader nasty gouge on her bicep.

That was enough to infuriate the demon. Brittney moved with snake-like quickness and seized Jamie and Lucio by their throats. She squeezed their necks until they both saw stars and their weapons dropped from limp fingers.

Lucio tried to struggle against the darkness closing in; his mouth gaped, desperate to suck in the tiniest breath, but Brittney's grip on his throat cut off all air. With his last bit of strength, he grabbed Jamie's hand, seeking a scrap of comfort at her touch.

Blackness enclosed him and he floated through the air, invisible wind seeming to riffle through his hair. Pain exploded in his back, skull, and shoulders as he crashed into a hard surface.

His heart ached as much as his body. All was lost. They'd tried to fight Brittney and her demon and had been swatted like flies. Now more people would die.

Lucio awoke sometime later, every bone in his body aching. His throat was on fire, but he was able to suck in greedy gulps of air.

Screams of terror and agony echoed around him, but he still felt triumph. As long as he and Jamie lived, there was hope.

Jamie.

Lucio opened his eyes and found himself lying against the bleachers. That's what had slammed against his back. He looked to his right and almost passed out again. This time from relief. His fingers were still entwined with Jamie's and she was coughing and rubbing her throat with her free hand.

He leaned over and pulled her into his arms, his eyes burning with tears. "I thought she'd killed us both."

"No, but she will if she sees that we survived." Jamie's voice was hoarse from being strangled. Angry red marks bloomed on her neck. They'd soon turn to bruises. "We need to try calling the light-bringer."

When Lucio released her, she scrambled in search of her purse. Somehow, the chain had stayed wrapped around her wrist. She opened it and Lucio reached in his pocket for the envelope that contained all the stuff needed for the probably hopeless ritual.

In tandem, he and Jamie pulled out their notes for the words to say and also found their offerings. Jamie had her star garnet—a better gift in Lucio's opinion—and Lucio had a polished amethyst because purple was his favorite color.

They placed the stones on the gym floor and made a circle of salt and marjoram around them. Then they joined hands and read the words.

"Oh light-bringer, creator of hope and beauty, please accept our offerings of nature's beauty and come forth to aid us against this entity of evil." The next words were in some other language that neither ever managed to identify, but they tried to read them, stumbling over the pronunciation.

Nothing happened.

Lucio's shoulders slumped. "I guess that's that."

Jamie's features settled into a stubborn expression. "Let's try again."

They joined hands, closed their eyes, and repeated the words, wishing hard for a miracle to come true.

Lucio opened his eyes and his heart sank to see the empty circle. "At least Brittney hasn't spotted us yet. Maybe we can escape again and try to get a SWAT team in here."

Bright light exploded in the gym. Everyone froze in terror, dreading whatever impossible, horrific thing would happen next.

A woman appeared in front of Lucio and Jamie. She was so beautiful that momentarily Lucio couldn't breathe.

Golden blonde hair cascaded in soft waves down her back. Her skin was flawless and her eyes were green as emeralds. Despite her casual outfit of jeans, halter top, and bangle bracelets, everything about her radiated that she wasn't human.

The woman knelt and collected the stones. She held them in her palm and inspected them closely. When she spoke, her voice reminded Lucio of his mother, or rather, the epitome of motherhood. "These are very pretty, thank you."

When she smiled, Lucio felt engulfed in soothing warmth.

Jamie recovered her voice. "Are you the light-bringer?"

The woman nodded. "Some use that name for my kind." For a moment, she looked sad, and Lucio's heart clenched. Then her serene smile returned. "How may I help you?"

She sounded so much like a saleslady that Lucio was momentarily stunned.

Jamie spoke up. "There's a demon inside that girl." She pointed at Brittney, who appeared to be frozen in place, staring at the light-bringer in shock.

The light-bringer followed Jamie's gesture and regarded Brittney with a severe frown. Then she nodded. "I will drive it out and help you to destroy it. Do you have weapons?"

Jamie and Lucio spied the chainsaw about twenty feet away by the overturned refreshment table. The sledgehammer *had* to be nearby. Unfortunately, Brittney was also at the refreshment table, and her blazing yellow eyes had sought out Jamie and Lucio.

He turned back to the light-bringer. "Our weapons are near the demon."

The light-bringer smiled as if that was a good thing. "That's convenient. Follow me. I'll protect you."

Even though the light-bringer was shorter than Brittney and looked delicate, Lucio believed the being was more than capable of protecting everyone here. He took Jamie's hand and helped her to her feet.

Slowly, they walked toward Brittney, staying a half step back from the light-bringer.

The demon cringed and snarled at the light-bringer. "Luminite," it spat. "What are you doing here? Your kind left Earth almost a millennium ago."

"I could say the same about your kind, Scarlionapskhis," the light-bringer said in a polite tone with a thread of steel. "I will ask you nicely to remove yourself from that girl's body and return to your realm. I am only asking once."

The demon spat again, and Brittney put her nose in the air, looking as imperious as when she was bullying Jamie. "Piss off. You can't stop me. You are weakened here because of the dearth of magic in this realm."

"Very well," the light-bringer said sweetly, though her green eyes began to glow. "I gave you a chance. Now suffer the consequences."

Wings burst from her back, a wide span of pearlescent feathers gilt with gold.

Lucio and Jamie gasped along with the rest of the surviving students.

"She's a real angel," Jamie breathed. Other people echoed the same sentiment.

The angel rose up in the air, her magnificent wings extended. She chanted words in another language that made Brittney flinch. The demon's flaming eyes flickered dully, then brightened again. Brittney's hands pushed forward, throwing an invisible force at the angel.

The angel rocked back and straightened one of her feathers with a look of annoyance. She cupped her hands and a ball of gold light formed. She thrust the ball at Brittney, who shuddered from the impact.

Britney's eyes shifted back to blue. She looked up at the angel with a pleading look. "Help me," she whimpered.

"That's why I'm here, bratling. I'm sorry this will hurt." The angel shaped her fingers like she was grasping the air in front of Brittney. She made a hard, jerking motion, and a black cloud poured from Brittney's mouth.

Brittney collapsed into a heap of bloody satin and tulle. The black cloud formed into a hideous horned beast with a twisted form and sharp, clawed hands. The beast cupped those clawed hands and formed a ball of flames. He threw the fireball at the angel, but she dodged it. Still, the edge of one of her wings caught on fire.

While the angel put out her wing, wincing in pain, the demon charged the angel. "I'll kill you and send you back to your home realm where you belong."

Jamie and Lucio held their breath, fearing for their savior.

The angel grasped the demon's wrists and they grappled and twisted. Lucio couldn't believe that the little angel had such strength. Her eyes glowed emerald flames as she chanted some words that made the demon release her and fall to the ground.

"You can't kill me, Luminite," Scarlionapskhis hissed, though his grinding voice sounded weakened with pain. "Your kind is incapable."

"That's true," the angel said, unfazed. "But I can transform you, and I can hurt you."

She thrust her palms forward and the demon cried out in agony. A cracking sound pierced the air as the dark creature twisted on the floor. Its shiny black flesh dulled, and the fiery light in its eyes dimmed to weak candlelight.

Still, the demon scrambled up from the floor and tried to charge her again. Instead of grappling with it again, the angel widened the span of her palms and created an invisible force field that the demon slammed into like a wall.

The angel turned around and faced Lucio and Jamie. "Now, you must kill it."

"Us?" Jamie squeaked.

"Yes. My kind can only create. We cannot destroy. I've transformed it into a weaker being, but it is still deadly. Hurry. I cannot hold this shield for long."

Jamie nodded and ran to the refreshment table. She grabbed the chainsaw and yanked the cord. The roar of the machine sounded so out of place what with the supernatural battle that was taking place. Lucio scrambled for the sledgehammer. He found it on the other side of the table. He turned to give Jamie a look of encouragement, but she was already charging to the demon. Lucio ran to catch up.

Jamie swung the chainsaw toward the monster's neck, aiming to get rid of it in one swing. It bent its head and the chainsaw glanced off its solid horns. Sparks flew and Jamie almost dropped the saw.

The demon lunged at her, but Lucio swung the sledgehammer and caught it on the jaw. It went hurtling backward and fell on the protrusions on its back. Jamie shoved the chainsaw blade in its heart, grinding and cutting through its rib cage. Crimson goo splattered everywhere, yet the demon still lived.

It reached for Jamie again, managing to scratch her shoulder. At Jamie's cry of pain, Lucio saw red. He swung the hammer again, caving in the demon's face. Jamie pulled the chainsaw blade from its ribcage and brought it down to the demon's neck, holding it steady as the saw cut its head off.

The demon melted into a puddle of goo. Brittney lay beside the puddle, sporadic shallow breaths hitching her chest.

Sirens sounded in the distance. Jamie and Lucio exchanged looks. "Figures that they come after everything's over."

They turned to the angel. "Thank you so much for helping us."

The angel surprised them by giving them hugs. As the angel's warm, loving arms enfolded Lucio's body, he fought not to burst into tears. She felt so much like his mother.

Jamie wiped away tears after the angel embraced her as well. Then she looked at them both and nodded with approval. She flicked her fingers and suddenly held their prom crowns.

The angel placed the crowns on Jamie's and Lucio's heads. "I am so happy to see a true bond. Such a thing is a precious rarity in this realm. It's a shame I have to make you forget me for I would so love to visit you again. I come to the area often, you see and—" She broke off and let out a sound of childlike glee. "Lilacs!" The angel rushed over to the wall and pulled down a small bundle. She buried her face in the little purple blossoms and inhaled deeply. "My favorite."

Lucio stared at her and blurted the question he thought the moment he saw her wings. "Is there a god?"

The angel looked up from the bouquet of lilacs and regarded him with a quizzical frown. She rubbed the burned edge of her right wing. "I don't know. I think there might be."

"How do you not know?" Frustration gnawed at him. "Aren't you an angel?"

"No. I'm something different from what any of your holy books claim. Why do you look so sad suddenly?"

"My mom..." He broke off with a strangled sob.

The not-angel's green eyes filled with understanding. She approached him and hugged him once more. "Energy can be changed, but not destroyed. She *is* somewhere, and she also remains a part of you." She looked around and frowned at the destruction and dead and injured people sprawled all over the gym floor and set down her bouquet of lilacs. "So much destruction. I will do what I can, then I must leave. The demon was right. I am weakening, and our fight accelerated the process."

She flapped her wings a few times, chanted in her silken language, and cupped her hands again. This time, a blueish purple orb formed in her hands. She thrust it outward and blue light encased the gym like a flash of lightning.

Then the not-angel picked up her bunch of lilacs, kissed Jamie on the forehead, and vanished.

Chapter Twenty-Six

Jamie blinked at the spot where the not-angel stood. Her forehead still tingled where the being had kissed her. Then she threw herself in Lucio's arms, suddenly unable to stop shaking.

The police burst through the door, no longer held shut by the demon. Jamie swayed and Lucio led her to one of the only chairs that hadn't been knocked over. They watched as someone rushed over to them, cut and bleeding, talking frantically and pointing at Brittney.

Time seemed to scramble as two of the eight police officers went over to Jamie and Lucio and questioned them. The place on Jamie's forehead where she'd been kissed burned as words poured out of her mouth beyond her control.

Brittney had gone crazy when Jamie and Lucio had been crowned king and queen, Jamie explained. She'd raved about how she'd killed their classmates in pursuit of the crown. No, they don't know how the doors had gotten stuck or what had caused the music equipment to catch fire and burn up the stage.

Someone had put out the fire, Jamie noticed as words poured out of her without thought. She stopped paying attention to what she was saying as she noticed some of the students who she thought had been killed were now alive and standing. People who'd been horrifically injured now looked fairly okay. The light-bringer must have healed them. Wasn't she supposed to forget the not-angel?

Not everyone was alive and well, though. Jamie saw the lifeless forms of Vanessa Ernst, Coach Kramden, Mr. Davis, Todd Banks, Joshua Mouline, and others she couldn't recognize because their faces were smashed, sliced, or burnt. Some were missing their heads.

Jamie's heart gave a twinge when she saw the corpse of Coach Kramden. He'd always been a major jerk to her every P.E. class, and yet he'd saved her life when Brittney had first attacked.

Later, she learned fifteen people had died in the chaos and forty people were wounded. Brittney was among the dead. Her heart had stopped from the demon being forced from her body, but of course, no one could tell the authorities about that.

Some people claimed to have had miraculous resurrections, or wounds that had been fatal that suddenly healed enough for them to survive. Jamie remembered the blue light the angel had cast through the gym and was overcome with awe. Thankfully, hers and Lucio's core group of friends had survived. Allison and Jason had fled when the disaster started, Drew suffered a broken arm, and Jane had a sprained ankle, but otherwise, they were fine.

Jamie finished her witness statement and so did Lucio. She hadn't heard what he'd said, but he seemed to be all right.

They were led to an ambulance, where a paramedic treated their various cuts and scrapes. They were covered with blankets as their vitals were taken. Both were diagnosed with shock, and had concussions. Each also had a necklace of bruises from Brittney trying to strangle them.

"Neither of you can go to sleep tonight," the medic cautioned. "People with concussions often don't wake up."

Jamie looked at Lucio and smiled. She knew what they could do to stay awake. Besides, after everything that had happened tonight, sleep wouldn't come easily anyway.

When the medic was through with them, they moved on since there was a line of injured people to treat. Jamie was happy to see Principal Cho was alive.

Lucio's dad and Jamie's mom were among the frantic parents waiting in the parking lot. Leigh and Mario found them, hugging them tearfully and asking for an explanation. Both insisted that they come home.

Lucio refused. "We never got our dance together as king and queen. Besides, the medic told us we needed to stay awake all night in case we have concussions. Both of you have to work tomorrow."

Mario nodded, but Leigh looked ready to argue.

Jamie spoke before her mom could shoot them down. "Please, Mom. What was supposed to be a magical night was ruined. We want to salvage what's left of it. And now that the killer has been caught, you don't have to worry about me anymore."

"Okay, but I'll *always* worry." Leigh nodded. "Go to your hotel room then. But get some clean clothes first. Your dress is covered with blood. I almost died of grief when I thought it was yours."

"We already packed clothes, remember?" Jamie said and hugged her mom good night. "I'll see you tomorrow."

When they were finally free, Lucio and Jamie had a huge meal at Denny's. They didn't bother changing clothes because they didn't want to get the clean clothes messed up with the blood and gunk on them. Obviously, they received a lot of stares at their bloody, ruined finery. Neither cared. There were other ravaged prom attendees there eating too.

Jamie devoured two eggs, a plate of hash browns, two biscuits with gravy, a chicken-fried steak, and two hot chocolates. Who knew that fighting a demon would give a person such an appetite?

When they got to the lovely hotel, they showered together. Lucio took the washcloth and gently washed every cut and bruise Jamie had, kissing each after it had been cleaned. She returned the favor, spending more time kissing his handsome face. As she scrubbed his back, Lucio spoke in a husky voice, "I'd make love to you here if I wasn't so afraid of slipping in this tiny tub."

Jamie nodded. "Shower sex is on my list for things to try with you. But I agree. I'm too shaky from what happened to get frisky yet."

After they were clean and dry, they changed into their pajamas. Lucio looked adorable in his black satin button-up shirt and pants. Jamie wore the nicest satin nightgown she owned. She went back into the bathroom to blow-dry her hair, and when she came out, she saw Lucio hanging up the phone.

"Who were you talking to?"

Lucio gave her a mischievous grin. "It's a surprise."

They lounged on the bed for a little bit and turned on the TV. Reports about the prom night massacre were on almost every channel. Some of their classmates talked to the reporters about how Brittney had super strength and could throw people. Others said she merely ran around, tipping over tables and sabotaging the music equipment and killing people through the strength of her rage. Several said that Jamie and Lucio had saved them by talking

Brittney down—or knocking her out—depending on who was talking. All agreed that Brittney died from a heart attack.

Only two people mentioned an angel and a demon.

Jamie grabbed the remote and turned off the TV. "I don't think I'll ever fully process the insanity of this night. I mean, we saw an *angel*. We hugged an *angel*."

"She told us she wasn't an angel," Lucio said.

"Yeah, but it's the closest word for her. I know the demon called her something else, but I don't remember what it was…" She trailed off and her heart thudded. "We killed a demon."

"Yeah." Lucio took her hand and stroked her knuckles with his thumb. "I don't think we're supposed to remember any of that. The light-bringer said that she was going to make us forget, but she must've gotten distracted by the lilacs. She was so odd. So beautiful and powerful that she seemed holy at times, but other times she was motherly, and then sometimes she was almost childlike."

"You noticed that too?" Jamie leaned on her elbow and stroked his hair. "She was incredible. And she said we had a true bond. I think that means that we're meant to be."

"I think so too. God, I love you so much."

"I love you too."

They kissed, gentle and tender at first, and then hungry and wild. Lucio broke away. He turned on the clock radio next to the bed and then got up. "Come here."

With a bemused smile, she rolled out of the bed and joined him. He grabbed his crown from the end table, placed it on his head, and then held out hers.

Jamie donned her crown and grinned with understanding. He really meant it when he wanted them to have their dance. The song on the radio, "The Safety Dance," ended, and the DJ came on. "Hello, night owls and survivors of the prom night massacre. I had a special request, and heard that the prom king and queen didn't get their last dance. Well, KMAX is going to give them their chance. Lucio Argento and Jamie Blair, this is for you."

The opening piano notes to "Total Eclipse of the Heart" came on and Lucio bowed and held out his hand. "May I have this dance, my queen?"

Jamie took his hand and put her other on his shoulder. "You called the radio station when I was drying my hair, didn't you?"

He grasped her waist and pulled her closer before turning them around. "Guilty."

She rested her head on his chest and closed her eyes, forgetting about the horrors of the night, and enjoying the secure feeling of being in Lucio's arms.

They danced for the whole song, and the power of Jamie's love and relief that they'd survived together made tears leak from the corners of her eyes. Thank goodness she'd washed off all her makeup and didn't have to worry about looking like a raccoon.

When the song ended, Lucio kissed her on the forehead like the light-bringer had. "I think it's so cute that you like this song and try to pretend that you don't."

"Damnit." She laughed. "How did you know?"

"You always smile when it comes on the radio, and sometimes I catch you mouthing the words."

"Here Comes the Rain Again" came on, and Lucio stroked Jamie's back in delicate motions that made pleasant shivers race down to her toes. Then he lowered his head, allowing his luscious curls to stroke her cheeks. His lips came down and worked magic with hers.

Feeling like she was going to melt, Jamie staggered back to the bed and pulled Lucio down on top of her. His tongue slipped into her mouth and she welcomed the onslaught. They kissed for a blissful eternity, and his hardness ground against the hot juncture between her thighs, working her into a frenzy. The sensation of sliding against each other with only thin barriers of satin separating them drove her wild in ways she couldn't explain.

Jamie pushed him up to unbutton his pajama top. Lucio obliged her and pulled off her nightgown. In moments they were naked. Lucio quickly grabbed a condom and put it on.

While he was sitting up, Jamie straddled his lap and slowly sank down on his length. The sensation of him sliding into her wetness made her moan. She wrapped her legs around his waist, working him deeper. That made him reach a spot that made her cry out in pleasure. She hugged him tightly as they rocked together. Jamie kissed him hungrily, making her feel like he was carrying her to new heights of paradise.

And he did. The climax rose with a deep, thunderous ecstasy that was almost unbearable, curling her toes as she moved with him and climbed higher. The pleasure plateaued, and she sank her teeth in his shoulder to muffle her cries and she went off the precipice.

Afterward, they lay down on the bed and cuddled. Jamie almost dozed, but Lucio gently shook her shoulder. "We have to stay awake. Remember?"

They gave each other gentle back rubs, massaging the pain from being thrown onto the floor and into the bleachers, and then there were the bruises from their final battle. Until Lucio reached the painful knots between her shoulder blades and in her lower back, she hadn't been aware of how sore she was.

They kissed each other's bruises and cuts, and that led to another bout of lovemaking, this time slow and gentle.

When they couldn't stay awake any longer, they snuggled under the covers.

"You know what I still can't believe?" Jamie murmured with a yawn.

Lucio chuckled. "Out of all the craziness that happened, I can't guess."

"I can't believe that Brittney summoned a demon and murdered people just to be prom queen." Jamie shook her head. "I mean, what did she intend to do with her life after she got the crown?"

"Nothing," Lucio said flatly. "The demon had full control of her. You saw. The thing would have blown up and massacred people anyway, probably at a different time, like at a pep rally or something, but it was inevitable."

"I know, but let's say she kept control over the demon. What would she do after that? Why was prom so important to her anyway?"

"Who knows? Maybe she would have gone to Hollywood and become an actress and killed her rivals so she could win an Oscar."

"Oh man, I could see that."

Lucio rose up on his elbow and stroked Jamie's hair. "You know what, though?"

"What?"

"Part of me is happy with how *some* things turned out. I wanted you to be prom queen in the first place. Even before I fell in love with you. And not only for revenge."

"Why?"

"Because you're the most beautiful woman in the whole school, for one thing." He stroked her hair, making tingles run across her scalp. "But also because you're smart and kind, and you deserved it the whole time."

"Well, I'm glad you won prom king," Jamie said. "But I still think our friends rigged the election."

"Who cares?" He lowered his head and murmured against her lips, "You'll always be my queen."

Epilogue

September 1987

Lucio unloaded the truck full of meat and produce, and organized everything in the new, larger freezers and refrigerators they'd had installed in Bava's. The one that had come with the property had been on its last breath.

Once he was done stocking the new inventory and checking off his list, Lucio went into the kitchen and paused, watching Jamie pull out a perfectly made *osso buco* and spoon the gremolada onto the shanks before placing the Dutch oven back into the industrial oven.

She'd accepted Mario's job offer and started working as a prep cook right after graduation. Within a year, she'd been promoted to one of the head chefs. She was also almost finished earning her associate's degree in business management with a scholarship she'd won. Some of the things she'd learned in school had already benefitted the restaurant.

Lucio had also gotten a scholarship. He assumed it had something to do with his and Jamie's efforts to stop Brittney, and because their witness statements had exonerated the school from any implications of wrongdoing. Though perhaps he was being cynical and the scholarship truly was for his improvement in grades during his senior year.

His scholarship was for a smaller amount than Jamie's, so he used it for a few business and accounting courses and didn't pursue a degree. Amteep Community College was much better at providing him a tutor and extra help with his dyslexia than Amteep High had been.

His father had also persuaded Leigh to come work for him, first as a server, then as head hostess, and now she was assistant manager.

The Shanty Bar had been heartbroken to lose her but couldn't match the wages Dad paid. He also threw out anyone who dared to try to grope her, unlike her last employer.

Lucio smiled. Now the family business felt more like one than when Bava's had been run by Dad alone, and when Lucio had helped out under protest.

Over the years, Lucio had several talks with his father and worked out his resentment. He wasn't sure if he'd ever completely forgive his dad for neglecting him for most of his childhood, but he could understand why he did it.

And now Lucio worked happily for the legacy that would be his one day, and then he could pass it on to his children. Children he'd have with Jamie, if his plans went right.

His heart swelled from love and pride looking at her. After waiting for her to put down the knife, he came up behind her and threaded his arms around her waist. Jamie spun to face him and lifted her chin, silently imploring him to kiss her. Lucio took her up on the offer and closed his eyes in bliss. Kissing her felt as good as it had that first time three and a half years ago.

"When is your shift over?" he asked when Jamie withdrew.

"Same time as yours, silly. I don't know what makes you forget the schedule right after your dad puts it up." She gave him an imploring smile. "Want to help chop garlic? We're running low and it's going to be a busy night."

Lucio opened the compartment of garlic heads and started peeling them. "I was hoping you'd want to go out tonight."

"That sounds awesome." Jamie's excited smile made him dizzy. "With school and work, it seems I only see you here these days. It's past time we have a night to ourselves."

"Exactly." But this night would be super special. "August through October are the worst, with no school breaks or the restaurant being closed. At least next month you'll have Thanksgiving break and Bava's will be closed the day before and the day after."

"That's right," Jamie laughed. "Most places in town only close for the day, but your dad needs the time the day before to prepare his big meal and then the day after to recover."

Lucio brought the subject back to tonight. "Anyway, there's a lake cruise tonight with dinner and fireworks, and I figured we could go, and then see *Hellraiser* at the drive-in."

"Mr. Hogadane and his fireworks." Jamie laughed at the town millionaire's tendency to light them off whenever he had the slightest excuse. "But seriously, it sounds like a dream date, even though it is starting to get chilly. Oh, you won't believe what I heard in school today."

"What?" Lucio settled comfortably beside her at the cutting board as they chopped the garlic cloves together. Although there was rarely interesting gossip at the college, there were often fun events, like operas, plays, art showings, and sometimes famous people came to speak.

Jamie's answer was none of those things. "The Alpha Lambda Fraternity and Pi Omega Sorority managed to rent the Raimi House for next month."

"What? But I thought the current owner refused to allow anyone inside that place."

"Apparently he needs the money to be able to afford to have the house demolished," Jamie explained. "Anyway, the reason the Alpha Lambdas and Pi Omegas are renting the place is because they're going to hold their initiation for new recruits on Halloween. The initiation will be for them to spend a full night at the Raimi House."

Lucio shook his head. Grief and dread darkened his happiness. "They're all going to die."

"That's what I said." Jamie sighed with resignation. "But lots of people have tried to talk them out of it, and that only made them more determined."

"Damn it. Maybe we can set up a rescue and first aid party to wait for those who make it out."

"I was thinking we could go in and rescue them."

"Absolutely not." Lucio took her arms and spun her to face him. He spoke low so no coworkers or customers could hear, but his tone was severe. "Sure, we have some experience fighting an evil force, but we had divine aid, and that demon was small potatoes compared to the Raimi House. If taking on a demon and healing people weakened the light-bringer, I don't think she could be a match for that house. Neither of us will set foot in the place, and that's final."

Jamie glared up at him. "I'm not sure I like you trying to command me."

"I'm sorry, I don't mean it that way." Lucio hugged her. "I love you and you are the most important person in my world. I don't think I could survive if I lost you."

"Okay." Jamie held up her hands in surrender after he released her. "We'll stick with your plan and have a rescue party outside. Maybe I can try to talk some of the new recruits into joining other fraternities or sororities."

Lucio's dad came in, interrupting their conversation. "I've decided to let you both go home early tonight." He winked at Lucio. "Hans wanted extra hours, so he's coming in a few minutes. Now you have more time to get ready for your special date."

Lucio sighed in exasperation. Could his dad make tonight's plan any more obvious? Jamie removed her apron and gave Lucio a suspecting smile.

Shit.

On their way out, Leigh told them loudly to have a wonderful night and then winked at Lucio.

Damn it! Dad had told *her* already?

Now Jamie's smile had widened further.

Face burning with humiliation, Lucio cleared his throat. "The cruise is at seven, so I'll pick you up at six-thirty?"

"Sounds great."

Even though Lucio took his time driving home, then showering and shaving, and making sure his nails were clipped and clean, the hours still crawled and the weight in the inside pocket of his leather jacket seemed to get heavier by the minute.

When at last he was able to get Jamie, he saw that she'd taken extra-special care with her appearance, so there was no way that she didn't suspect what was going to happen.

Her hair had been curled and then teased and sprayed out, making her look like a woman in one of the videos on MTV's *Headbanger's Ball*. Her eye makeup was vibrant and colorful, her lips berry red. The star garnet pendant he'd bought her for their first Christmas together hung between her luscious breasts.

She wore the blue crushed velvet dress that he'd bought her during their shopping spree back when he was trying to make her prom queen. The one that she'd complained about not being able to wear anywhere because it was too formal. There was a delectable slit on one side, going all the way up to her thigh.

"Lucio?"

"Sorry." He realized he'd been ogling her like the high schooler he used to be. "Your beauty will always entrance me." He hoped he didn't sound corny.

He took her hand and helped her down the steps of her mom's new house, a nice little bungalow on Burgundy Lane, not far from where he lived. Last year, Jamie and her mom had gotten the news that her father had died. Since the late Mr. Blair hadn't remarried, all his social security, a bit of insurance money, and some other funds had passed on to Leigh and Jamie. They'd left the trailer park as soon as they could. The neighbors who'd liked them had thrown a surprisingly large barbecue in celebration of the Blairs' escape from Springwood.

Lucio drove to the Lake Skeetshue Resort, used the parking garage, and took Jamie's hand as he helped her out of the car, and then they made their way to the dock where the cruise boat waited.

The *Mish-an-Nock* looked like an old-fashioned riverboat from a Mark Twain novel, only without a giant paddle. Instead, two large engines in the back powered the white and blue sixty-five-foot-long boat.

Jamie and Lucio spent some time on the back deck clinging to the railing and watching the huge spray of water on launch. They went inside where there was a fully stocked bar, and little round tables with narrow chairs.

Tonight, there was also a catered meal. The baked chicken wasn't as good as the dishes at Bava's but was still superior to most catered meals Lucio had eaten. The herbed potatoes were indeed delicious, but they both pushed away the broccolini, neither trusting the trendy, hybrid vegetable.

"Do you want to go to the upper deck and watch the fireworks?" Lucio prodded when they got their second glasses of wine.

His hands shook a little as they went up the narrow stairway. Nervousness gripped him as they waited for the fireworks.

Screw waiting. Lucio set his empty wineglass on a nearby table and took Jamie's free hand.

"Jamie Blair, you are the best thing that ever happened to me and..." he stumbled as he met her pale, almost golden eyes, that were now glittering with tears and the words he'd rehearsed vanished. His heart raced with panic that his memory lapse would ruin everything, but he pressed on. "Shit, I had a huge speech prepared and forgot most of it. What I mean is, I want to spend the rest of my life with you."

He got down on one knee and pulled the box from his pocket. "Will you marry me?"

"Yes." Jamie set down her wineglass, took the ring, and offered her hand to help him to his feet. She threw her arms around him and kissed him with more passion than he could bear.

When they caught their breath, she grinned at him. "I'm sorry your dad ruined your surprise."

Lucio shrugged and took her hand as explosions of color lit up the sky and reflected on the water.

"I don't care about that anymore. All I care about is that you said yes."

ABOUT THE AUTHOR

Formerly an auto-mechanic, Brooklyn Ann thrives on writing romance featuring unconventional heroines and the heroes who adore them. Author of historical paranormal romance in her critically acclaimed Scandals with Bite series, urban fantasy in the cult favorite, Brides of Prophecy novels, and the New Adult winner of the 2016 Reader's Choice Award Hearts of Metal series, she provides love for the broken and strange.

She lives in Coeur d'Alene, Idaho with her son, miscellaneous horror memorabilia, and a 1980 Datsun 210.

She can be found online at http://brooklynannauthor.com as well as on Twitter, Instagram, and Facebook.

For exclusive updates, sneak peeks, and giveaways, sign up for Brooklyn Ann's Newsletter.

Connect with Brooklyn Ann:

facebook.com/brooklyn.ann.7

twitter.com/Brooklyn__Ann?lang=en

instagram.com/brooklynann_author

www.ingramcontent.com/pod-product-compliance
Lightning Source LLC
Chambersburg PA
CBHW031331170626
46807CB00002B/641